Love At Last

by

Kate Sweeney

LOVE AT LAST
© 2011 BY KATE SWEENEY

ISBN 13: 978-1-935216-32-2

FIRST PRINTING: 2011

THIS TRADE PAPERBACK IS PUBLISHED BY
INTAGLIO PUBLICATIONS
WALKER, LA USA
WWW.INTAGLIOPUB.COM

- -

CREDITS

EXECUTIVE EDITOR: TARA YOUNG
COVER DESIGN BY TIGER GRAPHICS

ACKNOWLEDGMENTS

As always, thanks to Jule, my sister Maureen, and Tena for their great beta reading. I know it's not vampires and Irish goddesses, sis, but thanks for putting up with the romances, as well!

Thanks of course, to my editor Tara—what a treasure.

And last to Sheri Payton, my Intaglio buddy, who's teaching me the ins and outs of life in Louisiana—snake wrangling included.

Chapter 1

Beyond the blue horizon...waits a beautiful day.

The lively seventies rendition of the thirties song rang out as Allie danced around the kitchen while she mopped the floor. Her hips, which she hated, swayed rhythmically to the snappy tune. Allie sang out for all she was worth believing it could be true.

With that, the music stopped abruptly.

"For crying out loud, Allie," her husband called from the doorway as he flipped off the CD player. "Why don't you use your iPod with the headphones? I can't hear myself think."

Allie whirled around in surprise, then grinned, not wanting to break her good mood. "C'mon, Paul, dance with me."

She flipped the player on once again and held out her arms. Paul groaned as he held her, and after a few steps around the kitchen, he gently released her. For a moment, they looked into each other's eyes.

"Well," Allie said with a sigh, "that was painful."

Paul grimaced as Allie turned off the music. "Okay, Allie, I have work, you know that. You wanted me to stay home on a Saturday. So here I am. I'm sorry if I have work. Now, please, honey, just keep it down."

Allie narrowed her eyes at Paul's retreating figure and followed him into the den of their Oak Park home. "I just thought it would be nice to do something on a summer afternoon like a normal married couple. If we were ever that," she added sadly.

Paul groaned loudly as he sat behind his desk. "Allie," he started and took a deep breath. "I'm trying to make sure we're solvent in our old age."

"Good God, Paul. We're fine. Didn't we put two kids through college? Well, almost, Jocelyn will be done next spring."

"We?" He smirked. By the sick look on his face, Allie knew he realized his mistake.

Her eyes narrowed dangerously as she bore a hole into him. "Do not go there with me, Paul Sanders. Who worked her ass off for five years while a certain college grad looked for the 'perfect' job?" she asked slowly. "And who did this while she was pregnant?"

"Now in all honesty, Al, you weren't pregnant for five years." His grin faded while Allie continued to seethe. "I know you did. I'm sorry if that sounded harsh. I know you were a big help back then. I wouldn't have this job if it weren't for you." Paul tossed down his pen and looked up. Allie searched his face, saw the beginning of gray at his temples, and wondered when that started. She also noticed a trace of sadness in his eyes. "Were we ever that? Ya know—a normal married couple."

Allie sat on the edge of his desk and thought about it. She picked up his pen, toying with it before she said softly, "I think we were."

"Can we be again?" he asked, but before she could answer, he took the pen out of her hand and smiled slightly. "You're sitting on my paperwork."

Allie chuckled and scooted off the desk. She knew Paul really didn't want an answer, or perhaps he already knew what it would be. "Now why don't you go finish your dancing kitchen routine while I finish?" He concentrated on the papers in front of him.

"You're going to miss the beautiful day." She kissed the top of his head and walked out of the office.

"Hey, are you losing weight?" he asked.

Allie smiled and turned back. Maybe all that walking is doing the trick, she thought.

"Your hips don't look so big," he added and went on quickly when Allie glared. "I-I mean you're always complaining about your hips and..."

Allie held up her hand. "Don't overdo it, honey. Thanks."

She walked back into the kitchen and turned on the music

once again. Though now, it just didn't sound the same. She thought about how Paul was indeed missing the beautiful days and in the back of her mind considered her culpability. They were missing too many beautiful days, and she had no idea what to do about it.

With the house cleaned, Allie pondered what to do with the rest of her day; it was only noon. The sun was out and it was a gloriously hot August day. Paul still concentrated on his paperwork in the office, the door now closed. Allie flopped down on the couch and put her head back. The warm summer breeze blew through the curtains, and her mind wandered back to another warm August day when the children were so young.

Allie laughed as Jocelyn opened her mouth like a little bird. "Goodness, you're hungry this morning, sweetie," she said and offered another spoonful.

The toddler banged her spoon on the table with glee. "Okay, here it comes!" Allie announced.

Just then, another country spoke up. "Mama, me too," Nick called out as he watched. Allie noticed the frown and gave her five-year-old gentleman an indulgent grin.

"You want me to feed you, too?" Allie asked in amazement. Nick nodded quickly. "I just thought you were a big boy and didn't need to be fed like a baby, but okay…"

With that, Nick frowned deeper and picked up his spoon. "I'm not a baby, Mama," he said and dug into his Cheerios.

"I'm sorry, sweetie. You're such a big boy," Allie apologized as she wiped off Jocelyn's chin.

Nick nodded. "Joflyn is a baby."

"Yes, she is. That's why she's lucky to have such a good big brother."

That did it. Nick jumped off his chair and stood next to his sister. He took the paper napkin. "I do it."

Allie sat back and smiled as her young man wiped his sister's chin, nearly taking a layer of skin with it. "There, Joflyn, you messy."

Jocelyn scrunched her nose and giggled while Nick patted her head too hard. Allie winced and chuckled. "Thank you, Nick. You're a big help."

"Welcome, Mama. Can I go outside now?" He wiped off his chin.

"Sure, sweetie. Stay in the backyard. We'll be out in a bit." Allie kissed his cheek.

Nick pulled away. "Mama!" he argued and ran down the hall.

Jocelyn watched with interest as Nick disappeared. She looked back at Allie and struggled to get out of the highchair.

"Okay, little miss, hold on," Allie cooed and helped her down. She laughed as she watched her waddle after her brother.

Nick came running out wearing his Cubs hat and carrying the plastic bat. He nearly ran over Jocelyn, who teetered and promptly fell on her backside and let out a shrill cry.

"Nick," Allie scolded, and Nick stopped dead in his tracks.

"Mama, Joflyn always gets in the way," he told her, his baseball cap slightly askew.

"Nick Sanders," Allie said with her hands on her hips.

The little shoulders slumped, and he turned to Jocelyn. "C'mon, Joflyn, stop cryin'."

Jocelyn put her hands up and Nick dropped his bat and tried to lift her. Allie hid her grin as Nick groaned as he tried to lift Jocelyn. "Mama! Help!"

Allie ran over before Nick dropped poor Jocelyn on her head. She picked her up and handed the bat back to Nick.

"She's heavy, Mama." Nick dashed out the back door.

Allie shifted Jocelyn onto her hip and looked at her. "He's right. You are heavy." She then kissed her cheek. "But you have the sweetest cheeks."

As Allie walked outside, there stood Nick waiting with his bat on his shoulder. Allie placed Jocelyn in the sandbox and stood up with a groan.

"C'mon, Mama!" Nick called out.

"Okay, okay, hold your water." Allie mumbled as she picked up the plastic ball.

"Throw it," Nick said.

Allie waited and looked at Nick, who grinned. "Please..."

"Okay." Allie tossed the ball, and Nick swung and missed. "Almost, sweetie. Try again."

"That's okay, Mama. Papa said it's 'cause you're a girl." Nick handed her the ball, then dashed back to his spot.

Allie narrowed her eyes at him. "Is that what Papa said?"

Nick nodded quickly. "Girls aren't as good as boys."

"I'll have to have a talk with Papa," she mumbled and tossed the ball again.

Later that day, Allie had that conversation with Paul when he got home from work.

"He said that?" Paul laughed openly.

"I know it's not a big deal, but I don't want Nick thinking like that."

"Allie," he started. "It's sports. Men are better equipped for sports than women."

"Where do you get these things?" Allie raised an eyebrow and folded her arms across her chest. "And this comes from the voice of experience, oh, great athlete?" she asked, and he glared at her. "Or am I mistaken that your cousin Debbie has kicked your ass whenever you challenge her to a game of golf or tennis or one-on-one basketball or..."

"She's a freak of nature that woman." He turned on the television.

"And women should know their place, right?" Allie asked in a sad voice.

Paul sighed deeply as he flipped the channels. "I didn't say that, but—"

Allie held up her hand to silence him. "Our son will respect women, Paul Sanders."

"Wait a minute, Allie. I want Nick to respect women, too."

"Then don't make girls out to be weaker than boys. There's more to it than brute strength."

Paul hid his grin. "You sound like a lesbian feminist."

For some reason, Allie blushed. She saw Paul's lips twitch and shook her head. "Shut up. You know what I'm saying."

"I do. Really. I'll talk to Nick. Now where's my dinner?"

Allie glared at him. "We've already eaten. If you would get home at a decent hour, you'd eat, too. I of the weaker sex have laundry to do. It's fend-for-yourself night, Mr. Sanders."

The phone ringing shook Allie from her reverie. She let out a groan as she picked it up.

"Allie? Vicky. What are you doing? Rita and I are going to Market Days in Chicago, ya know, on Halsted Street. So come with us."

"I know where Halsted is. Market Days, what's that?" Allie asked.

"It's a street fair on the North Side, the gay district."

Allie raised an eyebrow. "Wow. You're very progressive there, Mrs. Belden." Allie chuckled. "Why Market Days?"

"Because they have all the shops set up on the street, and there are a ton of vendors. It's a beautiful day. Rita's meeting a few friends there, and it's something different on a Saturday. Mike is at the Cubs game with the kids."

Allie thought about it, looking at the closed door to Paul's office. "Okay. Come get me."

They strolled through the street shops and vendors. Allie ate a bratwurst while Vicky and Rita looked at jewelry.

"Allie, look at this!"

Allie strolled over and nodded. "It's beautiful." She looked around the busy Chicago street, now filled with vendors, and stopped when she caught the eye of a woman standing across the street, looking at her. The woman was tall with dark shoulder-length curly hair and smiling. Allie smiled, as well, and when the woman nodded, Allie did, too.

"Allie. What do you think?" Vicky was asking as she put the earrings up to her ears.

Allie turned her attention back to her friends. "What? Oh, great. Buy 'em," she said decisively.

Vicky laughed as she examined the earrings. "That's why I bring you along, Al. You cut through the crap and get to the important aspect. I will."

With that, someone roughly bumped into all three of them. Allie felt her arm roughly pulled, and suddenly, she was on the ground and her purse gone. "Hey!" she screamed from her sitting position, "he stole my purse."

Vicky and Rita were at her side, and in a blur, someone leapt over Allie. Her friends let out a screech as they watched. Just as quickly, a patrolman helped her to her feet. "He stole my purse," Allie said quickly and pointed in the direction.

"Stay put, ma'am," he ordered and took off.

"Geezus, Allie, are you all right?" Vicky asked, her brown eyes filled with concern and fear. "Shit. You scared the hell out of me."

Rita checked her for injuries. "Stupid fucker," Allie mumbled, and both women laughed nervously.

People had been milling around and offering assistance. Allie thanked them and took the offered bottle of water. Her hands were shaking horribly as she unscrewed the top, taking a long drink. What seemed like hours later, Allie spotted the patrolman and a woman walking toward them. It was the woman from across the street; she was a sweaty mess.

"Geezus!" Rita hung on to Allie and Vicky.

"Is this your purse, ma'am?" the patrolman asked and showed her the offering. Allie nodded mutely. "This woman helped. She tackled the poor guy." He motioned to the woman. "You'll have to come down to the station and fill out a report. Please check it and see if there's anything missing."

Allie, standing very close to her friends, opened the purse with shaky hands. After examining the contents, she nodded. "All here. Thank you." She looked at the woman, who nodded.

She was about five-ten. Her black hair was damp now, accentuating the waves and curls. She absently brushed said curls off her brow. As Allie watched the woman run her fingers through her hair, she noticed the streaks of gray throughout. What Allie really noticed were her eyes; they were slate gray.

"You're welcome," the woman said, smiling.

Behind her, Allie heard Vicky sigh, which she ignored.

"Well, Miss..." the woman started.

"Mrs. Allie Sanders," Allie said quickly. She glanced at Vicky and Rita, who were gawking at the poor woman.

"Mrs. Sanders, you'll have to come to fill out a report," the policeman repeated. Allie turned her attention to the policeman as he spoke. "You can do it in the morning. There's no rush."

"Thank you, officer." When she looked back, the woman had disappeared. "I-I didn't even get her name." Allie frantically looked through the crowd.

The patrolman shrugged and offered his hand and apology on behalf of the city of Chicago. Allie waved him off with a grateful smile.

"We need a drink," Vicky announced and dragged Allie by the arm.

They sat at the beer garden clutching their respective purses as they huddled together drinking beer.

Allie looked at Rita and Vicky and laughed. "My God, are we pathetic. We're grown women, and we're sitting here like scared rabbits."

Suddenly, they all burst into laughter. After a moment of hysteria, Vicky dried her eyes. "Well, your hero took off in a hurry. How about those eyes?" She fanned herself.

Rita agreed. "And that body. Holy shit, she must work out every day. Did you see those muscles?"

Allie nodded. "She's probably a trainer of some sort. No one has a body that trim by accident." She took a healthy drink from the plastic cup.

"She was one hot-looking woman." Vicky looked at both friends. "What? She was hot. Didn't you ever..."

Allie knew she was blushing and looked down at her cup of beer. "Ever what?"

Vicky rolled her eyes, and Rita gathered the empty cups and walked away. "Ever think about being with another woman?"

Allie did not answer. Instead, she leaned into Vicky. "Have you?"

Vicky blushed horribly and nodded but eagerly continued. "At the gym, there's this blonde. I know she's a lesbian. She's very 'out.' I've had fantasies about her and..."

Allie laughed with delight. "You're kidding! Does Mike know?"

Vicky winced and nodded. Allie was now astonished. If she ever had told Paul anything like that... She thought for a moment and wondered what exactly Paul *would* say. "What did he say?"

"What did who say?" Rita asked in full pout as she juggled three beers. "You talked without me."

Allie and Vicky laughed as Rita sat next to them. "What were you talking about?"

"I was telling Allie about my fantasy," Vicky said with a shrug.

Rita looked relieved. "Is that all? I thought it was something juicy," she grumbled and drank her beer.

Allie stared at both of them. "You too?"

"Oh, no, I don't, but I think it's cool that Vicky does. I hear Mike likes it," Rita said with a wink.

Vicky blushed and hid her face in her beer.

"What? What?" Allie begged like a kid in a candy store. "I definitely need to go out more."

"I told Mike about it and he got so turned on, we had to call my mother to come get the kids. He made some lame excuse, and God love her, she took them for the whole weekend," Vicky said and drank her beer.

"And?" Allie asked quickly.

Vicky looked up over her beer mug. "I was sore for days," she said happily.

Allie and Rita laughed as they drank. "I wonder what in the world Paul would do if I came home with a story like that," Allie said absently. She immediately wished she hadn't said that out loud.

Both women watched for a moment as Allie contemplated the idea.

"Paul would freak," Vicky said flatly. Allie nodded sadly.

Rita, however, was more optimistic. "I bet he'd be jealous and take you right there on the doorstep. Rip off your clothes and have his way with you."

Allie smiled gratefully. "Thanks, Rita, but it ain't gonna happen." She sipped her beer.

There was a time when Paul thought of her as a sexual being, but that was long ago and far away. Money was his sexual object now. He spent all his time at work making money. "When did he stop looking at me as a woman?" she thought. She was stunned to realize that unfortunately, she said that aloud. "I-I'm sorry, girls. I should never have said any of that. Paul is a good husband and father," she said honestly.

"I know. I like Paul. He's—" Vicky stopped and took a drink. Rita didn't say a thing. "Well, I think I'd better head home," Vicky said. "Enough excitement for one day, eh, ladies?"

Vicky pulled up to the brick bungalow. Allie glanced at her two younger friends.

"This was certainly an interesting afternoon," Allie said with a laugh, lightening the mood once again. "What'll we do next Saturday to top this?"

She left both women laughing as they pulled away.

Paul was watching the Cubs game when Allie walked in. "Hi, honey." She sat on the edge of his chair.

"Hi. How was the market? Get your hands on some good fruit?"

Allie laughed so hard she almost fell off the arm of the chair.

"What's so funny?" he asked seriously.

Allie dried her eyes, shaking her head. "Nothing. What's the score?" she asked, watching the game.

"It's the bottom of the eighth, and the stinking Cubs just might win a game. C'mon." He reached for the remote Allie had taken. "You love them as much as I do."

"Would you like a beer?" She headed for the kitchen.

As she grabbed two bottles from the refrigerator, she thought of what had happened that afternoon. Between having her purse snatched and Vicky's discussion of lesbians, her mind reeled with visions from long ago, visions Allie had tucked away since college. But now, she smiled slightly when she remembered the woman helping the policeman. Vicky was right—she was gorgeous.

As they watched the Cubs lose, Allie told Paul about the purse snatching. Paul nearly dropped his bottle of beer and looked up with concerned eyes.

"Did you get your purse back?" he asked in a worried tone.

Allie had the bottle to her mouth; she stopped and glared. "Yes, and I wasn't hurt at all. In case you were wondering."

Paul reddened and took a drink of his beer. "I-I figured you weren't. You'd have told me when you first got home. How did you get it back, honey?"

"A nice lesbian ran the thief down and tackled him. A perfect stranger risked her life. I wonder why."

"A lesbian?" Paul asked. "Just where were you today?"

"At Market Days on Halsted," Allie said, drinking her beer.

"That's the gay district."

There was a mixture of curiosity and hesitation in his voice that Allie ignored. "I didn't know that. It was Vicky's idea. If you can imagine that." She laughed as she remembered their conversation.

"Well, I'm glad you got your purse back and you weren't hurt. And I'm glad the lesbian caught the bad guy."

Allie watched Paul as he quickly finished his beer. "What's for dinner?"

That night, Allie lay in bed staring at the ceiling while Paul snored quietly next to her. She thought of the woman that afternoon. It was a brave thing for her to do. She looked over at Paul, then rolled on her side and watched him as he slept. He had certainly changed over the years, or maybe she had changed. She reached over and lightly touched his hair, and with a snort, he brushed her hand away in his sleep and rolled over.

Allie smiled sadly and patted his back, then rolled away and stared out the window at the dark quiet night. What was happening to them? When and how had they grown so much apart? She wanted to blame Paul and his obsession with his job and buying into the company. In the past ten years, he'd spent more time at the office downtown than at home. She'd like to think he neglected Nick and Jocelyn. If he were a bad father, it would be easy to lay this feeling of disconnect at his doorstep. But Paul was a good father.

She rolled onto her back and pulled the blanket up around her neck, knowing it wasn't all Paul's doing. Allie had changed, as well, and as the kids grew up, she and Paul grew apart.

"And here we are," she whispered into the darkness. Her gaze darted back and forth. "And just exactly where is that?" She had no answer, at least no answer she wanted to think about.

Chapter 2

Later that week, Allie finished her work at the art school. She loved her part-time job. It afforded her the time to do what she truly loved. And now with the day over, she headed for her favorite spot.

She sat by the Monet exhibit at the Chicago Art Museum and sighed happily as she gazed at the beautiful blues and lavenders. God, how she loved it here. It was quiet and peaceful. Smiling fondly, she remembered the many times she would come here when Nick was just starting school and Jocelyn was a baby. She'd drop Nick off and sit in this very spot, feeding Jocelyn and gazing at her beloved Monet.

Paul never quite understood her need for solitude and certainly didn't understand her love of painting. She gave it up so easily when they married. She then took the teaching position while Paul waited for the right job to come his way. For five years, she worked even while pregnant with Nick.

Finally, Allie gave up her position when Paul found the perfect job; he'd been lost in it ever since. Allie wondered what in the world motivated him, besides money, of course. Maybe it was his insecurity. He felt safe and in control when he had money. He wasn't always like that, she thought as she gazed at the artwork. However, at that moment, she couldn't remember when. Sighing heavily, she looked around the quiet exhibit as visitors absently milled about with brochures in hand.

Mostly tourists, Allie thought. It was August and the Chicago Art Museum was a big draw. As her gaze wandered, she blinked, and for some reason, her heart hammered in her chest so hard she thought she was having a mild stroke. Fine, she thought, menopause and heart palpitations.

It was the woman from the fair. She had just come into the room and was absently looking around. Allie buried her head in her purse and looked up to see a younger man following her. She took what looked like blueprints out of the man's hand and almost angrily perused them.

"I know what I'm doing, Inspector," he complained in a hissed whisper.

Inspector, huh? Allie thought.

The inspector looked around, ignoring him. "I'm not saying you don't, Brandon," she said seriously. Then she pinched the bridge of her nose in a tired gesture. "Did you even look at these blueprints?"

"Look, don't tell me my job," he whispered angrily. "You—" He stopped short of what he was about to say.

By his tone, Allie figured it would be a derogatory statement at best. She strained her neck to watch the exchange without looking directly at them; she almost passed out.

"Come with me," the woman shot back and marched in front of Allie.

Completely unnoticed, Allie watched as the angry young man followed until they stood out of sight behind a wall. Curiosity got the better of Allie. She bit at her bottom lip and nonchalantly walked over as close as she could to look at the other paintings. Oh, hell, be honest, Allie, you're a snoop, she thought.

"Look, junior," the inspector started in an angry whisper. "I don't give a shit what you think of me. I have a feeling it's only because your father was a battalion chief that you got this contract in the first place. I don't give a fuck..."

Allie's eyes grew as big as saucers; this woman was pissed.

"What I *do* give a fuck about is my job and this building. Look at the blueprints, Brandon. Look where you're planning to put the security and the electrical equipment. Do you *want* to start a fire in the Chicago Art Museum?"

Allie chuckled at the sarcastic tone; she heard the papers rustling.

"My father said you were like a man..." he spat back angrily.

Allie sneered at the young pup through the wall. There was a moment of silence.

"I had many conversations with your father." Allie heard a hint of affection in her voice. "I'm sure he wished he could have said the same of you."

Allie bit back a hearty bark of a laugh. Good for you, she said inwardly.

The inspector continued. "Now you listen to me. I'm a duly appointed inspector with the Chicago Fire Department. What I say goes. Now you fix this nightmare or I'll have my department so far up your ass you won't know whether to shit or go blind," she said in a low voice.

Allie frowned for a moment. Just what does that mean anyway? Although she didn't understand the sentiment, nonetheless, it sent a shiver right through her.

"I'll be back next Friday, same time."

Allie quickly turned to face the wall as she heard the inspector storm by her. The young man slowly followed, heading in a different direction.

"Wow!" Allie slowly made her way out of her haven. "What a show to look forward to next Friday. I should pack a lunch."

That night at dinner, Allie had just sat down when Paul asked, "Got any ketchup?"

Allie closed her eyes and was about to get up, then stopped. "Yes, we do."

Paul looked up from his plate. Allie placed the napkin in her lap and looked at him. "It's in the refrigerator. It's that big white thing in the kitchen where the beer is."

He sighed and tossed down his napkin. "You should take this act on the road." He disappeared into the kitchen.

When it seemed like he was taking much too long, she called out, "It's the big red bottle on the door."

Paul appeared and smiled sarcastically. "Very funny."

They ate in silence, Allie glancing at Paul from time to time.

15

She remembered when the kids were young, dinner was a special time. They'd discuss the day's events, and Nick and Jocelyn would retell their day at school. Sometimes Paul was there, but mostly, he worked late. And much to his credit, he made it up to them on the weekends. Time went by so fast, she thought. She looked at Paul once again while she ate.

"How was your day?" she asked.

Paul looked up, as if he just realized she was there. "My day?" he asked, seemingly surprised. "It was fine. Same ole, same ole."

Allie sat back. "Don't you ever get bored with it?"

"With my job?" He laughed. "Hell no, Al."

"You like it, don't you?" Allie asked; this seemed like the first time they had this discussion.

Paul thought about it and nodded. "Yes. I do. I love the challenge of getting the client. Making sure we do what they want." He nodded emphatically. "And keeping them. That's where the money is."

This was Paul's prime mover: money. There was nothing wrong with it, actually. It kept a roof over their heads and now, there were not the money issues they had when they were younger. Still, Allie couldn't shake the feeling she wanted more for Paul; she wanted more for herself.

"Don't you want more?" she asked softly.

"Like what?" he asked. "We don't want for much. The kids are grown. We're pretty much set financially. Well, almost."

What more did she want? By Paul's way of thinking, they were set. But lately, Allie felt unsettled in a time of her life when she should feel comfortable and settled. She would be fifty this year; Paul would be fifty-one. As she watched Paul eat dinner, she tried to visualize the rest of her life. She raised an eyebrow when he nearly emptied the ketchup bottle on his steak; she really tried harder then.

That Friday, Allie glanced at her watch as she strolled up the stairs to the art museum. Paul thought she was nuts to go back. What am I doing? She shook her head and laughed at her foolishness. Vicky would get a kick out of this.

As she stopped and turned to go back down the steps, she heard her name and knew the voice; it was Vicky waving like a fool. Oh, God...

"What are you doing in Chicago?" Vicky shook her head. "Why do I ask? It's your beloved Monet, am I right? In need of a fix?"

Allie laughed. Vicky knew her well, even though Vicky was a good ten years younger. "Yes. I thought I'd take a walk-through. What are you doing down here?"

"Mike's taking me out to lunch. Come with us."

"No, no. I'm perfectly content gazing at Claude for a while. Thanks, though."

They talked absently for a moment or two, then gratefully, Vicky kissed her on the cheek and walked away.

Allie waited until Vicky was out of sight; she grumbled as she glanced at her watch. She ran up the stairs and flashed her pass at the attendant. She was never so grateful for the healthy donation to Channel 11, the public station. She walked to the exhibit and quickened her pace. As she turned the corner, she ran full tilt into a brick wall that wrapped its arms around her shoulders.

"Geezus! Where's the fire?"

Allie shot a look at the bricks; it was her...she...whoever. Damn!

"Well, hello!"

Allie just blinked stupidly.

The inspector did not let go of her arms while sporting a dejected look. "You don't remember me? I'm insulted after retrieving your purse," she said with a sly grin.

"Oh. Yes, of course. How silly of me," Allie blustered, cursing her shaking hands. "You took off rather quickly as I remember. I didn't even get your name."

"Well, how silly of me," she countered. "Toni O'Hara. And I'm sorry I've forgotten your name."

Allie frowned deeply. "Allie Sanders. Mrs. Allie Sanders," she corrected herself.

Toni hid her grin and nodded. "Well, it's nice to meet you again, Mrs. Allie Sanders."

Allie wondered if she was making fun of her.

"Inspector O'Hara?" A voice called out from behind them.

Both women turned. A stout little man with white hair walked up to them. "Brandon, uh, Mr. Wiley is waiting for you," the old man said, chomping on a cigar.

Allie noticed Toni raise a dark eyebrow. "I'll be right there, Kevin. And Kevin?" She reached over, gently snatching the cigar out of his mouth. "We're in an art museum." He blushed to his roots and smiled sheepishly. "And you're my assistant. We're not on the back of an engine anymore," she whispered almost affectionately.

Kevin chuckled. "I wish we were," he whispered back and stuck the cigar into his breast pocket, then nodded to Allie. "Ma'am."

Allie noticed he gave Toni a fatherly glare. Toni turned bright red, which Allie saw, as well. Toni turned and swept her fingers through her thick graying hair.

"Well, where were we?" she asked, and Allie shrugged.

"You have to go see Mr. Wiley," Allie said evenly. "And I was just going to visit Mr. Monet."

Toni grinned. "Have coffee with me afterward? I should be done in a half hour."

"Oh, no, no. I have to get home." Allie stopped, trying to have her brain catch up with her mouth. "I have dinner to make."

Toni looked at her watch. "Um, it's only noon. What in the world are you cooking?"

Allie opened her mouth, then shut it quickly.

"How about this? You visit Monet, and if you're still here when I get back, perhaps you'll join me. If not, then it was nice being nearly run over by you, and maybe we'll see each other again," she said with a grin, then walked away.

Thirty-five minutes later, Allie stood to leave. Why should I care? It was Vicky—she started this ridiculousness, she thought. Good grief, I'm married with two grown kids, a house, and two cars. She chuckled at her menopausal hormones that flew all over the place. Still chuckling, she picked up her purse and headed out of the room. Once again, she hit the wall. Instinctively, she looked up into the slate gray eyes.

18

"This is getting monotonous," Allie said.

Toni laughed heartily, albeit breathlessly. "I'm sorry. I got caught up with..." She stopped and waved her hand. "Never mind. So were you leaving?"

"W-well, yes. I really need to go. I have so much to do. It was a nice offer, Inspector O'Hara." She stuck out her hand. "Thanks again for chasing that guy and getting my purse. It was very selfless. You firefighters are in a class all your own."

Toni smiled and took her hand. "It was my pleasure, Mrs. Allie Sanders. Goodbye." She let her hand go, then walked away.

Allie stood there and watched as Toni's tall frame weaved in and out of the museum crowd until she was no longer in sight.

Inexplicably, a feeling of regret swept through her; in the next instant, it was gone. She turned and headed home.

Chapter 3

"Where are you going?" Kevin asked, scratching his balding head.

Toni had slipped out of her uniform and into her jeans and black T-shirt. "The art museum." She stepped into her deck shoes. She looked in the mirror and ran her fingers through her hair.

Kevin eyed her suspiciously as he chomped on his cigar. "Since when do you like art?"

"Shut up."

"I knew it. It's that lady from last week. Am I right? I noticed a wedding ring."

"Yes, Kevin. She's married. I'm not looking for that," she said and continued, "I-I don't know. I just liked talking to her. She was kind and smart. I'm not looking for sex. I can get that anywhere."

"I suppose that's true, Antonia O'Hara," he said softly. "You have no problem with the ladies. Why don't you have some dame permanent-like?"

Toni gave him a disturbed look. "Dame?"

He waved her off. "Ya know what I mean. Maybe it's the job. A firefighter's a tough thing to get attached to. Too risky, too much worry. But you're an inspector now, with regular hours, well, except for the oddball fires. Why don't you settle down and find a nice woman?"

Toni laughed. "I'd love to, but I'm too old. Had my chances, Kevin ole boy." She ruffled his hair.

"Too old. You're only fifty, for chrissakes, and ya look like you're thirty." He shook his head.

Toni cocked her head and smiled. She walked over to her old friend and kissed his balding head. "You're too sweet, Kevin Murphy. You should have married my mother."

Kevin looked up with misty eyes. "I wish I did, but your old man beat me to it. If I wasn't on that fire run..." He took a deep breath. "Patrick O'Hara was one lucky sonofabitch."

Toni's face drew dark at the mention of her father. She caught Kevin's worried look as he quickly continued, "What's your plan with this married woman?"

"No plan. I just liked talking to her, that's all."

"You should leave it alone, Toni. You're gonna get burned."

Toni realized the truth behind his warning. She flounced into her chair behind her desk and put her head back. Although Mrs. Allie Sanders was nice, she was indeed married. Married women were nothing but trouble for Toni, so she swore them off years ago. They loved to escape, loved to experiment. Ordinarily, Toni was only too happy to oblige. However, her heart always got in the way, and by that time, the thrill was gone for the escapee, and that left Toni to berate herself for her blunder.

"Let's go get a beer," Kevin said, watching her.

Once again, Toni saw the worried look. She sadly agreed with a nod. "I'll buy."

They sat at the local watering hole that catered to firefighters. Toni absently ate the popcorn from the bowl and drank her Guinness.

"What are ya thinking?" Kevin drank his beer.

Toni shrugged. "Nothing, really."

"Okay, what is it about this woman? She's married."

Toni chuckled at his exasperated tone and slapped him on the back. "I know."

"I just worry, that's all. Ya need a keeper," Kevin grumbled.

Toni leaned over and kissed his ruddy cheek. "Thanks, Kev," she whispered. "But I don't need a keeper."

"Ya don't need," he said angrily, then whispered, "sex."

Toni laughed and drank her beer. "Well, I don't need a woman in my life, that's for sure. We both remember that nightmare."

She saw Kevin wince in understanding. "No offense, but she was a bitch."

Toni smiled sadly. "I was part of that debacle. It wasn't all Gina," she gently reminded him.

Kevin let out a rude snort. "No, but it was all *about* Gina. Don't deny it. You nearly left the fire department for that—"

"I know, I know. That's what I'm saying. I'm no good at the long haul." She pushed the empty pint away. The bartender gave her a questioning glance, and Toni shook her head.

"I'll have another." Kevin raised his empty glass. "You will be good at the long haul once ya meet the right woman."

Toni let out a heavy sigh. "I suppose."

Allie Sanders's smiling face flashed through her mind. What was it about that woman? Unattainable? Was that it? In the past, Toni had a propensity for going after that which she could not have. It constantly ended in heartache. Was that what she wanted from Allie Sanders? She couldn't help but think it was not.

"You're thinking about her again."

Kevin's warning voice brought her back to reality. She laughed at the truth. "Yes, I was." When she saw the concerned look once again, she quickly finished, "but not that way. I'm serious. I just think she was nice. No sex, no seduction, no flirting. Just a nice mature woman."

"Who's married," Kevin added and stole a side glance.

"Who's married," Toni agreed and threw her arm around his broad shoulders. "Now let's get out of here, you old woman, and get some sleep."

They stood outside in the warm late summer night. Kevin kissed her on the forehead. "Love ya," he whispered and walked away. "Go home. No gallivanting."

"Love you, too," Toni said. "You're a nag!" She watched him as he waved his hand in the air and walked out of sight.

"No gallivanting, eh?" Toni said with a raised eyebrow. She glanced at her watch—nearly eleven. I'm getting too old to be gallivanting. When did that happen? She pulled a sour face and headed home.

She slipped naked under the covers and stretched her tall frame. Her vertebrae popped and her knees cracked. All she needed was a snap, and she could be on the cover of a box of Rice Krispies.

After all the talk with Kevin, her mind wandered back to Gina Butler. Toni met her at a fundraiser about six—no, eight—years earlier. Flirting ensued, and they ending up in Gina's swanky apartment on Lake Shore Drive. The sex was raucous and lasted long into the night and the early morning. It was the beginning of a very bumpy ride with the egomaniacal Ms. Butler.

Gina was from a very wealthy Chicago family. Her father was a bigwig lawyer, and from the get-go, Toni felt out of place. However, Gina was a master of manipulation, and Toni allowed it. This was her culpability: She knew what Gina was doing and went along with it. Call it love, lust, call it insecurity, call it whatever. The only thing that was certain—Toni O'Hara allowed it. Several times, Toni had one foot out the door, tired of the bullshit, tired of the games. Something always pulled her back in to try again.

Now, for some obscure reason, she thought of her parents and shifted uncomfortably under the covers. There was no obscure reason—she knew what it was. She just didn't want to think about it again. She flipped on her stomach and punched the pillow. Don't start thinking about him now. She wrestled with the pillow and tried to dispel the visions of her father.

"Fuck him," she mumbled and yawned wildly. Mercifully, she faded off, but her sleep was uneasy, and disjointed dreams plagued her throughout the night.

She woke the next morning and looked at the clock on the nightstand. Grinning evilly, she poised her hand just above the alarm button. Just as the clock read 5:30, she hit the button, turning off the alarm before it went off.

"Ha! Gottcha again!" she said triumphantly and slipped out of bed.

After she showered and dressed, her stomach growled. She grabbed her keys and headed to her favorite spot.

She stopped at the bakery on Waveland Avenue. The

owner looked up as the bell signaled Toni's entrance. "Goot morning!"

Toni grinned like a kid. She loved Mrs. Walinski. "Hey, Mrs. W, how are the cinnamon rolls this morning?" She continued grinning when she heard the old Polish woman laugh.

Instantly, the laughter reminded her of Allie Sanders. Toni recalled how she was a quietly attractive woman with her sandy-colored shoulder-length hair and green eyes. Her kind smile was the first thing Toni noticed that day at the fair. She was laughing and joking with her friends, and her laughter pulled at Toni's heart. Damn it if she wasn't married.

"They are very goot," Mrs. Walinski was saying, shaking Toni from her musings. "Now sit. I get you coffee. You don't eat goot, Antonia."

Toni rolled her eyes and sat at the small table by the window. Mrs. Walinski set the steamy cup in front of her along with the huge pastry. Toni rubbed her hands together. "Mmm, you make the best cinnamon rolls."

Mrs. Walinski laughed and playfully slapped Toni on her shoulder. "Your mother made the best, but tank you, sweetie." She kissed Toni's head.

Toni looked up and damned the tears that sprang to her eyes. Mrs. Walinski smiled sadly and placed her old hand on Toni's cheek. "Do not cry. Eat…"

Toni only nodded furiously, trying not to cry. She took a healthy bite and watched Mrs. Walinski grin. "Is goot?"

"Is very goot," Toni said with a mouthful. "Sit with me, Mrs. W."

"Okay, is not busy yet. You are always the first customer." She groaned as she slipped into the chair opposite Toni. "Now tell me. How is Kevin Murphy?"

Toni took another enormous bite and washed it down with coffee. "Fine, fine. He asks about you, too." She wiped her mouth, stealing a glance at the blushing baker.

"He does not," she scolded but smiled slightly. "He does?"

Toni nodded. "Yep. If he weren't a late sleeper, he'd be here. I told him I'd bring something to the firehouse for him."

"I will get something to take to him. He does not eat too goot, either. You sit and enjoy," she ordered and walked behind the counter.

Toni chuckled like a kid. Although she knew Kevin secretly would always carry a torch for her mother—he truly loved her—Toni thought it would be all right to do a little matchmaking. Her mother, God rest her soul, wouldn't want two old friends to be lonely. Kevin should fall in love at last, Toni thought.

Toni smiled as she drank her coffee and looked out the window. The Rogers Park neighborhood had changed over the years from predominantly Irish and Polish to Hispanic and Asian. However, the essence of the neighborhood had always been the same. They looked out for one another. That was why Toni loved the small neighborhoods of Chicago. She looked around the bakery, remembering how she used to come here as a young girl. It was usually after her father went on a bender. Mrs. W. would sit her at this very table and give her a cup of coffee. Toni felt all grown up as she drank the adult brew. And for a little while, she felt normal. For a little while…

Suddenly, the angry feeling started deep in her belly. Visions of that asshole, her father… She shifted in her chair and drank her coffee. Shaking her head as if to dismiss him, she took another bite of the dwindling cinnamon roll.

"Here we go!" Mrs. Walinski said.

Shaken from her dark reverie, Toni looked up and grinned. Mrs. Walinski had two white boxes tied with string. "You give this to Kevin and tell him he must share with the others." She placed the boxes on the table. Toni smiled as she watched her gently run her fingers across them. "You tell him, Lidia Walinski says hello and do not be such a stranger in his own neighborhood."

"I will, Mrs. W.… Shit, I gotta go—"

"Stop with the swearing. How you going to get woman with a mouth like that?" she scolded and shrieked with laughter as Toni wrapped her arms around the ample waist and lifted her off the ground. "Let me go, you idiot!"

Toni twirled her around and easily set her down. Lidia laughed and put her hand to her hair. "You are strong as bull for a woman. Now get out of here and stop a fire."

Toni laughed and walked out, sending the bell tinkling merrily. She stopped dead in her tracks. "Shit!" she mumbled and walked back into the bakery.

Lidia Walinski had the two boxes of pastry in her hand, sporting a smug grin. "You would forget head…"

Toni laughed and kissed the old woman, grabbed the boxes, and dashed out the door.

Kevin sat behind his desk and cringed as he took a drink of stale coffee. He glanced at the treacherous coffeemaker.

Toni grinned as she watched from the doorway. "Why can't you get the hang of a coffeemaker?" She walked into the office.

Kevin looked up and laughed. "I don't know. Whaddaya got there?" he asked and licked his lips.

Toni set the boxes on his desk and handed him a large cup from Starbucks.

"Ah, Toni darlin', you're a grand gal," Kevin said in a thick brogue.

Toni snorted and sat at her desk. "And, Kevin darlin', you're full of shit."

"Stop swearing," Kevin said as he opened the boxes. "How are you ever…"

"I know, get a woman with a mouth like that," Toni finished for him. "That's exactly what Mrs. Walinski said this morning."

Kevin's head shot up. "Um, how is she?"

"She's fine. She asked about you again. She said you have to share." Toni motioned to the pastry. "She also told you to come around more often."

"She did?" Kevin asked, then cleared his throat.

"Why don't you?" Toni asked quietly as she concentrated on her paperwork. When Kevin didn't answer right away, she looked up. Kevin was frowning as he blew at the hot coffee. "Kev?"

He looked at her then and shrugged. "I dunno. She's a classy woman, widowed, and owns her own business, for chrissakes."

"So what?" Toni asked, honestly baffled. "She likes you."

"Ya think so?" He took a bite of the pastry. He rolled his eyes. "This is so good."

"Yeah, I think so. Don't you like her?"

All at once, her stomach started growling again. Even Kevin heard it. They both stared at her stomach.

"Geez, feed it before it explodes." Kevin slid the pastry box to the end of his desk.

Toni reached for the box. "Answer me. Don't you like her?"

"What's not to like? She's attractive, nice. She sure can cook. I just think—"

Toni looked up when he stopped abruptly. "What?"

"She's out of my league, kiddo."

Toni heard the disappointment in his voice. "Well, probably." She glanced his way. "She was telling me she's worried about the neighborhood."

"What's she worried about? What's wrong?" He sat forward.

"Oh, nothing, I guess. Mr. Su, you know the Chinese place with great egg foo yung? Well, evidently, somebody broke his window the other morning and Mrs. W. is worried—"

Kevin quickly stood. "Well, why the hell didn't you say this before? Christ, Toni, that woman is all alone, all the time. Damn it, O'Hara!" He grabbed his coat. "I'll be back."

Toni watched Kevin dash out of the office, mumbling all the way. She eyed the pastry box and grinned. "So easy…"

Across town, Lidia Walinski hummed quietly as she swept the floor in the kitchen when the last of the morning rush had dissipated. With that, she heard the little bell. "I will be right with you!" she called out.

She walked out of the swinging door to see Kevin Murphy standing there. Her heartbeat quickened when she noticed he was dressed in his fireman's uniform with his hat in hand.

He looked up as she walked out of the kitchen. Lidia saw the frown turn to a smile and smiled back. "Goot morning, Mr. Murphy."

"Good Morning, Mrs. Walinski. I was in the neighborhood—"

Lidia gave him a confused look. "You don't work today?"

Kevin blushed to his roots and laughed nervously. "Yes, what

I meant was, I was on my way to a…um…meeting, and I thought I'd stop by and say…er…hello."

Lidia raised an eyebrow and nodded. "Hello."

"Hello," Kevin repeated and swallowed.

They stood in silence for a moment. She sensed his awkwardness, and when he looked as though he might leave, she quickly said, "Would you like a cup of coffee? A piece of pie? I just made a nice pie with the rhubarb from my garden."

"Oh. Okay, sure. If it's not too much trouble," Kevin added.

Lidia smiled at his serious tone. "Is not too much trouble, Mr. Murphy. I am a baker, remember? Sit, please."

Kevin chuckled and sat at the small table by the window.

Lidia calmly walked back through the swinging door, let out a deep breath, and put a hand to her heart. "Oh, Got," she said and fanned herself with her apron. Trying to ignore her racing heart and her shaky hand, she quickly sliced two pieces of pie, one slightly bigger. She tore off her apron and ran her fingers through her thick white hair. She picked up both plates and took a deep confident breath.

"He is so cute," she whispered with a giggle. "And so it begins, Mr. Murphy."

Chapter 4

"You want to go where and watch what?" Allie asked, looking back and forth from Vicky to Rita as they helped her into her jacket.

"Mike is playing flag football in Grant Park. They're playing in the championship game. There's a men's and women's championship."

"I didn't know there was a women's league in Chicago," Allie said.

Vicky chuckled. "Well, they're women, but they're no ladies. Mike says they play tougher than most of the men do. I honestly think he's afraid of them."

Rita laughed along. "C'mon, it's Saturday, the last days of summer are waning, and it's beautiful in Grant Park. You've been moping around for weeks for whatever reason."

Allie felt the color rush to her face. She'd been illogically disappointed ever since she didn't see Toni O'Hara at the museum.

"We know Paul is working. Now we'll sit with the wives. I've got the vodka and lemonade." She held up the huge thermos and wiggled her eyebrows.

Allie gaped at them. "It's a Chicago Park District. You can't drink at—"

Vicky and Rita rolled their eyes and dragged her out of the house.

They set up their lawn chairs and watched the mayhem. "Good grief. I can't believe women play this game," Allie said as she watched the men flying around the field.

Vicky winced, as well, then looked behind her. "I wonder how the women play. Let's go watch them for a while," she suggested and quickly got up, pulling Allie with her.

Rita pouted. "I like watching the men."

Allie laughed at Rita, who with great intelligence, went back to retrieve the thermos.

It was indeed a beautiful Indian summer day. Not a cloud in the sky, though it had rained the previous night. Not much, just enough to make the playing field muddy. The three women made the incredibly short walk to the women's game.

Vicky stood between the two games, looking back and forth. "Hey, if we stand right here, we can see both games at once."

Allie raised a maternal eyebrow as Vicky sipped her drink.

"Don't be a dud, Allie," she said without looking at her.

"I am not a dud. I'll have you know, I can drink—" She stopped abruptly and blinked. The hammering started in her chest again—the onset of her mild stroke. There she was again.

Toni O'Hara stood thirty feet away from her. She was wearing what once was a white rugby shirt, the Chicago Fire Department emblazoned on the front and back. She wore green shorts and knee-high socks, her feet encased in heavy cleats. She had her thick hair pulled back in a ponytail. Some tall blond prepubescent-looking thing was wiping her face as Toni gulped the bottle of water. As she glanced over, she grinned wildly when she saw Allie. Allie, in turn, smiled and gave her a short wave.

Toni waved back and noticed Vicky and Rita, then looked at the men's game and nodded as if understanding her reason for being there. As if Paul would ever get dirty and play flag football, Allie thought. Well, maybe if it was for his job...

Allie cringed as Vicky's eyes widened. "Hero!" she screeched.

Allie looked around for a hole in which to throw herself.

Toni sported a lopsided grin, and to Allie's horror, she walked over. "Good morning, ladies," she drawled with a flirtatious grin.

Allie smiled weakly. Rita looked like she was drooling. "You have to admit she's gorgeous in a butch sort of way," Rita whispered in Allie's ear.

Toni glanced at Allie and nodded. Vicky stuck out her hand. "Save any damsels in distress lately?"

Toni wiped off her hand before taking Vicky's hand. "Nope. Not lately," she said as the blond woman walked up and draped her arm around her.

"Sweetie, they're starting. Can't start without the star." She ran her hand up and down Toni's sweaty back.

"The star, huh?" Vicky asked happily.

Allie saw the blush spread through Toni's neck as she chuckled. "Hardly. Well," Toni said and looked at Allie. "I should be going. It was nice to see you. We go out afterward if you and your husbands want to join us. We're going to The Shamrock Tavern on State—"

"That's where we're going, too," Vicky said, still grinning.

Toni's eyes never left Allie's. "Well…good. Maybe we'll see you there," she said as the blonde pulled on her arm.

"God, if only I were into women." Vicky sighed.

Allie laughed as she watched Toni. Rita laughed, as well, and whispered, "You're a slut!"

Vicky gaped in mock horror, putting a hand over her heart. "I am not."

Listening to her friends banter, Allie glanced back at the playing field to see Toni pluck the football out of the air and take off down the field. Allie gasped and winced openly as Toni's opponents tackled her, ripping the flag from her waist, but not before Toni tossed the football back to a teammate. This left her lying on the ground in their wake.

For an instant, Allie wanted to run out there. Toni slowly got up and shook her head rapidly, flexing her leg and rubbing her rear end. Allie smiled. *You're a bit too old for this, Inspector O'Hara,* she thought, noticing the much younger women running up and down the field. Toni looked to see Allie watching. Allie laughed and shook her head, while Toni grinned and shrugged, then ran down the field.

When the games finished, the Chicago Fire Department, both men and women, proved victorious.

Mike was grumbling as usual. "Shit, we almost had 'em."

Vicky hugged him around the waist. "Sure you did. You were the best, you know."

Mike smiled and kissed her nose. "I was, huh? Hey, I saw you talking to that woman. You know what that does to me," he warned playfully.

Vicky nodded wickedly. "Yep...so celebrate, Mr. Belden, but don't you dare drink too much," she warned as she kissed him deeply.

"There they go." Rita rolled her eyes.

"There's nothing wrong with that," Allie said, laughing as they walked to the car.

Allie glanced over at the other field and noticed Toni limping slightly as she walked next to the blond woman. They were talking, and the blonde immediately stopped. She looked irritated at Toni, who sported that damned grin and said something. The woman whirled around and took off in a huff, leaving Toni standing there shaking her head. Allie wondered what the exchange was about as she watched the much younger woman march off.

As they sat at the small table, Mike and his teammates licked their wounds. A few firefighters were doing a bit of bragging, and several of Mike's teammates were getting annoyed.

"God, men and their competitiveness," Rita groused as she ate the popcorn.

Allie tossed a few kernels in her mouth. "That's not only a male trait, Rita."

"True," Rita said, "but take a look at the women's table."

They all glanced at the other table. All the women were laughing and drinking. Then they collectively looked back at the table of men, who were drinking but definitely not laughing; they were still brooding.

As Allie sat with the other wives listening to the boasts of the winners and the complaints of the losers, she absently ate her popcorn and stole a glance across the bar. Toni stood there, one foot up on the bar rail, as she leaned in talking to the bartender. She said a few words, and he threw his head back and laughed uproariously.

"O'Hara, you're a wild one." The bartender laughed and walked away.

Toni laughed and shrugged as she drank her black beer, absently swiping her tongue across her mouth.

Allie heard Vicky groan and glared at her. "Will you stop with the groaning?"

Rita chuckled and Vicky giggled and leaned in. "I just called my mother. She's keeping the kids tonight."

With that, they all saw Toni saunter over with three pitchers of beer. She set them on Mike's table. "Please accept this, guys. My boys can sometimes be hard to handle," she said, glaring at her fellow firefighters. "And very bad winners."

The younger men hid their faces in their beer and Mike grinned. "Thank you. That was nice of you."

Toni nodded and turned to Allie's table.

"Have a seat," Vicky said.

Allie watched with amusement as Vicky glanced at Mike, who shook his head, wagging a finger at her. Ah, to be in love, Allie thought, smiling inwardly at her younger friends.

"Glad to." Toni eased herself into the chair, letting out a small groan.

Allie raised an eyebrow. "Sore?"

"Completely. I have to learn when to quit. Every year, I say it's the last."

Several wives and husbands said their goodbyes. It left Allie, her friends, and Toni.

Vicky leaned in. "So, Toni, what do you do for a living? Do you fight fires?"

"Not anymore. I'm an inspector now. It's less wear and tear on the old bones," she said as she drank her beer.

All three women snorted. Toni grinned at their disbelief. "What?"

"How old are you? Thirty-something?" Rita asked honestly.

Toni laughed out loud. "Wow, you made my day, Rita. Are you married?" she asked with a sly grin.

Rita laughed. "No, and I don't walk on your side of the street."

"My misfortune." She winked.

Vicky sighed openly and Allie smiled as she drank her

beer. She couldn't blame Vicky. Toni was indeed charming. She absently ate the popcorn, not really paying attention.

"How's Claude?" Toni's voice was low as she leaned into Allie.

She chuckled quietly. "He's doing well, thank you."

"You really like to sit there, don't you?" Toni asked, sounding completely intrigued. She pulled her chair in, letting a grunting firefighter by.

"Suck in it, O'Hara," he growled playfully, slapping her hard on the back.

Allie winced at the playful encounter. "To answer your question, Inspector, yes, I do love to sit there. It's very cathartic for me. Why? Is it unusual?" she asked; she knew she had an edge to her voice. Paul's inability to understand her basic need was like a raw nerve, but she really didn't need to take it out on a stranger.

Toni raised an eyebrow. "Not at all. Everyone has a special place for solitude. Mine is Lake Michigan, right at sunrise or looking at the horizon at the end of the day. I understand," she said softly, then shrugged and drank her beer.

"Beyond the blue horizon…" Allie sighed openly as she toyed with her mug of beer.

Toni grinned and lifted her beer and sang along, "Waits a beautiful day."

Allie's mouth dropped in surprise. Toni picked up a piece of popcorn, aimed, and tossed it into her open mouth. Allie nearly choked as she laughed. "If we know that song, we're showing our age."

Toni laughed. "Now tell me. Why the museum?"

"When the kids were small, I would just sit there for hours, just staring and—"

Toni ate some popcorn and waited. "And what?"

Allie shrugged. "Dreamed, I guess," she said with a grin and looked into the gray eyes.

"Whaddya dream about?" Toni gently prodded.

Allie thought about it as she nibbled on the popcorn. "Ya know, I don't remember. I guess I dreamed of being a famous artist."

"You paint?" Toni asked, completely enthralled. "I have a hard time with color by numbers."

Allie let out a genuine laugh, and Toni laughed along with her. "Yes, I paint. I used to teach full time, believe it or not."

"Why did ya quit?"

Allie fought the urge to compare this woman with her inquisitive daughter when she was a child. "I had children."

"I like the way you're smiling right now," Toni blurted out and continued, "It seems to come from your soul. How many?" Toni asked as the waitress brought an enormous plate of nachos.

Allie raised an eyebrow. Toni sported that damnable grin. "I ordered them, sorry. I'm starving. Dig in." She handed her a small plate, then one to Vicky and Rita.

"So?"

"Oh, two. A son, Nick, and a daughter, Jocelyn," Allie said proudly as she blew at the hot cheese.

"Jocelyn, that's a beautiful name. Does she want to be an artist when she grows up?" Toni asked, taking a healthy bite.

Allie laughed and wiped her mouth. "She *is* a grown adult, as is Nick."

Toni blinked stupidly. Then her gaze darted all over Allie's face and body. Suddenly, Allie felt extremely uncomfortable. She was aware Vicky broke her conversation with Rita, and both women now listened.

"I'm serious," Toni said, sounding every bit of it.

"So am I," Allie said emphatically and took a drink of her beer. "God, I'm having a good time. I haven't had nachos and beer in ages." Hips, the hips, she thought. She didn't care. Not tonight.

"Are you trying to tell me that you look as good as you do and you have two grown children?" Toni asked.

Allie heard her incredulous tone and could feel the color rush to her face at the compliment. Her hand instinctively went to her hair. "That's because I'm like a Monet painting. The farther away, the better I look." She noticed Toni wasn't laughing, just staring with an odd look on her face. "It was a joke."

Vicky cleared her throat and called out, "Husband!"

He looked up curiously. "Yes, wife?"

"Now. We need to go home...now!" she said quickly and stood.

Allie, knowing why Vicky was leaving, felt the color rush once again. She avoided Toni, who was still watching her.

"Bye, guys," Mike said to the men at his table and grabbed Vicky's hand.

Allie gaped at Vicky and Mike. "You're my ride." She tried to sound nonchalant, but she was painfully aware of Toni's eyes on her.

"Inspector O'Hara? Take Allie home?" Vicky called out as Mike yanked her out the tavern door.

Toni blinked and looked away from Allie; she nodded and waved. "Sure, no problem."

"Hey, wait a second." Allie called out in vain, but the heavy door slammed on Vicky's laughter. She nervously looked back at Toni. "Y-you don't have to take me home. I can drive with Rita..." She looked at her other friend. Rita was flirting with a firefighter, totally oblivious and in a tonsillectomy duel.

Toni looked on, as well, and laughed. "I don't mind, Allie. I think Rita is otherwise engaged."

They walked a couple of blocks to Toni's car. Allie noticed her slight limp and chuckled.

Toni glared at her. "Do not laugh. I think I broke something of extreme importance."

"I'm sure that girl could tell you what," Allie said and had no idea why she emphasized "girl."

Toni let out a low laugh. "She's part of the reason."

"Why didn't she come to the bar?"

"We, um, we had a disagreement."

"About her curfew?"

Toni stopped, and for a second, Allie thought she had overstepped her bounds. Then to her relief, Toni laughed. "No, that wasn't it."

Allie glanced up at her new friend as Toni opened the door, then gently closed it after Allie slipped into the passenger seat.

She watched as Toni got in and started the car. As she pulled away from the curb, Allie gave instructions.

"So, Allie. Short for Alexandra?"

"Nope."

Toni frowned and grunted. "Alexis?"

"Ice cold."

Toni was undaunted.

"Alice?"

"Wrong."

Silence fell, and Allie glanced at Toni, who was scowling, her gaze darting back and forth.

"Aha!" she said triumphantly, then stopped. "No, that can't be." She took a deep breath.

Allie gave her an incredulous look and laughed. "Good grief, you're a competitor."

Toni shot her a quick look. "I am not. I'm…I'm playful," she countered playfully. "Now keep quiet. I'm trying to think."

Allie hummed a little as she looked out the window.

After a few more minutes, Toni grumbled. "Oh, all right. I give…"

"Alana," Allie said in a quiet voice.

"That is a beautiful name. Who are you named after?" Toni asked, mirroring Allie's quiet tenor of her voice.

"My grandmother. She was born in France. So were my parents. Jocelyn is named after my mother," Allie said quite easily. She shook her head, trying to remember the last time she talked to anyone about her children. She looked over at Toni, who was smiling while she watched the road. "It's easy to talk to you," she admitted.

Toni glanced and grinned. "I know. I feel the same way. I-I like talking to you, Alana. You don't mind if I call you Alana, do you?"

Allie couldn't help but hear the hopeful sound in her voice. "No, I don't mind at all," she said. "This is my house on the left. The brick bungalow here."

Toni nodded and pulled into the driveway. They sat there for a moment in silence.

"Well, Inspector…"

"Hey, if I can call you Alana, can't you call me Toni?" she asked with a grin. "I mean, I risked my life to save your purse and all."

Allie laughed and nodded. "I have a feeling you're going to use that excuse quite a bit… Well, good night and thanks for the ride, Toni," she said and opened her door.

Toni quickly reached across and placed a hand on her forearm. Allie stopped and felt the warmth spread down her arm.

"Maybe I'll see you at the museum."

"Toni, I—"

"Wait. I'm just saying for a few laughs and some coffee. We're both grown women. I like your company as a friend, that's all. I like you," she said honestly. "No flirting, no seduction."

Inwardly, Allie wasn't sure if she was relieved or not. This suddenly weighed on her mind as feelings from long ago drifted through her. "Maybe I'll see you at the museum. I-I go on Tuesdays and Fridays… Maybe." She quickly exited the car.

Feeling every bit as she did when she was seventeen and coming home late after a date, she quickly walked up the front walk, knowing Toni watched her.

Chapter 5

"So?" Vicky asked as she slipped into the booth.

Allie gave her an indulgent smile. "So…what?"

"So did Inspector Gorgeous make a pass at you?"

"Vicky! It was over a week ago. Of course not. Geezus, she was a perfect…well, she was very considerate. We talked about the kids. She then dropped me off. Sorry, there's no story there for you. You and Mike are going to have to find another avenue, kiddo."

Vicky laughed. "You have to admit she's gorgeous. Rita is right, though, in a butch kind of way. I mean, she has to work out constantly. Did you notice those thighs? Or those biceps? Whew!" she said, fanning herself.

"You're insane." Allie looked at the menu, though she wasn't reading it. "I've got one hour, then back to school. Classes start in two weeks. I can't believe the summer is gone, and I have not seen one Cubs game." She pouted seriously as she examined the menu.

There must have been something in the air. Instinctively, Allie looked up, somehow knowing Toni would be there. And there she was. She had ordered a coffee to go as she stood by the counter of the small deli. She wore a pair of black slacks and shoes, very work-like. She had her white long-sleeved shirt rolled up to reveal her trim forearms. Allie noticed the gold insignia of the Chicago Fire Department on the collar of her starched shirt. She wore a pair of aviator sunglasses, and her gray-streaked dark hair seemed tousled and unruly. Allie laughed quietly for some reason at the impatient posture. Toni did indeed remind her of Jocelyn.

Though Allie did nothing to attract her attention, Toni immediately looked in her direction, noticed her, and smiled. Allie smiled back and waved.

Vicky followed her gaze. "Shit, she's here."

"Will you stop? My God, Vicky. She's a friend, will you relax?" Allie said in a calm voice. "What is it with you and this woman?"

"Hi, gals." Toni grinned and snapped her fingers as the coffee spilled over the edge of the cup. Allie laughed and handed her a napkin. "Thanks. How are you?"

"Fine, Inspector," Vicky said with a sly grin.

Toni raised a wary eyebrow and looked at Allie. "Alana. How's Claude these days?"

"He's well, Toni. Thank you."

Vicky glanced at her watch. "Shit! I gotta get the kids. Sorry, Al..." she said and kissed her cheek. She stood next to Toni and looked into her eyes. "Ahh... See ya, Inspector." She sighed, then dashed out of the deli.

"May I?" Toni gestured to the empty booth.

"Sure. I see you're in uniform. Busy day?" Allie asked as the waitress brought her lunch.

Toni glanced at it and licked her lips. Allie gave her a curious look. "Did you eat?"

"Uh, well, I have to be in court. It's right across the street," she said as she eyed the sandwich.

Allie gave her a smirk and cut the sandwich in half. "Here, I don't want you fainting in front of a judge."

"That would never do. Thanks, are you sure?"

"Do I look like I'd miss half a sandwich?" Allie placed the half on her plate.

"You look fine to me. Thanks again," she said absently as she took a healthy bite. In three, she had it done.

Allie was astounded. "You eat like Nick. You'll get indigestion," she scolded as Toni gulped her coffee.

"Sorry, but there was a fire last night, and I was at the scene till four this morning. Had two hours sleep, and I've got to be in court."

Allie noticed the tired circles under her eyes. "Why?"

"I have to go periodically. Building codes, specs...you'd be amazed at how many assholes try to bend the rules. I'm on this month, we alternate."

"Well, you look very professional," Allie said as she drank her iced tea.

"Hmm. They wanted me to wear a skirt. I laughed in their face. Do you know the last time I wore a skirt?"

Allie chuckled and shook her head.

"Fifteen years ago. My father's funeral," she said definitely.

Allie blinked. "I'm sorry," she said softly.

Toni nodded emphatically as she gulped her coffee. "Me too. I hate heels."

Allie gaped at her. "No. I meant about your father."

"Oh. Thanks, but he was an asshole. I have to run. Look, I have two Cubs tickets. I won them off a lieutenant at the Twenty-third..."

"What was the bet?"

"Long story. Wanna go?"

"Are you nuts? The Cubs, yes," Allie said quickly.

Toni laughed. "I knew you were a Cubs fan. Great. I know it's the last minute, but I just got the tickets yesterday. Can you get away tomorrow? It's a one thirty game. Can you take the day?"

Allie thought sadly, the day? Saturday? Why not. "Sure. Paul will be working."

"Wonderful," Toni exclaimed and glanced at her watch. "Shit. I'm gonna be late. Okay. I'll come get you at noon, right?" She stood and finished her coffee. "Thanks for the sandwich. It hit the spot."

"You're welcome, see you then. Quit running!" Allie laughed as Toni stopped running right as she got to the door.

To her amazement, Paul walked in just as Toni dashed out. He held the door for a redheaded woman and another man. "Paul," she called.

He found her and smiled, looking as surprised as Allie. He pointed to the counter and Allie nodded. He said something to the woman, then made his way to Allie's booth.

"This is a surprise. What are you doing here?" he asked.

"I'm eating lunch," she said. Paul still looked confused. "Ya know, from my job? Teaching?"

Paul's face reddened. "I meant here." He looked back at the counter. "I'm with some associates."

"I gathered that, honey."Allie watched the redhead and the other man as they paid for the lunches. Allie grabbed her purse and slid out of the booth. "Well, I don't want to be late for class. Be home for dinner?"

Paul waved to his friends and looked at Allie. "What? Oh, I'm not sure. We have a client in. I'll call."

"Okay. Have a good rest of the day."

"You too, Al." He kissed her cheek and walked away. "Call ya later."

"Oh, I'm going to the Cubs game tomorrow," she called back.

Paul turned and grinned. "I'm jealous, you brat."

"Box seats. I'm impressed," Allie said as they sat on the third-base side three rows behind the dugout. She glanced around Wrigley Field. "God, I love this park."

"Me too. I practically grew up here. Got Ernie Banks and Ron Santo to autograph a baseball when I was eight." Toni whistled for the beer man. After ordering two, she grinned at the vendor, slipping him a folded bill. "Don't be a stranger, pal."

He nodded and winked as he walked away, calling out his ware.

Toni handed the beer to Allie and noticed the smirk. "What?" she asked in a helpless gesture.

"I'll get the next one," Allie assured her.

Toni nodded in understanding. "Dutch date, huh? Okay, no problem. Although if we were dating, I'd be buying, toots."

"Toots? I'll bet you win a great many hearts with that one."

Toni looked at her over her sunglasses and flashed that damnable grin. "You have no idea," she said in a low growl.

Allie said nothing further on the topic and concentrated on her beer. By the third inning, Allie was cursing up a storm. She jumped up and yelled, "My mother hits better than you!" As she sat down, she noticed Toni staring wide-eyed. "What? She does." She drank her beer. "God, they make me so mad. They break my heart every year."

"But not as much as the sixty-nine Cubs. You're too young, but they truly broke a few thousand hearts, including mine. I cried for a week."

"I know. If the Mets never win another game, I'd be in heaven," Allie agreed.

Toni laughed openly and raised her beer. Allie laughed along, then stood and yelled at the next batter. She looked down to see Toni looking up at her, grinning. She then took a drink of her beer and a bite of her hotdog.

As Allie sat, she noticed Toni had mustard down the front of her white tank top. She narrowed her eyes at Toni, who wore a Cubs hat on backward, aviator sunglasses, and mustard. It was now on her mouth and chin.

"I can see that you're single." Allie offered the napkin.

Toni blushed and took it, then noticed her tank top. "Oops. Wanna bite?" she enticed, and Allie licked her lips. Toni waved the hotdog in front on her. "It's *so* good and tasty, especially with a beer..."

Allie opened her mouth to say yes, and Toni quickly shoved it in, laughing hysterically at Allie with mustard now on her blue blouse. Allie quickly ate the hotdog, glaring at Toni. "You idiot. Do you have any idea how much it's going to cost to clean this? This is linen, you dope."

Toni threw her head back and laughed again. "Who wears linen to a Cubs game? I'll have it cleaned. Sorry, Alana, it was just too good to pass up."

By the fifth inning, Toni bought a bag of peanuts. Allie rolled her eyes as she sipped her beer. She watched Toni out of the corner of her eye as she took a peanut and popped it into her mouth, shell and all. She then proceeded to suck all the salt off and take it out of her mouth, open it, and eat the peanuts. She tossed the shells aimlessly at her feet.

After several peanuts, Allie figured Toni must have felt the eyes of scrutiny upon her. She stopped in mid-lick and looked at Allie.

"That is disgusting."

Toni laughed and continued. "I love salt."

"You love beer, hotdogs, and nachos. It's only the fifth inning. What, don't you want a frosty malt?"

Toni's eyes lit up as she frantically looked around. "Thanks for reminding me." She looked for her new favorite vendor.

"No, I don't want some," Allie lied as Toni placed the ice cream on the wooden spoon.

"Alana, open wide." She pressed the chocolate malt to Allie's lips.

Allie rolled her eyes and opened her mouth. "Hmm." She let out a throaty purr.

Toni immediately stopped grinning. "Okay, um, all done," she said quickly and ate the rest.

"I don't get any more?" Allie asked in full pout.

Toni laughed nervously, her face bright red. "I think not."

"Good. I can barely fit in this seat anyway," Allie said lightly.

Toni tossed the empty carton on the growing pile at her feet. She turned in her seat to face Allie.

"That's the second time you've made a comment about how you look. Stop it, will you? I happen to think like your husband. You look great. Your body shows your life and love. You've had two children and your body is beautiful because of it. So please, stop talking like that."

The man in the seat behind leaned in between them. "Did I come to a baseball game or *Oprah*?"

Toni turned in her seat. "*Oprah*, now mind your own business. Can't you see the Cubs are losing?"

Allie chuckled but looked down at her hands. "How do you know my husband thinks like that?"

"Well, because he loves you. You—not just your body, which changes throughout your life. He loves your soul. So should you," she finished quietly.

Allie looked into the gray eyes that bore into hers, seemingly willing Allie to believe. "Thank you," she whispered.

"You're welcome. Now…I need a pretzel."

"It's a combination of too many hotdogs, too much beer, and too much sun," Allie scolded as she held the wet cloth to Toni's forehead.

"Don't forget the frosty malt." She groaned.

Allie shook her head. She took the cloth away and doused it with water from the bottle. "You eat like an eighteen-year-old, but you have the digestive system of a…well, whatever your age is."

Toni was sitting on the hood of her car in a pathetic pose. "Fifty." She groaned and held her stomach.

Allie was amazed. "Hell, you don't look it."

"How old are you? I'd say maybe forty, and that's only because you told me you had two grown kids," she asked, fighting the wave of nausea.

"I'll be fifty next July," Allie said in an even voice.

Toni shot her head up and dropped her mouth. "Fifty? That's impossible!"

Allie nervously looked around. "Thank you, now that all of Wrigleyville knows. Sit still." She placed the cool cloth behind her neck. "Is this how you wow the women, Inspector?"

Toni chuckled pathetically. "The secret's out." She sat there for a few moments as the crowd dissipated. "I'm okay." She slid off the hood of her car.

Allie gave her a wary glance. "You need to get out of this sun. Even for early September, it's warm. I'm not too familiar with this area. What do you suggest? What's the closest?"

"Well, there's a bar just down the street, but—"

"Fine, let's go. You can get some more water in you."

"But—"

"Toni, quit arguing. C'mon."

They walked down Clark Street, and Toni stopped at the entrance to the bar. "Alana, this place might not be…"

Allie looked in. It was relatively empty with the door open. "This is fine and you look a little pale."

Allie guided the ill woman to a small table by the window. As she got Toni in a chair, a man stood behind them. "What's wrong with your fella?"

Allie heard a low chuckle from Toni, which she ignored. Allie looked up into the bluest eyes she'd ever seen. "He-she's had a bit too much sun. Can we have some ice water, please?"

The young man patted her arm. "Sure, honey." He looked at Toni and shook his head. "The big butch," he admonished quietly.

Allie turned five shades of red. Now she knew what Toni meant.

"The bigger they are—" he said.

"The harder they hit." Toni growled.

The young man put up his hands in defeat. "Bet she's a pussycat between the sheets," he whispered to Allie, who smiled weakly.

Toni lifted her head. "I tried to explain."

Allie sat next to her and held the cloth against her forehead. "Hey, I'm a grown woman. Wait till Paul hears I spent the afternoon in a gay bar with a gorgeous lesbian." She stopped when she realized what she said.

Toni smiled but mercifully said nothing and lowered her head in her hands. Allie was grateful for the dim lighting.

"He'll be all jealous, and that's when you assure him you love him. Then he'll get all manly and sweep you into his arms and carry you off to bed," Toni mumbled as Allie gently rubbed her back and held the cloth against her forehead. "If you came home to me with a story like that, that's what I'd do anyway."

Allie smiled at Toni's romantic side. She stared out the window and wondered just what Paul would do. What would Allie want? She looked down at Toni's head and reached out to touch her hair.

"I'm okay now." Toni looked up and took the cloth out of Allie's hand. "Thanks."

"You're welcome."

"Feeling better?" the young man asked. "How about a cocktail? Or more water."

"Water is good."

They sat for a moment in silence. Allie glanced around the bar; there were a few patrons sitting at quiet tables away from the bar. Mostly men, though Allie did see two women sitting at the table by the window. They laughed and kissed each other; they held hands and seemed like they were having a good conversation. A pang of jealousy swept through Allie—she and Paul had not had a good conversation in years. She looked at Toni and realized she had talked more to this woman than her husband.

The drive home was quiet. Allie stole a glance at Toni now and then, knowing she was embarrassed. Toni and Allie stood by the car in Allie's driveway. "God, I'm so sorry. Geez, I feel like an idiot."

"You were at a fire till four in the morning. You could have canceled. I'd have understood, for heavensake. You only had two hours of sleep."

Toni shrugged and kicked at the tire. "Shit, I almost puked."

Allie hid her grin. "It's okay. What are friends for, if not to be there when they vomit?" Both laughed as Allie continued, "Now stop it. I'll feel bad if you keep blaming yourself. It was a fun day."

Toni snorted. "Some fun."

"It was. Where else would I be asked to dance by a transvestite in the middle of the day?" she asked, and Toni laughed quietly. "I had more fun than I've had in quite a while, Inspector O'Hara. Now you go home and get some sleep. I'll talk to you next week." She fought the urge to kiss her pouting cheek.

Toni looked up then and smiled. She reached in her wallet and handed Allie a card. "Take this, please. In case you need to get a hold of me for something."

Allie looked at the card. "Thanks. Now get going. You still look pale," she said in a worried voice.

"It was a great day, Alana. Best I've had in years," she said as she got in behind the wheel.

Allie heard the sincerity in her voice. Toni pulled away before Allie could say another word.

Chapter 6

"Did the Cubs win?" Paul asked as he buried his head in the refrigerator.

"Do you really need an answer to that?" Allie remembered the last part of her adventurous day. Allie was staring at nothing as Paul talked about work. She blinked a few times. "I'm sorry, honey, what?"

"I said it'll only be for a few days. Our client wants to show us the facility in New York. I'll leave Tuesday and be back Friday night," he said as he opened the bottle of beer.

"You never had to travel before."

"Well, it's part of owning your own company, and I can't very well say no," he said defensively. "Christ, Allie. It's my job."

"Whoa." Allie was shocked at his response. "I'm not complaining. I was just stating the obvious."

Allie watched as he paced back and forth; it reminded Allie of a caged tiger. "What it is? Why are you getting so irritated?"

Paul stood and ran his fingers through his thick graying hair. "I'm not angry."

Allie quickly walked over to him and put her hand on his shoulder. "Honey, please talk to me."

He avoided her gaze.

"What's wrong?"

Paul sighed and shook his head. "Nothing, really. I'm just tired, that's all." He smiled and kissed her lightly on the lips.

"C'mon, let's go to bed. You do look tired," she offered and turned off the lights. "You've been working too late at night. You need to relax."

As they climbed the stairs, Paul said nothing, but Allie could feel the tension emanating from his body. Once they were in bed, Allie lay on her side away from Paul. She felt the bed move as Paul slipped over behind her.

"Are you asleep?" he whispered and moved his hips against her.

Allie felt his arousal and desperately wanted to be aroused, as well. It had been so long since they'd had sex or any kind of intimacy. She knew it was bad timing, but Allie was trying to remember when the last time was. As Paul pulled her toward him, Allie looked up into his eyes.

"It's been a while." She really wanted to talk to him, to understand what was wrong. She reached up and touched his cheek. "What's wrong?"

"Oh, for chrissakes," he said angrily. "Can't we just have sex? Do we need to talk?"

"No, we don't need to talk, sweetie. I—"

Paul smothered her next words with a bruising kiss as he slipped between her legs. For the first time since they were married, Allie felt extremely uncomfortable. "Paul, no..."

He pulled back, breathing heavily and sporting a confused look. "What's the matter?"

"The matter?" Allie pushed him away. She struggled to get out from under him and the sheets. "I'd like to know that myself." She threw on her robe.

Paul ran his fingers through his hair and flopped on his back. "It's this menopause thing, right?"

For a moment, Allie was stunned, then she laughed. "Yes, that must be it. It's just me and my menopause." She angrily tied her robe and flipped on the light. Paul shielded his eyes and groaned. "What else could it possibly be?"

"Fine." Paul rolled over.

"Oh, no. Not this time, Paul Sanders." She walked over and turned on the light by his side of the bed.

"Damn it, Allie. I have to get some sleep."

"A second ago, you wanted sex."

"Yeah, well, that's not gonna happen now, is it?" he asked angrily and punched his pillow.

49

"It's been a long while since we've been intimate. And I'll be honest, this is the first time..." She stopped and sat on the edge of the bed. "I don't know. What's happening to us? It seems all you care about is your job and nothing else. Now out of the blue you want to have sex, and—"

Paul rose up on his elbow. "And you don't. Why? Look, I know I haven't been attentive and I've spent a good deal of time at work, but..."

Allie looked at him as he seemed to gather his thoughts. "But what? Please talk to me."

Paul looked into her eyes. Allie was shocked to see them misty. "I don't see the same look in your eyes. I haven't for a long time now."

Allie swallowed and said nothing, but she quickly stood and walked over to the window, her arms folded across her chest. Paul's next words tore through her heart.

"I know I'm a dope as you say, Al. I know. But a guy likes to feel his wife wants him, too."

After a moment of silence, Paul turned off the light. Allie looked out the window into the darkness, then walked down the hall to Jocelyn's room.

She lay in the bed staring at the ceiling. She closed her eyes, trying to remember the time when she and Paul were first married and happy. It was a hard vision to conjure. She remembered when they met in college. Paul Sanders walked right up to her while she sat on the park bench, sketching, and asked her out. That was it. They dated and married a year or so after graduation.

She remembered them making love in their first apartment and closed her eyes. But the vision faded quickly. Then suddenly, Toni O'Hara's face, with the goofy grin, popped into her head. Allie chuckled softly when she remembered how sick Toni had gotten from eating everything in sight at the Cubs game. And in the next instant, Allie felt a surge of arousal that came from nowhere. She clenched her legs together to alleviate the sudden incessant throbbing. Oh, God, don't do this to me, she begged and hugged her pillow—the urge to touch herself was overwhelming. In a moment, she gave into her arousal and slipped her fingers between her legs. With her eyes closed, she envisioned Toni's fingers on her, then her mouth. Oh, what am I doing? she asked herself.

The vision of Toni lying between her legs was overpowering. She felt her body begin to shake as it had never before. She felt strong but soft hands all over her, touching her, caressing her. Her fingers entwined in black, silvery hair as Toni's tongue danced through her.

"God Almighty!" she screamed into her pillow as her orgasm ripped through her.

She pulled her hand away before she gave herself a heart attack. Oh, my God, she thought as her heart beat rapidly. Guilt then washed through her. She had a husband down the hall, and she was sleeping in her daughter's bed. She had the best orgasm of her life, unfortunately self-induced, and she was fantasizing not about her husband, but about another woman.

She felt the same guilt nearly thirty years ago in college, before she met Paul. There was another who wanted Allie's affections, but it was a woman who proclaimed her love. Confused and totally out of her element, Allie ran; she ran from her kisses and words of love right into Paul Sanders's awaiting arms.

Allie shot out of bed and paced back and forth, much like Paul had earlier that night. Is that why she married Paul? Is that how it was? She sat on the edge of Jocelyn's bed and buried her face in her hands.

"God, what's happening?" she whispered. She sighed and crawled into bed, hugging the pillow.

The next morning, Allie whisked the sheets off the beds and tossed them with the other laundry, trying desperately to forget the entire night. Paul was already gone to work before Allie woke. She knew he wasn't much for talking, and he probably wouldn't want to revisit the topic again. She also knew it would be up to her if there were to be any resolution to what Paul had said and how he felt. She tried to dismiss the pained look on his face.

"It would have been much easier if he was being a jerk,"

Allie said as she finished making the bed. Out of the blue, she had a sudden craving for chocolate. "Now what? At least I'm not pregnant."

Though she smiled as she remembered being pregnant with Nick and Jocelyn. With Nick, she craved shrimp and pizza. It was hard to keep the weight off. With Jocelyn? She laughed openly as she took the laundry to the basement. It was macaroni and cheese; she couldn't get enough. With Jocelyn, it was downright impossible to keep her weight down.

After her birth, between running Nick to school, taking care of the house, and a newborn, Allie shed the weight quickly. Bounding up and down the stairs ten times a day helped.

She piled the sheets into the washing machine and flipped it on. Leaning against it, she wondered where Paul was all that time. Work, she thought, that's where.

Once the children were born, she supposed Paul figured his duty was his job. He fathered children, Allie took care of them. But she never had to insist or pester Paul when it came to family vacations. Paul might have been a workaholic, but he did find time for the kids.

Paul wasn't always into his job. In the beginning, before the children, he laughed and enjoyed life. Their sex life was...she stopped and thought about it. She tried to remember what their sex life was like. Certainly, they did it often. From the bedroom, to the shower, even in the kitchen. Paul was patient with her, as she never had been with anyone else. Once again, the memory of Sue's lips on her flashed through her mind. God, it'd been thirty years, and she and Paul certainly had shared more than the brief interlude of kisses she shared with another woman. Why then was it this memory that surfaced now?

Allie shook her head as she took the clothes out of the dryer and sorted them. Why did Paul marry me? she wondered as she folded the towels and stacked them in the basket. He took control, strategically organizing their dating, engagement, and finally their marriage. Allie was somewhat overwhelmed. She remembered talking to her father, who offered the typical advice: He's your man. Feed him, look nice for him, and keep the house and the kids. You're lucky to be married and not alone like your sister.

Her mother, on the other hand, told her: Don't lose yourself in anyone. Have babies, love them, and teach them to be self-reliant, kind, and compassionate. Her mother was a passionate Frenchwoman.

Allie was confused and allowed Paul to control everything. It wasn't until recently, maybe five years or so, that Allie took charge of the checkbook and the household finances. Paul had commandeered that, and it was Jocelyn, at the age of sixteen, who looked at Allie and said, "Mom, you're Dad's partner. What will you do if, God forbid, something happens to him? How will you take care of everything?"

Allie was ashamed of herself that Jocelyn had to tell her this. However, her shame quickly gave way to self-respect and taking care of the household account, which she wanted to know. Paul was surprised but gladly sat down one Saturday morning, and by late afternoon, Allie knew how to keep the household finances as well as Paul. For the first time in their marriage, Allie felt like a partner, not just a mother or housekeeper.

Speaking of housekeeping, she thought with a smile... She finished the laundry and hauled it upstairs. There were too many questions about their relationship lately. Too many questions Paul needed to answer—that they both needed to answer.

As she prepared dinner, she heard the back door open.

"Paul? In here, honey," she called out as she chopped the tomatoes. She looked up to see Paul walking into the kitchen, pulling at his tie.

"Hey, Al," he said as he looked at the mail.

"How was your day?" Allie opened the refrigerator.

"Fine, grab me a beer, will you? I need a shower." He tossed the mail on the table.

Allie handed him the icy bottle. "How about a nice warm bath?"

"Nah, a quick shower is all I need." He kissed her head. "Smells good, what's cookin'?"

"Pork roast," she said and walked back to the sink.

Over dinner, Allie looked down at Paul, who ate heartily and just about finished. "Can we talk about last night?"

Paul had his fork in his mouth; he raised an eyebrow and Allie had to laugh. He looked like Nick. After swallowing, Paul took a drink of wine. "Okay."

Allie heard the resigned tone and shook her head. "It's not an execution, Paul."

Paul chuckled grudgingly but said nothing, so Allie continued, "I've been thinking all day—"

"So unlike you," he mumbled into his glass.

Allie chose to ignore the sarcasm. "Did you mean it?"

Paul toyed with his wineglass and nodded. Allie waited and raised an eyebrow. "Care to elaborate?"

With that, the phone rang. Paul grinned and jumped up. Allie glared and drank her wine. In a minute, Paul came back and sat. "I have to call John at home in a few minutes. It's about the merger."

"What merger?" Allie asked.

Paul gave her an impatient look. "Does it matter?"

"Shouldn't it?" Allie retorted.

He tossed down his napkin, drained his wineglass, refilled it, and set the bottle down.

"Yes, sweetheart, I'd love another glass of wine," she said evenly. She reached over and picked up the bottle and poured herself another glass.

"Allie, you've never cared about my work. Why are you asking me now?"

"I always ask how your day is."

"That's just the obligatory question. You know what I mean. You know how much I love my company, but you never take an interest in it."

Allie felt her anger rising. "And you've cared greatly about my passion for my painting."

Paul started to argue and stopped. This was one thing about Paul—he admitted when he was wrong. He was not like other men, or women for that matter, who stubbornly and arrogantly kept up the argument, even though they were wrong. He took a long breath. "It seems perhaps we're both at fault," he said in a quiet voice.

Now it was Allie's turn. She had to agree. It was both of them. At that moment, she and Paul seemed so far apart.

"You know. The children are gone. It's just you and me now, sweetie. We need to find out what we want out of life."

As Paul opened his mouth, his cell phone went off. "I gotta take this." He quickly stood and walked out as he answered the call and Allie's question, as well.

Allie took a deep, resigned breath and looked around the dining room. "Well, that went well. Dinner was excellent, Allie. Thank you, Paul, I love to cook, you know, and I know a pork roast is one of your favorite meals." She raised her glass to the vacated seat. "I aim to please!"

Later that night, Allie was already in bed when she heard Paul come up from the office. She heard the familiar sounds of him getting ready for bed. First, his wristwatch made a noisy clang on the dresser. Then his shoes made a thud as they hit the floor. His slacks and shirt were next. She heard the muffled noise of them hitting the chair next to the bed as he made his way to the bathroom. Upon return, he sat on the edge of the bed and Allie shook her head. Okay, now the alarm clock.

He set the clock with its little beeps and clicks. Setting it precisely for six thirty-five, not six thirty, but six thirty-five on the dot. And does he wake up at precisely six thirty-five? No, he's up at six twenty and goes into the shower. The damned thing goes off, and I have to jump and turn it off, she thought.

Paul slid into bed and Allie felt him get settled and heard the sigh. In a matter of minutes, she heard the snoring.

After an hour of staring at the ceiling, she got out of bed and slipped into her robe. She walked downstairs and put the kettle on for tea. As it started whistling, she made a cup of strong tea and grabbed her sketchpad and pencil.

She sat at the kitchen table and stared absently drawing, something she'd always done that relaxed her. She smiled as she drew Nick's face and Jocelyn's. She didn't even realize what she had done until she was finished. She blinked and looked at the pad. She had drawn Toni O'Hara's smiling face, as well. She smiled and drank her tea as she looked at the drawing. After a few minutes of sketching, she held the drawing at arm's length.

The three faces smiled back at her. She remembered Nick in his youth when he tried to fly off the couch. Well, he was Superman, after all. Unfortunately, Superman required ten stitches. Jocelyn? Well, she tried to nurse Mr. Bear back to health after he fell off his bike. Allie knew then her only daughter would go into the medical field. She was due to graduate next spring with a degree in nursing.

She then looked at Toni and laughed out loud when she remembered how sick she made herself at the Cubs game. What a nut, she thought. She also tried to ignore her fantasy about her. She took the drawing and carefully placed it deep between the sheets of the pad for safekeeping.

Chapter 7

"Frank Sinatra or Nat King Cole?" Allie asked.

"Frank Sinatra."

"Okay. Ella Fitzgerald or Judy Garland?"

"Doris Day."

Toni didn't notice the scathing glance from across the table. She was fighting with the shell on the Dungeness crab. The crab was winning.

"Doris Day was not an option," Allie reminded her as she easily cracked open the shell.

This irked Toni to no end as she frowned childishly and continued to struggle. "Doris Day is always an option," Toni countered seriously as she watched Allie pull out the delectable morsel, dipping it in the hot melted butter. Allie rolled her eyes dramatically as if savoring the taste. Toni pouted as she watched.

Allie smiled and gave her a smug grin. "Need some help?"

Toni narrowed her eyes at her. "No, I don't," she said with maniacal glee and raised the small wooden hammer. "I'll do this my way."

Allie visualized the crab flying all over the restaurant. "Give me that!"

Toni obliged and handed over the murder weapon.

"Here, you baby." She switched plates with Toni, who grinned happily. Allie placed the plate of crab in front of her, free of shells.

Toni ate her fill of crab and patted her stomach. The waiter brought out the key lime pie, and she rubbed her hands together; she dug into the pie with gusto.

"So, no date tonight, Inspector O'Hara?" Allie asked as she ate her dessert.

"Nope," she said between mouthfuls. "I'm free as a bird." She finished her pie, then watched Allie eating hers. "No husband tonight?"

"Nope. Paul is in New York. I will never eat a full meal when I'm with you," she said evenly and pushed the pie in front of Toni. "You're good for my waistline."

"Shut up about your waistline, you look fantastic," Toni said and dug in.

Allie took the opportunity and watched her. Toni O'Hara was in tremendous shape. Tall and lanky with the longest legs Allie had seen. She smiled remembering her father's words. "She has legs that go all the way to the floor," he would joke about Allie's mother, who was tall like Toni. Toni wore no jewelry to speak of, just a small silver chain with a Celtic cross. A simple watch and no rings. Allie knew Toni was not a fashion hound by any stretch of the imagination.

When asked to this expensive restaurant, Allie took all day trying to figure out what to wear. She smirked now, looking at Toni devouring the key lime pie. She wore a white T-shirt under a black v-neck sweater with the sleeves, as usual, pushed up nearly to her elbows. Her silvery-streaked raven hair, all over as usual, looked as if she used her fingers for a comb. She wore a pair of black jeans and cowboy boots. Allie eyed the black leather jacket. Her mind went back to earlier in the evening when Toni came to pick her up. Allie had watched her come up the front walk and had to admit the woman looked sexy in black. Sexy? Allie asked herself.

"*Hello.*" Toni waved a hand in front of her face.

Allie blinked. "I'm sorry, what were you saying?"

"I asked you, Ella or Judy?"

"Oh, Ella Fitzgerald," she said obediently and drank her coffee. "So tell me the truth. Doris Day because of her voice or..."

Toni wriggled her eyebrows, answering her question. Allie laughed and shook her head. "So." Allie dug the crab out of the shell and dipped it into the butter.

"So buttons," Toni said, doing the same.

"Tell me about your past loves."

Toni looked up and sported an amused grin. "No."

Allie laughed outright. "Why not? You know about mine. As meager as it is."

Toni sat back and took a drink of wine. "I've sown my oats, let's leave it at that."

Hearing the playful tone, Allie took that as her cue to continue their banter. "I'm sure you have exploits—"

"Yes."

"And you're not going to tell me? And I thought we were friends. C'mon. Have you ever been in love?" Her grin spread across her face as she looked at Toni, who immediately stopped the banter. All at once, Allie felt as though she was being intrusive.

"Sure," Toni said softly. "I'm just like anyone else. I've been in love."

Allie didn't know what to say to the pensive woman sitting across from her. Toni stared at her wineglass, seemingly lost in her past. Nice going, Sanders, Allie thought.

Toni looked up then and smiled sadly. "But I fell in love with a snake that bit me in the asp."

Allie blinked for a moment, then saw the crooked grin and laughed. "You are an asp."

"Thank you." Toni raised her glass to Allie's.

After dinner, they walked along Michigan Avenue, and while Alana window-shopped, Toni had her hands in her pockets not saying much. She liked the comfortable silence she shared with Alana. She didn't feel as though she had to make conversation or flirt or try to impress her. She liked this "friendship" thing they had going. Lost in her musing, she realized she was walking alone. She stopped and looked back at Alana, who was gazing in a store window.

"Whatcha lookin' at?" Toni ambled back and stood next to Alana as she looked into the art gallery. Though closed, there was a billboard stating the Van Gogh exhibit that week. "Ah, art. I should have known," Toni said affectionately.

Alana chuckled and started walking again. "It's a beautiful night, isn't it?"

Toni had to agree, it was a cool autumn night.

"Look at that moon," Alana sighed. The full harvest moon was rising between the tall Chicago buildings. "I can barely see it for the high-rises."

Toni glanced around. "Come with me." She walked to the curb, let out a shrill whistle, and hailed a cab.

"What are you doing?"

"You'll see," Toni said with a childlike giggle and pushed her into the cab.

The cab let them off, and they walked down Navy Pier to its end. Lake Michigan spread out before them as the moonbeams rested on the waves.

"You have a romantic soul," Alana said as she looked out over the lake. "I can't believe you have no one in your life."

Toni turned to her. "Hey, I have plenty..." She noticed the motherly glare.

"Someone to tell your troubles to, not just share a bed," she scolded gently.

Toni took a deep breath and said nothing. There was a moment of silence. "I have you," she said in a low soft voice. "You're probably my best friend. I'm fifty and I can honestly say I've never felt more at ease with anyone."

Alana smiled slightly. "I feel the same way. I'm glad we're friends, true friends."

Toni nodded and turned her attention back to the moonlit lake. They stood in silence for a moment.

"But you are an asp."

Toni pulled Alana away from the pier. "C'mon, let's get you home before you hurt yourself."

The next day, Allie had just finished the last class of the day when her cell phone went off. She smiled when she looked at the caller ID.

"Hello, schoolmarm," Toni drawled into the phone.

Allie laughed, juggling her phone as she walked through the school parking lot. "Hi. What's up?"

"Well, I know you said your husband was out of town, and last night was fun. I thought if you weren't doing anything, well, maybe..."

"I've just finished my day. What did you have in mind?"

"How soon can you be ready?"

Allie stopped in the middle of the parking lot. "I'm in the school parking lot. Ready for what?" she asked tentatively and heard the laughter on the other end.

"Just be ready by five. And wear something like you had on last night."

"What?" She looked at the phone. "Toni, what are you hatching in that brain?"

Toni laughed again. "Nothing. Just be ready by five. See ya," she said and hung up.

Allie was ready by the appointed time. "Okay, where are you taking me?" Allie asked as Toni drove into the city. She looked... well, she looked good, Allie thought.

Toni wore a pair of tan slacks and deck shoes, no socks. A navy blue cotton shirt, sleeves rolled up, of course, neatly tucked into the belted slacks. She peered at Allie over her sunglasses.

"It's a surprise," she said in that low voice.

Allie tried to ignore the hammering, which started again.

Toni pulled onto Michigan Avenue, and Allie noticed she stopped by a crowd that had gathered. Toni pulled up sporting a grin. She hopped out and a valet opened Allie's door. She tossed her keys to the young man. "I know the mileage, so no joy riding," she said seriously and slipped the valet a folded bill. He grinned and winked.

Allie was just looking around, saying nothing. Then it dawned on her. She looked at her grinning friend.

"Surprise!"

"Toni, we're going to the exhibit?"

"Yep. Just so happens, I know the owner of this gallery. So when you stopped here last night, I had the idea. I've never been to an exhibit. Jane assured me this was going to be a big one," she said with a shrug.

She saw the amazed look on Allie's face as they made their way inside. Toni had to admit she didn't have a clue about art. She picked up two glasses of champagne and handed one to Allie.

"Free drinks and eats," she exclaimed happily.

"Now I know why you came." Allie sipped the bubbly spirits.

Toni's hearty laugh echoed throughout the hall. She cringed as heads turned. "Sorry," she whispered.

"Well, well," a woman's voice called out behind them.

Allie was about to turn when she noticed Toni's face pale dramatically. She said nothing as she watched the very elegant woman saunter toward them.

"Gina, what a surprise," Toni said, gulping her champagne.

"I could say the same for you. How are you, Toni?"

Allie took a step back and watched. Toni looked sad, hurt, and pissed all at once. The transformation was astounding. Gina grinned like a cat as she took the glass of champagne out of Toni's hand and took a drink. Allie raised an eyebrow watching the arrogant exchange. This woman then handed the fluted glass back to Toni and kissed her cheek.

"It's been a long time." Gina wiped the lipstick off Toni's cheek with her fingertips.

"Not long enough," Toni said and pulled back.

Allie knew Toni tried to sound light and uncaring, but her voice was anything but.

Gina laughed slightly as she ran her fingers through her blond hair. Allie noticed the dazzling bling—the woman had rings, bracelets, and a dress Allie knew did not come off the rack at Marshalls.

"Don't be cross, Toni. I never expected to see *you* at an art exhibit."

Allie raised an eyebrow and watched as Toni turned a nice shade of crimson and avoided her curious glance.

Gina gazed at Allie with mild amusement. "You must have some hold on her." She looked Allie in the eye.

Allie raised the other eyebrow and sported a smug grin. "No, not really. I like art, and Toni was kind enough to bring me."

Gina pasted on a smile and nodded.

"Gina, this is Alana. Alana, Gina is an old friend," Toni said.

Gina held a limp hand out to Allie. "Don't be modest, dear. I never could get Toni out of bed long enough to drag her to an art gallery," Gina said with a sly grin and looked at Toni.

Toni gulped down her glass of champagne and took another off the tray as the waiter walked by.

"Are you bragging or complaining?" Allie asked.

Gina's smile turned into an evil glare. She reminded Allie of Cruella DeVil; she just smiled sweetly.

Toni sputtered and choked on her champagne. "Well, this was fun. Like slamming my head in a car door. We'll have to do this again real soon. Goodbye, Gina," Toni said and steered Allie away.

"It was a pleasure, Gina," Allie said over her shoulder.

Toni laughed softly as they made their way into the exhibit. "Sorry about that."

Allie shrugged. "It's none of my business. You're not responsible for the actions of former bed partners—of which you have many, I'm sure."

Allie hoped Toni knew she intended that to be a joke. However, when an awkward silence followed, Allie knew she had been judgmental. "God, I'm sorry. I have no right to make any comments about your life," she said, completely apologetic.

"Forget it. I have no secrets with you. Like I said last night. I've sown my share of wild oats. You were bound to meet one sooner or later."

Allie reached over and placed her hand on her forearm. "You owe me no explanations. You're a grown woman with a healthy sexual appetite. There's nothing wrong with that."

As they walked through the art gallery, Allie stole a glance at Toni's somber face. "Was she the snake?"

Toni grinned reluctantly and nodded. Allie could feel the sadness emanating from Toni's body. She easily wrapped her hand around Toni's forearm. "Well, let's forget her. Let me tell you about Vincent," Allie said lightly, easing the tension.

"Okay, schoolmarm. I'm all ears," she said with a smirk. "Get it? Van Gogh, all ears?"

"Yes, I get it, O'Hara." Allie grabbed two glasses of champagne. "Here, you need this." She looked around. "Now where is the guy with the tray of hors d'oeuvres? You look like you're going to keel over from hunger."

The evening was delightful. Occasionally, Allie would find Toni watching her while she talked with a few people. "Are you bored? We can leave."

"Are you kidding? You look too happy talking about God-knows-what. You go be artsy. I'm very content watching you have fun, as long as I..." Toni stopped the server with the champagne tray and the server with the hors d'oeuvres.

After the exhibition, Toni glanced at Allie now and then as they walked side by side down Michigan Avenue.

"Thank you, Toni. That was a wonderful evening. It was a thoughtful thing you did," Allie said as they strolled down the avenue.

"My pleasure. I know you love art. However, the night is not over, Mrs. Sanders." Toni pulled Allie into a bistro.

The restaurant was cozy and warm as they sat at a table by the window. "So when does Paul get back from—New York was it?" Toni asked as she ate the decadent chocolate cake.

"Tomorrow," Allie said. "And I feel guilty."

"Why? You're not doing anything wrong."

"I know. I feel guilty I haven't really thought about Paul for two days. But he had to see some big client. I don't know."

Toni had the fork in her mouth and took it out slowly.

"He's been working so much lately. I'm afraid he'll have a stroke. He comes home late, so tired sometimes."

She watched Toni, who shrugged but said nothing.

"You're trying to be nice and not tell me you hear the irritation in my voice. And you're hesitant to ask because you're not sure if you wanted to get into a discussion about my marriage." Allie looked at Toni. "Right?"

Toni laughed. "Right. But I am here for you. So say whatever you like. He's trying to make a good life for you."

Allie groaned loudly. "We have a good life. We have two kids that we put through college, who are normal well-adjusted people, both of whom I'm extremely proud. We have a nice house, a nice car, a nice nest egg, a nonexistent sex life..."

Toni's eyes widened, her fork still in her mouth.

Allie gazed out the window, then took a deep breath of resignation, and looked at Toni. "You look like an owl with a fork in its mouth." All of a sudden, Allie started to laugh. "You should see your face."

Toni now started chuckling. Soon, both women tried to contain their laughter. "Well, you shocked the shit out of me, woman." Toni wheezed as she dried her eyes.

Allie banged on the table in a fit of laughter. In a few moments, the wave of hysteria died. Allie dried her eyes. "God, that felt good. Thank you."

"You're welcome. Laughter is good for the soul," she agreed. "Can I finish my cake now?"

"Yes, you may." Allie sighed happily and sat back.

Toni ate the remainder of her dessert in silence, stealing a glance at Allie as she stared out the window once again. "Whatcha thinking about?" she asked softly as she drank her coffee.

"Oh, I don't know," Allie said in a pensive voice. "When you were young, did you ever think what you'd be doing when you were fifty?"

"Yep. I thought I'd be dead."

Allie laughed and stirred her coffee. "I'm serious."

"So am I," Toni said. "I never thought I'd live to be fifty. As a kid, when my folks were fifty, I thought they were so old. I never thought I'd be *that* old."

Allie nodded in agreement. "And look at us now."

"No shit. We're just two old fogies, schoolmarm," Toni said with a wide grin. "I feel like it in the morning, let me tell you."

"Too much flag football?" Allie asked with a teasing grin.

"No, smart ass. Fighting too many fires." Toni stared at her coffee cup.

"Were you ever hurt?" Allie quelled the urge to reach over and brush the wayward lock of hair off her brow.

"I almost quit the department about eight years ago. I was in a relationship, and we used to argue about me being a firefighter. And to answer your question. Yes, the snake woman you met."

"Was it too dangerous a job for her?" Allie prodded.

Toni let out a rude snort. "Gina was not worried about my health. Her worries were more along the lines of appearance. Being a woman and a firefighter didn't look good to her family and friends."

"I don't get it."

Toni laughed quietly. "Gina came from money, scads of money. Tons of money. So much money—"

"Cut to the chase, O'Hara," Allie said dryly.

Toni laughed once again. "It was not refined. She wanted me to quit."

Allie gaped at her. "And you thought about it?"

"God no, but it was weighing heavily on my mind, and I wasn't focused. That's not good when fighting fires. I paid for it," Toni said with a shrug.

"How bad?" Allie asked. For some reason, seeing Toni's strong body in pain made her stomach clench.

"I zigged when I should have zagged," Toni said with a grin. She stopped when she saw the serious look on Allie's face. "I took a wrong turn on a stairwell and fell through to the first floor. Broke a leg, an ankle, a few ribs, and my wrist." She stopped and shrugged. "You see, Alana, a fire is a living thing. And when you don't give it the respect it deserves, it will let you know. But I'm fine now. Bones heal."

"What happened to Gina?" Allie drank her coffee.

"She never…"

"Never what?" Allie asked softly.

Toni looked into her eyes and smiled sadly. "She never came to visit me in the hospital. I was in for two weeks, then home convalescing for a few more. I'm not a baby, and I don't need to be taken care of, but shit…" She shrugged. "Anyway, when I told her I wasn't going to quit, she had enough."

"She didn't deserve you."

"Thanks, but I can be a pain in the arse. Come on, I'll take you home before I spill my stupid guts about my entire life." Toni hailed the waiter.

"Would that be so bad?" Allie asked.

"Yes," Toni assured her with a laugh and pulled Allie out of her seat. "Besides, I have a busy day tomorrow and a date tomorrow night, so I need my rest."

Allie stopped and looked up at the laughing gray eyes but said nothing. Toni cocked her head. "What?"

"Nothing. Who's the lucky woman?" she asked as they walked to the car.

"Remember Miss Flag Football on Saturday?" Toni wriggled her eyebrows.

"The prepubescent blonde?"

Toni laughed heartily. "I'll have to remember that one. Yes, her. So you see where I need my sleep?"

Allie laughed along and slipped into the car. "Don't forget the Geritol."

Chapter 8

Toni tried to peel Carol off her body. "Carol, Carol, I need to breathe, sweetie," she said in a coarse voice.

Carol lifted her lips from Toni's and pulled back, grinning. She then kissed Toni's soft firm breast, her teeth raking across the hard nipple.

"Ahh!" Toni cried out as Carol's fingers traveled south.

Toni instinctively parted her legs as Carol quickly entered her. Toni arched her back in surprise, her hips moving in rhythm. She sighed and closed her eyes. Suddenly, once again, and for the umpteenth time in the past few weeks, Alana's face crowded her mind. Damn it. Go away, she begged inwardly.

It was no use. As she neared orgasm, Alana was the one making love to her—it was Alana's face she saw. Alana's body she felt pressing close to her.

"Yes!" Toni cried out as her body shuddered. She arched her back and cried out, "God, Alana!"

Well, that went well, Toni thought now as she remembered her blunder. Never had she seen a woman so angry. Toni O'Hara had been slugged before for various reasons. Never had anyone hit her square in the face like Carol had that morning. She gingerly felt her jaw, knowing the bruise was starting.

"I think she loosened a tooth." She shook her head. She stood on her fourth-floor deck, overlooking the Chicago lakefront. I have the best orgasm I've ever had, she thought, and I have to be fantasizing about a married woman and a good friend. She let out a dejected sigh as she drank her coffee.

To get her mind off her debacle, Toni thought of the upcoming holidays and her siblings, Matt and Fran. She grinned and grabbed her cell. She'd call her younger brother first.

"Hey, sis."

Toni could hear the smile in his voice and grinned. "Hey, Matt. How goes it?"

"It goes well. If it would stop raining."

"Hey, nobody twisted your arm to move to Seattle, pal. Well, maybe Sheila's dad."

Matt laughed and agreed. "The money was too good. You know that. Besides, it's better than a Chicago winter. So how are you? How's the fire inspecting business?"

"It's good, unfortunately. Less wear and tear on my body, that's for sure. So what are you and Sheila doing for the holidays? I haven't seen you or our sister in three years. I thought—"

"I'd love to, but I really can't get away this season. I'll be working the whole week of Thanksgiving, and at Christmas, we're going to Florida with Sheila's parents."

Toni smiled sadly. She couldn't blame Matt. Since their mother died four years before, Toni tried to keep all of them together. However, she couldn't blame them for wanting their own lives. Neither younger sibling loved Chicago as Toni did. When Matt married three years earlier, his father-in-law offered him a great job in rain-soaked Seattle. The same happened with Fran, but she wound up in Boston with her husband, Lou. Toni was happy for them; she missed them but couldn't deny their happiness. Their childhood wasn't so happy, and they deserved their own lives.

"Florida? Good for you, sun and beaches."

"Yep, two weeks of nothing to do. We'll be out there for New Year's, too."

Toni fought the lump she felt in her throat. "Well, you have a great time. You deserve it."

"Thanks. Hey, what are you going to do?"

"Oh, I'm spending the holidays with Kevin."

"Good. Well, I gotta get going…"

"Sure, sure, Matt. Give Sheila my love."

"Will do. We really have to get together soon. I miss you."

"Miss you, too."

"I'll see ya."

"I love you."

He had already disconnected.

Toni called Fran but got pretty much the same result. She was having her in-laws over for Thanksgiving, then going to her sister-in-law's for Christmas. Toni set the phone down and got a cup of coffee that she took onto the deck. She blew at the steamy cup and shivered, pulling the big sweater around her. As she gazed at Chicago's skyline and the lake, not surprisingly, she felt lonely. She loved the holidays, and she really thought this year, Fran and Matt might be able to come home. The fact that neither invited her out there was something that Toni put in the back of her mind.

They needed their lives away from Chicago to feel normal. Toni saw that and honestly couldn't blame them. They were young and only caught the tail end of their father's abuse. Toni, however, caught the brunt and gladly took it. She would rather he beat her than her mother or the younger ones. God, how she hated him. And, God forgive her, how glad she was that he was dead.

She grabbed her keys, feeling restless, as she always did after thinking about her father, and headed out. She walked the neighborhood and came to the familiar bakery. Taking a deep happy breath, the smell of freshly baked goods filled her senses. The wonderful sound of the tinkling bell brought Lidia Walinski through the swinging door.

"Hi, Mrs. W.," Toni said with a grin.

Lidia wiped the flour off her hands and smiled. "Antonia. What brings you down here this time of day, hmm?"

Toni shrugged. "I dunno. Just walking, I guess."

The old Polish woman gave Toni a skeptical look. "Sit, I get you something." She gently pushed Toni into the nearest chair, then disappeared into the kitchen.

Toni glanced around the bakery and smiled. She loved it here. She felt safe, content. This shop was a constant. "Ya know, Mrs. W.," she called out as she looked around, "you should make this into a coffee shop. Sell those smoothies and juice and put more tables in here. You'd get more of the younger crowd."

"You and your coffee houses. I am too old to be changing." Lidia walked up to the table with a small plate.

"Never too old to change, Mrs. W. A few tables here, a nice little coffee bar in the corner. It could work." Toni licked her lips. "Kolachkies."

"Not kolachkies," Lidia mimicked her. "You Americans. It's kolachky."

"Tomato, tomahto. Are they apricot?" Toni asked with glee.

Lidia nodded. "Yes, just for you. And Kevin."

Toni had the cookie in her mouth as she gave her a curious look. "Kevin, is it?"

Lidia grinned and nodded. "He came by last month to see if I was all right."

Toni swallowed and grinned sheepishly. "Really?"

"Yes. It seems he got the idea that Mr. Su down the street had a window broken, and he was worried. I wonder where he got that idea."

Toni shrugged and continued eating. "He was worried about you. So? What's happening?"

"Nothing. We went out for dinner and a movie."

Toni was wild-eyed. "Really? That's good?"

"That's very goot. Now eat." She reached over and pinched Toni's cheek. "You big lovable buttinski." She gave her cheek a playful slap.

Toni grimaced and flexed her jaw.

"What are you doing for Thanksgiving?" Lidia asked quietly.

Again, Toni shrugged.

"Have you talked to Matt and Fran?"

Toni nodded as she ate. "They got plans."

Lidia leaned in. "They have not invited you yet?"

"They're so busy, Mrs. W."

"Do me one favor?"

Toni noticed the tentative posture as she wiped the powdered sugar off her mouth. "Sure."

"I will be going to my sister's for the holiday. Would you see that Kevin…?" she asked as she dusted off her apron.

Toni grinned. "Of course, I will. I think he might be with his brother, but don't worry. He won't be alone for the holidays."

"And neither will you. Thank you, Antonia. You make me feel much better for leaving."

After her fill of cookies and coffee, Toni promised once again to take care of Kevin while Lidia was gone.

"And who is taking care of you?" Lidia asked with a stern look.

Toni felt her bruised jaw and chuckled. "Right now, I'm better off on my own. It's much safer that way. I think I'll head over to my office. I've got a ton of paperwork I'd like to get off my damned desk before the holidays. If you see Kevin, tell him I'm there. See ya, Mrs. W. And thanks."

Toni sat in her office shuffling papers. "God, I hate paperwork. It was much more fun fighting fires. Hmm. I'd like to torch this desk."

As she sifted through the tidal wave of papers, her mind wandered to Alana. She wondered what she was doing. She'd been to the museum a few times and thought stupidly Alana would stop by. Toni hoped everything was all right between Alana and Paul. Although, Toni had no room to talk. Her jaw still hurt from the right cross from Carol. She still couldn't believe she was fantasizing about Alana. Actually, she could believe it; it was just such a bad idea.

With that, her phone rang. "Inspector O'Hara." For an instant, there was nothing. Then the familiar voice called out, and Toni smiled instantly.

"H-hi. It's—"

"Alana? Hell, how are you?" Toni leaned forward in her chair, knocking over the cold cup of coffee. "Shit…" she cursed as she scrambled.

"Am I interrupting?"

"No, no. I spilled my coffee," she explained with a chuckle.

She heard Alana laugh quietly. "How are you?"

"Fine, fine. How are you? How's Claude?" Toni asked as she mopped up her mess. She tossed the coffee-saturated paper towel at the wastebasket and missed. As she moved to pick it up, she nearly pulled the phone cord out of the wall.

"He's fine."

"I-I went to visit him a couple times," Toni said, struggling with the wastebasket.

"You did?"

Toni heard the smile in Alana's voice and grinned. She sat back in her chair and rocked. "He asked about you, thought you'd be by for a visit." Toni played with the phone cord. She heard Alana's soft laughter.

"Claude misses me?"

"Yes. The poor man is high-maintenance." Toni chuckled.

"I sincerely doubt that. Claude strikes me as a self-sufficient, smart, savvy…guy," Alana said.

"So enough about Claude. To what do I owe the honor of your call?"

"Well, I thought…well, I have to call the kids, but I'm sure they're coming in for Thanksgiving, and I'm throwing a little party on that Wednesday night. Just family and a few friends, and I thought if you weren't busy, perhaps you'd like to stop by."

Toni immediately sprang forward in her chair but didn't answer.

"I know you must be busy, so if…"

"I'd love to. What time?" Toni asked quickly. She thought she heard a sigh of relief.

"How about seven? Don't bring a thing. I'll have everything," she assured her. "You can bring a date if you like. Just not the snake woman."

Toni laughed at the idea. "Definitely. Okay. Thanks, Alana. Thanks for thinking of me."

There was another pause. "Is everything okay, Toni?"

"Right as rain. See you in a couple of weeks…Wednesday," she said and rang off.

Toni sat back as she gently set the phone down. She looked up to see Kevin standing in the doorway. "Hey, Kevin," she said quietly as he walked into her office and sat down.

"Hey. What are your plans for Thanksgiving? Are Fran and

Matt coming in?" he asked. "Hmm. I can tell the answer by the look on your face."

"You great mind reader. But you're right. They already have plans. Fran's in-laws are coming in, and Matt's working and can't get away, but he's taking Sheila to Florida for Christmas." She leafed through her files.

Kevin nodded. "Well, you'll just have to make dinner for me then."

Toni shot a curious look his way. "What about your brother?"

"Nope, he decided to go up to his sister-in-law's in Wisconsin. They asked me to go along, but I hate to travel. So I thought we'd have something together unless you got something going."

Toni smiled. "No. With Fran and Matt busy…well, hell, you can't be alone on Thanksgiving," she said. "Besides, a certain baker is worried about you."

Kevin's grin spread across his face. "Oh, yeah?"

"Quit grinning, you look like a pumpkin."

"You make a list. I'll buy the food, you cook."

"It's a deal."

It might be a good holiday after all, she thought. Toni knew how much Alana loved her children, so she hoped Alana's kids were coming home for the holidays. She actually looked forward to meeting Alana's family. This should prove interesting, she thought, and started on her list.

Chapter 9

Allie smiled at the idea of Toni coming to her home for a holiday party. As she dialed the number, she continued smiling when she heard Jocelyn's happy voice.

"Hi, Mom. Of course, I'll be home for Thanksgiving. I'm flying in Wednesday." Jocelyn squealed with delight. "But I do have a favor. If you can't, that's fine. It's just that Marcie isn't going home for Thanksgiving and—"

"Of course, you can bring her. I remember Marcie." Allie was elated. "Honey, I'm so happy. What time? Are you flying into O'Hara?"

Jocelyn laughed. "No, but we're flying into O'Hare."

Allie pulled the phone away from her ear and looked at it. "What did I say?"

"You said O'Hara." Jocelyn was still laughing.

Allie looked to the heavens, feeling her face redden, but she laughed along. "And no, I haven't started on the holiday punch."

"You'd better wait for me. I'll be there at five in the evening. I can't wait to see you. It's been four months! How's Dad?" Jocelyn asked quickly.

There was a moment's hesitation. Paul and she had not been so talkative since their dinner discussion the previous month.

"Mom? Is everything okay?"

"Yes, honey. It's fine."

"You don't sound sure." Jocelyn was silent for a moment. "Mom..."

"What, sweetie?"

"Can I say something? I-I don't mean to bring anything up on the holidays…"

"You know you can say anything to me. You and I have always been open. What's on your mind?"

"I don't know when this happened, but I've noticed a change in Dad and you. Maybe I'm reading too much into things. And I don't…I just see you both changing. I can't put my finger on it. I'm sorry to bring up something like this right before the holidays, but it's been in the back of my mind for so long now."

Jocelyn's observation stunned Allie.

"Mom?"

"Oh, sorry, sweetie. And don't worry about anything. Maybe your father and I are just getting to know each other all over again. We don't have you and Nick to take care of now…" She wasn't sure what else to say. "Well, enough of this kind of talk. We'll talk about it—"

"Over a cup of hot chocolate."

Allie smiled as the tears welled in her eyes. "You remember," she whispered.

"Of course I do. I was seven, and John Downing broke my heart." Jocelyn stopped; Allie heard her sniff. "Any problem can be solved through talking and a good cup of cocoa. That's what you always said."

Allie wished it were that easy now.

"So is Dad still working like a jackass?"

Allie raised both eyebrows. "Jocelyn Celeste, he is still your father."

"C'mon. Tell me."

"Yes, but not like a jackass. We'll pick you up Wednesday. I love you."

"I love you, too. Quit crying," she said and hung up.

Allie rubbed her hands together in anticipation. "Next, Nick."

"Can you come, Nick?" Allie asked hopefully. She heard his hesitation and the shuffling of papers.

"I have a ton of work. I don't know if I'll be able to get away," he said honestly.

Allie shook her head. "Listen to me. I love you very much, but if you become a workaholic like your father, I'll shoot you," she said in a firm quiet voice.

"Mom…" he said in a warning chuckle.

"I'm serious. You're young and alive. If you choose this life now, you'll never get out from under it. Money is not the answer. Life and love is, please remember that, sweetheart."

"You sound like the ghost of Christmas Past," he said affectionately.

Allie laughed along with him. The laughter died down, and Nick cleared his throat.

"Is everything okay, Mom?"

Allie now hesitated for a moment. First Jocelyn, now Nick. She hoped this was not going to be the topic of conversation for the holidays.

"It's not, is it? What's he doing? Working like a fiend?"

"Now you sound like Jocelyn."

"How is Jossie?"

"If you come for Thanksgiving, you'd know," she countered and smiled at the sound of Nick's laughter.

"Okay, I give. I'll be there. I'll call you with the flight information," he said, laughing. "Mom?"

"Yes, sweetie?"

"I love you, you know," he said quietly.

Tears sprang into her green eyes. "I love you, too. It's the most important thing, sweetheart."

"I know. I'll call you later in the week. Bye..."

Allie hung up and smiled at the phone. Though she knew they were grown and had their own lives, she adored the fact that her children wanted to come home.

Two weeks went by much too quickly for Allie. *What was I thinking? Having a party and picking up the kids on the same day?* She struggled with the groceries, letting out a deep groan as she set the last bag on the counter.

Thirty minutes later, she had everything put away and started on the house. She flipped on her music and grinned wildly as her song rang out. *Beyond the blue horizon, waits a beautiful day...*

Two hours later, she was done—exhausted but done. Autumn decorations filled each room. Allie had placed the last of them out when Paul walked in the door.

"Hey, honey, just in time. I need help with the tablecloth," she said and kissed him.

"Hi. God, I'm tired. What time are the kids getting in?" He set down his briefcase.

"Well, you're elected to pick them up. Gratefully, your intelligent son got a flight that gets in nearly the same time as Jocelyn's. So you have just enough time to jump in the shower and head to O'Hara...O'Hare," she said, shaking her head. She heard the groan. "C'mon now, honey, it's Thanksgiving. You remember we're having a party tonight, right?"

"Yes, I remember."

Allie watched him curiously. She walked over and felt his forehead. "Are you feeling all right?"

He quickly took her hand away. "I'm fine. I've been working all day, and I don't relish driving in this sleet to the airport." He walked upstairs.

Allie felt the air leaking out of her holiday balloon when the phone rang. "Hello?" she said with a heavy sigh.

"Good grief. Who died?" Vicky's voice rang out.

Allie laughed. "Sorry."

"What time does this clambake start?"

"Anytime after seven and the kids will be home, if Paul decides to join the living and pick them up." She tried not to sound completely irritated. "Are you bringing the kids?" Allie asked as she took the lace tablecloth out of the drawer.

"That depends on who else is going to be at this party," Vicky said evasively.

Allie stopped and looked to the heavens. "Get a sitter."

She heard Vicky chuckle on the other end. "You invited Inspector O'Hara...good! See you at seven-ish," Vicky said and hung up.

"She is a lunatic," Allie conceded and set the phone on the desk.

Allie shook her head as she watched Paul walk out as if he were going to the gallows when he grudgingly left to pick up Nick and Jocelyn.

An hour or so later, Allie heard Jocelyn calling her from the living room. "My God, that was fast." Allie ran out from the kitchen as her children hugged the life out of her. She was grateful to see Paul smiling as he watched. Jocelyn's friend Marcie stood behind them.

"God, you two feel so good. How was the flight?"

Jocelyn nodded happily. "Fine. It only took two hours, and that's even stopping in Milwaukee."

Allie grinned as she watched Jocelyn's blue eyes dance with happiness. "Are you taller? Your hair seems lighter, and you've cut it. I love it."

Jocelyn ran her fingers through her hair. "I did cut it, but I'm gonna let it grow back."

"Hey, Mom. I missed you," Nick said.

"Oh, I've missed you, too." She looked at Nick, who was hanging up their coats. He looked the same, more like his father. His soft hazel eyes smiled as he kissed her.

"Man, what smells so good?"

"I'm making a few things for the party. Vicky and Mike are coming. So is Rita and her firefighting date," she added, and both siblings sported confused looks. "I'll explain later. Oh, and Toni O'Hara, you don't know her. She's a friend of mine. She works for the Chicago Fire Department."

Jocelyn laughed. "She's not Rita's date, is she?"

Paul snorted. "She could be," he added dryly.

Jocelyn glared at her father and grabbed Marcie's hand. "Dad, Mom, you remember Marcie."

Allie glared at Paul, as well, then smiled and took Marcie's hand. "Yes, Marcie. How are you?"

"I'm doing well. Thanks for inviting me, Mrs. Sanders. I won't be much trouble. I've got an aunt I'd like to see on Friday."

"It's no trouble at all, honey. You can stay here or at your aunt's. You know you're welcome."

"Thanks again." She turned to Paul. "Mr. Sanders. Nice to see you again."

Paul had the decency to redden as he took her hand. "It's nice to see you, as well." He let go of her hand. "Well, who'd like something to drink?"

"Nothing for me just yet, thanks," Marcie said.

"Me either, Dad."

"I'll help you, Dad." Nick followed him to the kitchen.

"Marcie, my dad didn't mean anything."

Marcie held up her hand. "No worries. I know he didn't. Your dad is cool, Jos." She turned to Allie, her big blue eyes sparkling. "So who is this firefighter Toni? I'm assuming she's a sister."

Allie laughed. "Yes, she's gay and way too old for you."

"Now, now, Mrs. Sanders," Marcie scolded playfully.

"How did you meet her?" Jocelyn asked.

Paul came out of the kitchen along with Nick, each holding a glass. Allie told them how she came to meet Toni at Market Days. All three were enthralled by the story.

"She chased him down? No shit," Nick said.

Jocelyn watched her mother. "Well, then I'm glad you invited her. I'd like to thank her for coming to your rescue." Jocelyn put her arm around her mother's waist. "Now what's to eat?"

Allie got them settled into their old rooms and gave Marcie the sofa sleeper in the den. When she came out, she looked at Paul, who did not look in a festive mood.

"What's the matter?" Allie asked. "Is everything all right at work?"

Paul nodded. "It's fine, Al." He took a deep drink from his glass. Out of the blue, he leaned over and kissed Allie on the cheek. "Happy Thanksgiving, sweetie."

Allie pulled back, and again, she saw sadness mingled with fatigue when she looked into his hazel eyes. Allie was about to say something when the timer went off in the kitchen. "Oh, hell," she said. Then the doorbell rang.

"I'll get it!" Nick called out.

Paul laughed quietly and pushed her toward the kitchen. "I'll go take a quick shower."

Nick opened the door to see an attractive older woman standing there, hands full of some type of floral arrangement hidden by the wrapping. Nick noticed the genuine smile and smiled back. The woman juggled the gift and offered her hand.

"You must be Nick. You're just as your mother described you."

Nick laughed and took the hand, surprised at the warmth and strength behind the shake. He returned it in manly fashion. "Thanks, but my mother is a little prejudiced." He blushed as he stepped back. "You must be Toni. C'mon in."

Toni stepped in and wiped her shoes on the mat. "Some weather," she grumbled.

"Toni." Allie walked into the living room, drying her hands on a towel. "You're right on time, Inspector," she said warmly as Toni grinned and offered the gift.

"You didn't have to do that," she said. "But I'm glad you did. I love getting flowers."

"Good. I didn't know what to get, but it was nice of you to invite me to a family gathering." Toni handed her coat to Nick. "Thanks."

"It's beautiful," Allie exclaimed as she unwrapped the flowers. It was an autumn arrangement in an adorable woven basket.

"Whew! I'm glad you like it. I have no clue about these things. A friend of mine owns a shop on Halsted. Now *he* knows these things," she said and winked.

Allie laughed and nodded in understanding.

Toni looked up as a young woman walked into the living room. She blinked twice. "You have to be Jocelyn. Your mother should be a writer instead of an artist. She has described you two perfectly." Toni offered her hand.

Jocelyn smiled and took the offered hand. "Thank you. It's nice to meet you, Ms. O'Hara."

Toni waved her off. "Oh, God, please. Call me Toni. I feel old enough as it is."

"This is my college roommate, Marcie."

Toni put out her hand. "Nice to meet you, Marcie."

"Same here." Marcie shook her hand and held on to it for a moment longer before letting it go.

As Toni and Allie exchanged quick glances, Allie then saw Jocelyn give them a curious smile.

"What can I get you to drink, Toni?" Nick asked, rubbing his hands together. "I'm the bartender tonight."

Toni laughed. "I'll have a beer. Whatever you have is fine."

"Coming right up. Marcie, you ready now? Why don't you come with me and make a decision?"

Allie noticed the flirtatious grin on her son, and they headed off to the kitchen. For a moment, Allie, Toni, and Jocelyn stood in silence until Jocelyn laughed.

"I'd better go tell Nick that Marcie would have a better chance with you, Toni. My poor brother is barking up the wrong lesbian."

Toni let out a whooping laugh as did Allie as Jocelyn disappeared into the kitchen.

"I take it your daughter knows about me?" Toni asked.

"Yes, do you mind? I—"

"Of course not. I'm glad you feel comfortable with it. Thanks for inviting me, Alana. I mean it."

"Well, I talk so much about my kids I thought you should put a face with the names," she said. She was inexplicably happy right now as she looked up into Toni's gray eyes.

Nick handed the black ale to Toni, who raised an eyebrow. "Guinness? How did you know?" She looked at Nick, who shook his head and pointed to his mother.

"You were drinking it after that football game…" Allie started.

"Football?" Jocelyn asked in complete amazement as she and Marcie joined them.

"Flag football," Toni said. "But it still gets rough."

"Marcie plays on the team at college."

Marcie grinned. "Yep. It's brutal."

"I hear ya," Toni agreed. "But you're much younger than I am. I think it was my last season," she said and rubbed her backside.

Allie laughed openly as she remembered that Saturday not too long ago. "You looked exhausted after that game," Allie said. She noticed the astonished look on her children's faces. "What?"

"I don't know which is more amazing," Jocelyn said. "That a woman plays football—"

"Or Mom went to watch," Nick finished for her. There was an instant delay. "I choose Mom watching," Nick said deadpanned.

Paul walked into the room while they continued laughing. "Well, the party must have started."

Allie was glad to see he had showered and changed and appeared ready to have a good time. "There you are. Come here, I want you to meet…"

Paul walked up to Toni. "Yes, I've heard the story. It's nice to meet you, Toni. Paul Sanders," he said evenly. "Thanks for helping Allie."

Toni looked him in the eye. She had been smiling as he approached. "It's a pleasure to meet you, as well, Paul. It seems as though I know all of you," she said warmly and offered her hand.

When Paul hesitated for the slightest instant, Allie held her breath. Then he reached out and shook Toni's hand. Mercifully, the doorbell rang and the party started. Soon, everyone had arrived and the cocktails flowed, as did the hors d'oeuvres. Allie dashed to the kitchen and peered in the oven.

"Can I help?" Toni asked in a low voice.

Allie jumped up and laughed. "Good grief, don't sneak up on me like that. Yes, get that plate over there on the sink, will you? I had no idea everyone would like these so much. Thank God, I made enough."

Toni quickly retrieved the plate and brought it to her side. "They're delicious. Now tell me what the deal is with Vicky."

Allie turned bright red and blinked. "D-deal?" she asked with a weak grin.

Toni narrowed her eyes in suspicion. "She's been at my side since she arrived." She ran her fingers through her thick hair. "Not that I mind having a pretty woman at my side. However, she makes me nervous with her husband right there. I have a feeling she's…" She stopped and leaned against the sink.

Allie arranged the appetizers on the plate. She got another

Guinness and poured it, handing it to her friend. "Okay. Let me explain. She'll kill me, but you have a right to know."

Toni took the offered stout, took a healthy gulp, and listened.

"See, Vicky, well, she and Mike. See, they like...Vicky, well, Vicky has this thing about," she stumbled and stopped.

"Lesbians?" Toni offered.

"Yes," Allie said in a relieved voice. "Thank you. You understand."

"No, not really."

"Oh, do I have to spell it out?"

"Spell it out? Alana, you haven't completed a full sentence," Toni argued with a grin.

Allie took a deep breath. "Okay. Vicky and Mike have very good sex when Vicky fantasizes about other women. Okay?"

Toni threw her head back and laughed. "You're kidding?" She laughed and shook her head in disbelief. "Well, I'm glad I can contribute to somebody's good sex life."

Allie laughed along but saw a trace of sadness in the gray eyes. She picked up her glass of wine, took a drink, and watched while Toni stared at her glass. Allie wasn't sure if she wanted to get into a discussion about Toni's sex life. She remembered her own fantasy a few weeks back. Still, she didn't like the sad look on her face.

"Everything all right?" she asked tentatively.

Toni blinked and looked up. She gazed into Allie's eyes and smiled. "Everything is fine," she said in a low soft voice. She then eyed the plate and reached out.

Allie pulled the plate back and Toni pouted severely. "Oh, here. You child." Allie offered the plate.

Toni grinned like said child and took one, popping the crab cake in her mouth. She rolled her eyes dramatically. "Man, those are good," she exclaimed with a mouthful.

She took another as Allie waited patiently. "I have other guests," she reminded her.

Toni grinned evilly and taunted her friend with the tasty morsel. "Yum. Want some? It's so good with a glass of wine," she teased and put it to Allie's lips.

Allie rolled her eyes and opened her mouth. Toni placed it into her mouth and Allie bit down and grinned as she pulled the entire morsel into her mouth. Toni's finger followed innocently.

For a nanosecond, both women blinked as Toni's middle finger lay against Allie's warm lips. Toni then snatched it away as if burned.

Allie quickly chewed the crab cake, and as they both turned, they saw Jocelyn and Marcie standing in the doorway with an empty tray. Allie saw Jocelyn's curious look—again. And Marcie's stupefied look, but she was also smiling.

"We, um…" Marcie started and looked at Jocelyn.

Jocelyn blinked. "Oh, yeah, we…" She stopped and held out the empty plate to Allie.

Toni gratefully took another crab cake and said, "You gals better get these away from me before I eat the entire tray."

Mercifully, Jocelyn said nothing; perhaps she and Marcie didn't see Allie practically sucking on Toni's finger. But by their reactions, Allie figured that wasn't the case. Allie avoided Toni completely as she scooted around her and grabbed the empty tray from Jocelyn.

"Hey, Mom, is it okay if I have a glass of wine? I'll be twenty-one in three months," she asked. "And Marcie is already twenty-one and Nick is…"

"Um, sure. Have whatever you like, sweetie," she said.

"Sweet!" Jocelyn headed for the bottle of wine on the counter. Toni shifted out of her way.

Allie quickly filled the tray with the remaining crab cakes. As she walked toward the kitchen, she turned to see Jocelyn taking a sip of wine.

"What are you doing?" Allie asked seriously.

Jocelyn blinked. "Y-you said I could have some."

"I did not," Allie argued.

"Mom, yes, you did." Jocelyn looked at Toni, who chuckled quietly.

"Yes, you did," Toni assured her flustered friend. "Mom."

Marcie nodded, as well.

Allie glared at Toni, then at her laughing daughter. "It was a mistake for you two to meet. I can just feel it." She sighed and walked through the swinging door.

"So, Toni? You're a lesbian firefighter?" Marcie asked.

Jocelyn's eyes grew wide as she drank her wine.

"Guilty on both counts, kiddo. But I'm an inspector now. Take it slow with that wine. I don't want your mother mad at both of us," Toni said to Jocelyn as she laughed.

"I understand Mom told you she paints? She never talks about that. I wish she'd start again," Jocelyn said seriously.

"Why did she stop?"

"Well, she never had time. Two kids, teaching, taking care of all three of us," she explained in a sad voice. Then she smiled. "She used to take me to the art museum when I was a little girl."

"I know." Toni smiled. "Monet."

Jocelyn cocked her head and glanced at Marcie. "You seem to know a good deal."

"Yes. Your mother and I have had wonderful talks. How she used to take you after she dropped Nick off at school and sit for hours."

"That's right," Jocelyn said, amazed at the information Toni had.

"So you're studying to be a nurse," Toni said, and Jocelyn nodded. "Your mother says when you were a little girl you used to nurse your stuffed animals." Toni grinned as she sipped her beer.

Jocelyn blushed. "God, I'm going to kill my mother."

Marcie laughed. "I hadn't heard that one."

"Don't be angry," Toni said with a laugh. "Your mother loves you very much. I love to hear about your antics as kids."

With that, Nick came into the kitchen. "Hey, what are you three talking about?" he asked as he eyed Toni's dark beer.

"Have one. There's plenty there, and I've just about reached my limit," Toni offered.

"Mom's been storytelling, Nick," Jocelyn informed him.

Nick cringed and drank the stout beer. "Oh, God, what did she tell you?"

"Nothing much. Nice scar on your chin, though," she said into her glass.

Nick blushed to the tip of his nose. Jocelyn squealed with laughter. "I don't remember," he grumbled.

"I do!" Jocelyn insisted.

"Shut up, Jossie," he warned playfully.

Marcie leaned into Toni. "This is fun. I'm an only child."

"So you were your parents' favorite?" Toni grinned and drank her beer. Marcie feigned indignation.

Nick and Jocelyn were still bantering, so Toni and Marcie leaned against the counter and watched the sibling exchange.

"You tried to fly and jumped right off the couch," Jocelyn said, laughing. "You tripped and your pants came off!"

Nick avoided Toni's face. "They did not!"

"Did too!"

"Well, how about you? Talking to your teddy bear after the 'accident,'" he countered sarcastically as he laughed.

Now Jocelyn avoided Toni, who just watched the happy bantering.

"Seems Mr. Bear fell off his bike," Nick said, trying not to laugh.

Jocelyn glared. "Your face…"

"Your mama's face," Nick mumbled.

Jocelyn was hiding her amusement. "Well, at least he kept his pants on."

Toni laughed, snorting beer all over the kitchen as she started choking. Brother and sister roared with laughter. Nick slapped Toni on the back.

"Put your hands up over your head," Jocelyn ordered.

Toni coughed and raised her hands, while Nick helped to beat the cough out of her.

"What in the hell did you do to her?" Allie's voice called out.

Allie ran to Toni, who was trying to catch her breath.

"She snorted beer through her nose," Nick said quickly and slapped her back again.

"Nick, honey, you'll break a vertebrae." Allie gently pushed him away. She looked at Toni whose face was finally a normal color.

Toni took a deep breath and blinked. "Wow. I was choking," she said seriously.

Allie raised a disturbed eyebrow at all three of them. "I'm not going to ask what you children were doing."

"I'm innocent," Toni said, causing Nick to spew his beer all over the kitchen.

Someone pushed the kitchen door, sending Allie flying into her children and Toni. Paul winced as he poked his head in. "Sorry. The natives are getting restless for more food."

He walked into the kitchen and glanced at Toni, who smiled. Allie commandeered Nick, Jocelyn, and Marcie to help bring out another tray of food and refreshments.

This left Toni alone with Paul—and an empty glass.

For a moment, neither said anything. Then Paul cleared his throat. "So you're a firefighter?"

"An inspector now. Less wear and tear."

"I bet," Paul said, fixing another drink. "Live in Chicago?"

"Yep. Have an apartment a few blocks off the lake."

"Must be a nice view." He leaned against the counter swirling his drink.

"It is. It's beautiful even in the winter." Toni smiled. "If Chicago in the winter can be beautiful."

Paul chuckled. "Well, at least the Cubs can't be losing."

"Oh, Paul. They'd find a way."

They laughed, easing what little tension there was. Toni crouched down and looked in the oven. "Wonder if they're done?"

Paul looked, as well, and opened the oven. He took the pan out and set it on the top. "Allie is a good cook. I hope these won't be missed." He picked up a mini eggroll and tossed it back and forth in his hand, blowing on it at the same time.

Toni laughed as he tossed it to her. She blew on it a couple of times before taking a tentative bite. "Alana is a very good cook."

Paul glanced at her while he ate. "Alana?"

Toni stopped in midchew but said nothing.

"It's a beautiful name," Paul said, watching her as he drank. He reached over and tossed her another eggroll.

Toni nodded as she caught the hors d'oeuvres—she believed she caught his meaning, as well.

"What are you two doing?" Allie asked. "Hey! Quit eating those." She grabbed the pan off the stove and slid them onto a serving tray. "You're as bad as the kids."

As Allie whirled around to leave, Nick burst through the swinging door, catching Allie, who juggled the tray. Paul ran over in time to save the appetizers. Toni leaned back and laughed while she watched.

"Sorry, Mom…" Nick said with a sheepish grin. "I just got a call from Scott, you remember him? Well, he's in town, too, and there's a party Friday night…"

"Oh, Nick. I thought we'd do something together while you're in town," Allie said.

"Like what?"

"Well, I don't know. Go downtown, see the Christmas decorations," Allie offered with a hopeful look.

Toni saw the hopeful, but disappointed look from Allie. "Um, if you want, I have four tickets to the first show of the Nutcracker at the Auditorium. One o'clock, front row seats."

Allie raised an eyebrow. "Win them off of the same lieutenant?"

Toni laughed. "No, they were given to me, but I have to work shift Friday. You're more than welcome to them, if you like."

Nick's eyes lit up as he looked at Allie and Paul. Toni noticed Paul's frown.

"I was supposed to stop in at work Friday," he said.

Allie sighed and Nick groaned. "Dad. Jossie and I never see you or Mom. And it'll be perfect because I think Marcie is visiting her aunt Friday. It's a holiday."

Paul nodded reluctantly. "Okay." He looked at Toni. "Thank you. How much?"

Toni shook her head. "I didn't pay for them. So I can't take your money."

Paul looked uncomfortable and Allie stepped in. "You come over for dinner, and I'll feed you. How's that?"

"Better than money," Toni said with a smile.

"Great!" Nick said. "Thanks, Toni. I'll go tell Jossie." He looked at his mother. "Then Friday night will be free?"

"Yes, you're off the holiday hook. Go…"

After Nick left, Allie looked at Toni. "Thank you."

"My pleasure," Toni said. "Happy Thanksgiving."

As she drank her beer, she noticed Paul watching both of them.

Chapter 10

"Paul, the kids are only here for the holiday weekend. You said you weren't going to work," Allie insisted.

"I can't help it, Allie. This is a big client."

"Like the one in New York," she asked softly.

Paul whirled around to her. "What's that supposed to mean?"

"Nothing. It's just lately you've been gone so often. We don't talk anymore. Why?"

"Did we ever? Really?"

Allie let out a disappointed sigh. "Perhaps you're right. I had the kids and the house. You had your work. Now with the kids gone…"

Nick interrupted her as he poked his head into their room. "Hey, it's almost time to leave."

Allie looked at Paul, who rubbed his forehead, then chuckled. "Okay, we'll be out in a bit." He frowned and shook his head. "I need to make a call. I'll be right down, Al."

"It'll be fun," she whispered.

Paul just nodded as he reached for his phone.

The Nutcracker was a holiday delight. Allie, Nick, and Jocelyn had a wonderful time. Paul looked as happy as he could. Allie just didn't get it.

As they drove home, they turned down a North Side street and stopped at a red light. Allie absently looked at the Christmas decorations, already displayed. She then looked in a bakery shop window and was shocked to see Toni sitting there, alone and drinking coffee. The car pulled away, and Allie craned her neck to see Toni until she lost sight of her.

Kevin Murphy looked in the bakery window and shook his head. He walked in and wiped his shoes.

"I thought you'd be here. Thanks for the leftovers. I love turkey." Kevin sat across from Toni, who looked up and smiled. He looked around and Lidia walked out from the kitchen holding a pie and three plates.

"Yeah? Good," Toni said. "I thought I did pretty well for my first time making a turkey." Toni drank her coffee.

"Well, how was your holiday?" Lidia asked.

Toni smiled as Kevin stood and offered Lidia a chair. "Thank you, Kevin Murphy."

Kevin sat and watched Toni. "What is it with you and these coffee shops? You're still hanging out at them all the time."

"This is not a coffee shop, is bakery," Lidia scolded as she sliced the apple pie.

Toni shrugged. "I don't know. You know I used to all the time when I was a kid. It felt safe."

Kevin chomped on his cigar. He understood exactly what she meant. When Pat O'Hara went on a bender, Toni would take the brunt of it, then he'd pass out. Once she was sure the little ones and her mother were safe at their grandmother's, Toni headed for the coffee shop—oh, sorry, bakery. Many times, Kevin would find her there, sporting the bruise of the week. God, Kevin hated Pat for his abusive behavior toward his oldest child. She took many a beating for her siblings and their mother.

He remembered one time in particular when Pat, in a drunken stupor, went after her with his belt. The poor girl had welts on her back so thick...he shook his head sadly. He looked at Lidia and knew she was thinking the same thing by her teary expression.

Toni looked up at Kevin and smiled sadly. "I hated him for it, too, Kevin," she whispered into her cup. "But I never let him touch Mom or the kids. I would have killed him myself if that scaffold hadn't."

Kevin shuddered at the dead calm voice. He believed her.

"Hey, didn't you win tickets in the raffle?" he asked, changing the topic.

Lidia placed the pie in front of both of them and listened.

Toni grinned, then cleared her throat and concentrated on her pie. "I did. Gave them away. What was I gonna do with four tickets to the stupid Nutcracker?"

Kevin eyed her suspiciously but said nothing.

Lidia would not let her off so easily. "Who did you give the tickets to?"

Toni frowned and pushed her plate away. "Nobody."

Kevin hid his grin at the childish sound in her voice.

"Tell me or no more kolachky," Lidia warned.

"I'd tell her if I was you." Kevin ate his pie.

Toni folded her arms across her chest. "Who cares? I didn't want 'em, so I gave 'em away. Shit!"

"Stop with the swearing, and tell me."

Kevin looked at the woman he thought of as his daughter. "You gave them to the museum woman, didn't you?"

Lidia frowned in confusion. "What museum woman?"

"I did not!" Toni argued and glared at Kevin.

"What museum woman?" Lidia insisted again.

Kevin smiled slightly. "Yes, you did."

"What museum woman?" Lidia asked with frustration and tapped her fork on the table.

Toni took a deep breath and tiredly rubbed her face. "I met this woman, and she's very nice and very cultured and—"

"I like so far, and what?"

"Very married," Toni said.

Lidia sat back. "That's no goot."

Kevin nodded in agreement. So did Toni. Lidia watched her carefully. "Tell me about her."

Toni smiled then, and Kevin and Lidia exchanged glances. "Her name is Alana Sanders. She's an art teacher. She has two great kids, both adults. She lives in Oak Park and has a nice little bungalow. She loves Monet and her children. I wanted to take Alana and her kids to the Nutcracker. I toyed with the idea all week. But I knew Alana was having trouble with her husband,

Paul. It was a better idea to give them the tickets. I thought...I dunno, maybe it would help."

Lidia watched as Toni stared at her cup. "I really like this woman as a friend, and I don't want to ruin that. I've never really had a friend like her. She—"

The bell above the door rang, and Lidia looked up to see a woman standing there. She had blondish hair and green eyes. She was looking at Toni, who had her back to this woman.

Lidia watched as Toni immediately sat erect and whirled around in her chair. "Alana!"

Lidia looked at Kevin, who nodded slightly.

"Hi. I-I was in the neighborhood," Allie said and chuckled. "That was lame." Toni shot out of her chair as Allie walked up to the table. "Am I interrupting?"

Kevin stood. "No, no, sit. We were just talking about you—"

Toni and Lidia's eyes bugged out of their heads. "Yuletide, yuletide. We were talking about Christmas," Toni said quickly. "Alana, you remember Kevin, and this is Lidia Walinski, the owner of this bakery and a good friend."

Lidia smiled kindly at this woman who had Toni so flustered. She shook hands and noticed how soft her hand was. "You have gentle hands, Alana."

"Thank you, Mrs. Walinski," she said and sat down.

"Please, call me Lidia."

"I don't get to call you Lidia," Toni said seriously.

Lidia still looked at Alana. "No, you don't." She cut a piece of pie. "Would you like a piece of pie, Alana?"

"Please, thank you." Allie glanced at Toni. "So you were talking about Christmas? Good, then I can join in. Thanks for the tickets. It was a nice holiday treat," Allie said as she watched Toni.

Lidia stood. "Well, I have bread to make for tomorrow. Kevin Murphy, why don't you come and help?" She pulled him out of his seat.

Toni smiled as she watched their retreat.

"I like her," Allie said.

"She's great, like family. So is Kevin," Toni said. "Well, I'm glad you used the tickets. Did you use all the tickets?" Toni asked absently as she played with her fork.

Allie smiled. "Yes, even Paul went along. It was a nice time. The kids told me to tell you thank you and maybe they'll see you at Christmas." Allie watched her tentative posture. Toni seemed withdrawn and quiet, very unlike her.

"I'd really like that," Toni said softly. "I like Jocelyn and Nick. I see so much of you in them," she said almost to herself.

"That was a nice thing to say," Allie said. "Would you like another piece of pie?"

Toni leaned back and grinned, rubbing her hands together. "Yes, ma'am."

"So you had to work today? Seems like a short day," Allie asked pointedly as she placed the plate in front of her. She noticed Toni avoiding her face.

"Um, yeah. I switched with someone. Last minute," she said with a shrug and buried her head in her plate.

"Hmm. That was nice of you."

Again, the shrug.

"I'd think you would have seniority."

"Yeah, well, Chicago politics. No biggie." She avoided Allie completely as she ate. When she looked up, Allie was watching her. "Hey. Did you do something to your hair?"

Allie frowned and gave her a suspicious look. "Nope."

"Oh, well, it looks nice," she said with a smile.

"Thanks."

Allie dropped the topic. They ate their dessert in silence until Kevin walked out covered in flour.

"That woman is a maniac in the kitchen. I'll see ya later," he said and walked out.

Lidia was right behind him laughing. "He is no goot in kitchen. I sent him home. Now," she said and sat down, letting out a relieved sigh. "My feet are killing me, and I have pies to make."

Allie grinned. "I can help."

Lidia gave her a curious look. "Goot! Come with me," she said and stood. "You too, Antonia."

Toni groaned as she stood. "Kevin got to leave."

Allie and Lidia laughed and pulled the reluctant Toni along. It was like an assembly line. Toni peeled, Allie sliced, and Lidia supervised.

"You're doing very goot, Alana. Antonia, not so much."

Toni glared at her and wiped the flour off her shirt. "This is not my forte, Mrs. W."

"This I can see. Now tell me about yourself, Alana. Antonia says you have two beautiful children."

Allie glanced at Toni, who frowned deeply as she concentrated on her peeling skills.

"Yes, Nick is twenty-four, and Jocelyn will be twenty-one in a few months," she said with a grin as she rolled out the pie dough.

"And you adore them," Lidia said wistfully as she watched them work together.

"And I adore them," Allie said, still grinning. She thought of Paul and her smile faded.

"But something is wrong?" Lidia asked.

Toni was oblivious. She was still trying to peel the apple without taking half the apple with it. Lidia rolled her eyes.

"Well. No, everything is..." Allie said and stopped. She rolled the dough harder with the rolling pin.

Lidia watched curiously as Allie frowned deeply. "Alana, you must either tell me or stop abusing my pie dough."

Allie stopped and blushed horribly. She wiped the hair off her face with the back of her hand.

"Come and sit by me. We have to wait for slowpoke to peel." Lidia patted the chair next to her. Allie obediently sat and looked at her hands. "Now tell me what is troubling you, darling."

"I feel like a fool. I shouldn't burden you with my marital problems," Allie said in a small voice.

"Treat me like therapist," Lidia offered with a smile.

"That might work," Allie said with a weak chuckle. So she told a relative stranger about her trouble with Paul. She was hesitant at first, then the floodgates opened.

"I don't know when it happened."

"What?" Lidia asked softly.

"When we became strangers. I told myself it was because of the kids and Paul's obsession with his work. I had the house, the children. And suddenly, one day I'm sitting across from the man I married, and I realize twenty-five years have gone by, and I don't know who he is, or..."

"Or who you are?" Lidia offered.

"No. I know who I am." Allie realized she didn't sound very convincing, going by the skeptical look on Lidia's face. Hell, she didn't sound sure to herself.

"It is hard when children are gone from nest. Mother hen does not know what to do with herself or the coop."

Allie sat forward. "That's just it, Lidia. I know what to do. I went back to teaching art. I gave up my passion, and I raised the kids and took care of the house and Paul. It's just lately, I feel like something is gone between Paul and me. Maybe it was never there. I don't know." She sat back.

"Why lately?" Lidia glanced at Toni, who just now finished one apple; Lidia sighed.

Allie watched Toni. "I'm not sure. I feel restless. Anxious, you know?" Allie looked back to Lidia. "Like I'm going to jump right out of my skin."

"Menopause?" Lidia asked with a grin.

Allie laughed outright. "Well, there's that, too. But I don't think that's it. This has been a long time lying just beneath the surface. I think it's coming to a head because frankly, Paul and I have no reason to avoid the issue now." She looked at Lidia. "Paul is a good man. He's a good father and a good provider. And he is a good husband. I think it's me."Well, it has been my experience in these matters it's never just one person when two are involved." Lidia reached over and patted Allie's hand. "If you are partners in goot times, you are partners in not so goot. And if it does not work, you are partners in that, too." She wagged her finger in Allie's direction. "About this I am right."

Allie smiled. "I agree with you. Although Paul seemed always busy with his work, he truly found time for the kids. We always made a point to go somewhere during the summer.

Nothing expensive or elaborate, just made sure we were together. We thought it was good for the kids."

"It seems you are right. He is goot father. They will remember that and that you are goot mother. That will never change in their hearts. No matter what happens to you and Paul."

Tears sprang into Allie's eyes. "I know."

Lidia patted her hand once again. "Well, you have goot friend in Antonia. She is goot."

Allie still watched Toni. "Yes, yes, she is."

"Hey! I got it!" Toni announced and held up the peel. She saw the sad look on both women's face. "What's wrong?"

Lidia groaned. "Nothing, but you need to leave my kitchen before something bad happens," she said and stood. "You are like Kevin. Get out."

"B-but…" Toni said as Lidia ushered her out of the kitchen.

"Alana, take this woman home, please." Lidia kissed her lightly on each cheek. "You are goot woman, too."

Tears sprang to her eyes as she hugged Lidia. "Thank you so much for listening."

"I pray for you," Lidia pulled back, "that perhaps at last, you are happy. And Paul, too."

"Hey, don't I get a hug?" Toni opened her arms.

Lidia pulled Toni down to her and kissed her on the forehead. "Go home."

They stood outside the bakery. Allie chuckled and reached up to wipe the flour off Toni's cheek. "You're a disaster in the kitchen."

"You should have seen the kitchen after I made a turkey." Toni laughed and stood there until Alana was finished. She looked down into the green eyes and smiled. "Thanks."

"Can I drive you home?" Allie pulled her coat around her.

Toni shook her head. "No, thanks. I live just a couple blocks away. I like to walk. Clears my head. Let me walk you to your car, though."

Allie laughed and pointed to the van right in front of them. Toni laughed along.

"Well, good night. Thanks again for the tickets. It was the sweetest thing anyone has done for me and the kids in a long while." Allie slipped in behind the wheel.

"Then I'm glad I got to do it. Good night, Alana." Toni gently closed the door.

Through the window, Alana smiled and waved, then pulled away from the curb.

Toni pulled her collar up around her neck and headed home.

Chapter 11

"C'mon, I'm going Christmas shopping and you're coming along." Allie pulled Vicky and Rita out of the van.

What a disaster. After a day of fighting the Christmas crowd, Vicky suggested a drink. "And I know just the place."

They walked a few blocks, and Rita stopped short. "Vicky, it's a gay bar," she said seriously.

Allie looked around.

"It is?" Vicky asked innocently.

Allie groaned. "You're evil," she insisted as Vicky laughed and pulled them into the small bar.

The clientele, mostly women, lined the oval bar. The music was not as loud as Allie had expected it to be. Though she had no clue what she expected. Vicky walked up to three empty seats at the bar.

"Vicky, hi!" A young bartender smiled as Allie and Rita exchanged glances.

"Hey, Tammy."

"What'll it be?" Tammy glanced at Allie and Rita. She raised an eyebrow and looked back at Vicky with a small grin. Allie frowned and looked down at Vicky.

"Gin and tonic," Allie ordered as she tried not to be obviously looking around. She remembered then, long ago in college. Susan's plea: Come with me, I think you'll like it.

Allie never did, and she never saw Susan again. Why must that memory come back to her now?

Rita obviously didn't care, she was gaping. "Um...oh. A cosmopolitan."

"I take it you've been here before?" Allie asked dryly as the bartender came back with their drinks.

"Well, kind of," Vicky offered.

"Kind of? You've either been here or you haven't," Rita countered.

"Well, then yes, I've been here. But just a couple times. It's much nicer than a regular bar. No men pawing all over you."

"I like men pawing." Rita looked at Allie. "Don't you?"

"Not particularly," Allie said quickly while looking around. She saw the curious looks from both friends. "What?"

"Nothing," Vicky said with a chuckle.

Allie continued to scan the bar when in the corner she saw her. The hammering started when Allie saw Toni shooting pool with some younger woman who was so close to Toni, she could have been in her back pocket. Toni didn't seem to mind one bit. And it wasn't the blonde from the football game.

Allie tried to look away but couldn't. She was fascinated. Toni was sporting a very sexy grin as she whispered something in the woman's ear. The woman closed her eyes, and Allie could almost hear her groan as she leaned into Toni's body.

Toni set the pool cue down and pulled the woman into her arms. Allie now couldn't look away even if she wanted to, which for some reason, she did not.

They were alone in the corner. Toni kissed the woman deeply, and Allie's mouth went dry as Toni slipped her thigh between the woman's legs. Toni gently rocked into her, and Allie swore she could feel the woman shiver. Well, good Lord, Allie thought.

Then, Toni quickly backed the woman up against the wall and held her hands above her head with one hand. Toni, her back now to Allie, lowered her head to the woman's neck. Allie swayed slightly and blinked as she watched Toni slowly, sensually move her hips into the limp woman. She then saw Toni's hand slip under the sweater and hold the woman's breast. Allie would attest to anyone she actually felt Toni's warm hand on her breast.

She was so aroused she didn't know what to do or where to look. Okay, shit or go blind, shit or go blind—she repeated it like a mantra. Now she knew what that saying meant. She quickly slid off the barstool on shaky legs.

"Restrooms?" she asked in a squeaky voice.

As she splashed cold water on her face, Allie took a deep quivering breath. Good Christ, that was steamy. She looked at the other women in the bathroom. There were two kissing in the corner. She absently watched as she washed her hands. The tingling sensation rippled through her body. She thought about the fantasy of a month earlier, she visualized Toni...

Just then, two more young women walked in the bathroom, holding on to each other and kissing. Allie looked around. Is there something about this bathroom? Shaking her head and tossing the paper towel in the basket, she headed back to the table. "I wanna go home."

As she hurried out the door, she ran into a brick wall. Oh, God, please no, she begged. He wasn't listening, or He was laughing too much.

"Whoa, sweetheart," the familiar voice cooed.

The arms wrapped around her shoulders, and for an instant, Allie leaned into it.

"You all right, miss?" Toni's soft voice asked in the dark hallway.

Allie looked up, and Toni's eyebrows shot to the top of her head. "Shit!" Her voice came out in a shrill squeak.

"Hi," Allie offered weakly.

Toni was still holding on to her and staring like a deer caught in the headlights. "Shit!"

"Um, you already said that." Allie bit her bottom lip.

"Alana? What the...shit?" As if she just realized she was holding Allie, she dropped her hands to her side. "My God, I think I'm having a stroke."

Allie sported a sheepish shrug. Toni swallowed, trying to compose herself. "What..." She stopped and took a long breath and let it out slowly. "What are you doing here?" she asked quickly and looked around. She took Alana by the elbow and led her to the jukebox in the corner.

"I...Well, Vicky..." she started.

Toni frowned deeply. "Vicky? What are you doing?" she asked again, this time more firmly.

Allie heard the accusatory tone. She bristled instantly. "Just what do you mean?"

Toni glared down at her. "Vicky comes here for one reason. I've seen her. Now you're here."

Allie's mouth dropped. "How dare you! Get that tone out of your voice. We came in here for a drink…"

Toni rolled her eyes and snorted.

"Don't get sanctimonious with me, O'Hara. I came in here innocently because of Vicky. You're the one having sex in a public place. Geez! Why didn't you just strip her and take her on the pool table?" Allie cursed the vivid mental picture that flashed through her mind.

Toni was seething with anger. "Get out of here and go home," she ordered through clenched teeth.

Allie saw red. "Don't you dare tell me what to do. I'm a grown woman," she said just as angrily.

Toni rolled her eyes and grabbed her elbow. Allie yanked it away, and in doing so, she caught Toni on the cheek with her ring.

Toni stifled the cry of pain as she went reeling into the jukebox. Her hand went to her cheek as Allie saw the trickle of blood.

"Oh, God." Allie reached for her.

"Shit, Alana," Toni whined as the tears stung her eyes. "Geez, I'm bleeding!"

"Oh, you big baby. Come in the bathroom," she ordered and pushed Toni through the door.

Toni was blinking and bleeding as Allie gently pushed her against the counter. She took a few paper towels and ran them under the cold water.

A few women walked in and laughed. "That's it, sweetie. O'Hara likes it rough." They laughed and walked out.

Toni glared at the retreating figures.

"Friends?" Allie placed the wet towel on her cheek, just below her eye.

"No," Toni said quickly.

Allie said nothing as she held the towel in place.

Toni looked at her. "Sorry," she mumbled. Allie grunted but said nothing. "I'm sorry," she insisted.

"Okay, you're sorry."

Allie was unaware that she was standing between Toni's legs as Toni sat on the counter. Toni had her hands resting on her thighs, and when Allie pressed the wet cloth to her injured cheek, Toni jumped, her hands instinctively moving to Allie's hips.

"Hold still."

Toni obeyed and just looked at Allie. "I really am sorry. I had no right. You just floored me. Never in a million years did I expect to see you in a gay bar."

Before Allie could respond...

"What the hell is going on?"

Toni leaned to the side, and her eyes widened in horror.

Allie looked over her shoulder at the woman Toni had been fondling moments before.

"Get your hands off her hips!" the woman roared.

"My hands...? Oh, shit!" Toni removed her hands from Allie's full hips quickly. She pushed Allie away and slid off the counter.

Allie took the bloody towel away. "You're still bleeding, sugar," Allie cooed and batted her eyelashes. Toni shot her a look of horror.

"Sugar?" the woman screamed.

It was then Allie noticed how young the woman was. That was the second woman Toni was with who looked like she just got out of college.

"Mandy, don't jump to conclusions. Alana is an old friend..."

Allie snorted as she washed her hands. Toni glared at Allie for an instant, then chuckled. Allie shot a look at Toni and couldn't help it, she started laughing, as well. It was an odd situation, Allie had to admit.

"Toni O'Hara, you can go straight to hell," Mandy said.

"As I'm sure I will. I'll save you a seat," Toni said, her lips twitching.

Mandy turned on her heels and marched out. They stopped laughing and stood there in awkward silence.

"It stopped bleeding. I think you'll live," Allie said, breaking the silence.

"Thanks." Toni chuckled and gingerly felt her cheek. "So, um, just what did you see out there?"

Allie enjoyed the squirming posture. "Enough," she said and looked into the gray eyes.

Toni grimaced and shook her head. "Well, I deserve this. I'm sorry I accused you. I know you'd never do what Vicky does. I'm not judging her. I just know you're not like that, and when I saw you and you mentioned her, I—"

"Got all manly on my ass." Allie tried to sound tough.

Toni now turned so red Allie almost laughed openly. Toni only nodded and ran her fingers through her hair. "Boy, that just doesn't sound right coming from an art teacher."

Allie laughed quietly as did Toni.

"I'd better get back," Allie said.

"You go ahead. I'll wait here for a bit."

"Why?"

"I don't want them thinking you…I mean, you don't need any gossip."

Allie smiled affectionately and placed her hand on Toni's arm. "Thanks, Sir Galahad, but I'm a grown woman, and I don't care about gossip. You're my friend," she said firmly. "We'll go out together. Don't ever feel like you have to sneak around or hide. Don't ever do that. Not for me or anyone."

Toni gazed at her for a moment. "Thanks. You're a good friend," she said and opened the door. As Allie walked by, Toni whispered, "With a wicked left."

Allie barked out her laugh as they walked back to the bar. Vicky and Rita nearly fainted as they walked up to them.

"W-well, Toni. How are you?" Vicky looked from her to Allie and back again.

"I'm doing well, Vicky. How are you? How's Mike?" Toni hailed the bartender and ordered another round.

"He's well. The kids are good. We were just Christmas shopping."

Allie smirked at the nervous tone in Vicky's voice.

Toni nodded and laughed quietly when she noticed Rita gawking. Vicky nudged Rita in the ribs, nearly knocking her into another woman.

"Oh. Hi, Toni," Rita said. "Nice place."

Allie sipped her gin and tonic. What an odd day, Allie thought. From Christmas shopping to a lesbian bar. Oh, well.

"A penny for your thoughts." Toni leaned into her.

Allie laughed. "I was just thinking how my life has changed since I met you."

Toni raised an eyebrow and took a drink of her beer. "Badly?" she asked tentatively.

"God, no. For the better," she blurted out.

Toni blinked in surprise. "Well, that's good to know. Though I'm not sure Paul would agree."

"Well, Paul doesn't agree to much these days. And I don't know what to do about that."

"I caught a little of what you and Mrs. W. were talking about. Do you think a counselor might help?" Toni leaned on the bar.

Allie thought about it. "I don't know. It couldn't hurt, I suppose. I just can't see Paul talking to a perfect stranger about our problems." She looked at Toni, who looked deep in thought. "Thank you, O'Hara."

Toni smiled. "What for?"

"For being a good friend when I needed it."

"You're quite welcome. I'll try always to be here when you need me."

"That's a great comfort, and I'm not being overly dramatic when I say that."

In the background, Nat King Cole started singing *The Very Thought of You*. For a moment, Toni looked like she might ask her to dance. Allie for some reason was sick to her stomach as Toni gazed into her eyes and smiled. "I hope I'm not being out of line, Alana..."

Allie laughed nervously. "Unfortunately, it probably will be."

Toni laughed along. "Well, since you're here..."

"Toni, dance with me," a voice came from behind her.

Toni blinked, "Oh, no thanks, Sheri…"

"Oh, come on. I know you love this old shit."

Allie watched as the woman pulled Toni out onto the dance floor. As Allie knew she would, Toni danced perfectly to the gentle strains of Nat King Cole.

While Toni danced, she looked over at Allie, who was looking in her eyes. Toni swallowed and maintained eye contact with her throughout the rest of the song.

When it finished, Sheri kissed Toni on the cheek and walked away. Toni, still looking at Allie, walked back to the bar. She said nothing as she took a healthy drink of her dark beer, nearly draining the glass in one gulp.

Allie watched her but said nothing, as well; she had no idea what to say. Visions of long, long ago flashed through her mind. Scenarios she had long since put to rest, or so she thought. She too took a long drink. "I need to go home," she said in a quiet voice.

Toni nodded. "I can take you," she offered and stared at her glass.

"No, thank you. Right now, I think I just need some air, and I need to—" She stopped and laughed nervously. "I'm not sure what I need anymore, but I need to get out of here. Good night, Toni."

She didn't wait as she quickly walked out of the bar. Vicky called after her.

"Go with her, Vicky, see that she gets home all right," Toni said and turned back to the bar.

Chapter 12

"Well, help me," Toni said impatiently as she ran her fingers through her hair, wishing she cut it when she thought of it last week. It was getting far too long for her.

Kevin rolled his eyes. "I don't know what your teacher wants for Christmas. Are you even sure you should be buying her something?"

"She's my friend. Friends do things like this for each other," she said angrily and glanced around the crowded store on South Michigan Avenue. "At least I think they do. Now she's an artist, for chrissakes. I want to get her some art stuff. It's Christmas, and I want her to be happy."

It then caught her eye. Toni slowly walked up to the counter and blinked. "That's it."

Kevin looked and blinked, as well. "You can't afford that, and there's no way you should be even thinking about something like that." He pointed to the diamond ring.

Toni rolled her eyes. "Not that, you dope. That." She pointed to the advertisement on the counter. "Let's go…"

Thirty minutes later, she was grinning like a fool. Kevin chomped on his cigar and shook his head. "She'll like it, right?" Toni asked and stopped grinning. "Shit, what if she doesn't?"

Kevin pulled her along. "She'll love it. When are you going to give it to her? Christmas is only a few days away."

"Well, she's busy with her family, so I don't want to bug her. Besides, Paul doesn't seem thrilled with me. I don't think he's a homophobe, though. He really seems like a good guy. Anyway, Alana doesn't need that during the holidays."

"What's he like?" he asked as they walked down the busy holiday street.

"We only talked for a few minutes in the kitchen, ya know. Jobs, Cubs. But he said something."

"What?"

Toni laughed at Kevin's rough tone. "No, not like that. He made a comment on how Allie was a good cook. And I said, yes, Alana was. He questioned me calling her Alana but just said it was a beautiful name. I got the message, though."

"Hmm. Jealous husband?"

"I'm not sure jealous. I think he just wanted to let me know he was still her husband. Ya know, he looked kinda sad. I hope everything is okay between them."

"Do you really?"

"Yes, I do. Oh, I think Alana is beautiful inside and out, but I really do like her and I don't want to ruin that. I do miss her, though, haven't seen her in a couple weeks. When we talk on the phone, she seems okay. Damn, I wish I could see her face. I can tell in her eyes if she's happy."

Kevin gave her a worried glance. "Toni," he started.

Toni heard his worried voice. "You worry too much," she said and slapped him on the back. "C'mon, let's get some Christmas cheer at Kitty O'Shea's."

Kevin rubbed his hands together. "Now you're talking."

As they strolled down the street, Toni saw Alana coming the opposite way. She grinned and waved. Alana saw her and smiled, as well. Toni then saw Paul, who was scowling and holding boxes. She couldn't blame the poor guy.

"Hey there! Christmas shopping?" Alana asked.

"Something like that." Toni introduced Kevin to Paul. "We were just finished and heading for a little cheer, care to join us?" Toni looked from Alana to Paul.

Alana gave Paul a hopeful glance. "Why don't you go with them?" Paul said. "I have to stop at the office. I'll catch up with you in an hour or so."

"The office? On a Sunday?" Alana stopped short. "Fine." She looked at Toni. "Where were you headed?"

"Kitty O'Shea's, just down the street," she said. "In the Hilton."

Paul stood and juggled the boxes. Toni offered her help. "I'll take them if you want."

"Thanks," Paul said, and Toni took each box.

"Good grief, what did she buy?" Toni asked.

Paul wiped his forehead. "The store."

"You don't have to do that, Toni. We can take them to the car." Alana glared at Paul.

"It's no problem, really." Toni glanced at both of them.

"Why do that?" Paul asked. "It's five blocks away. I'll catch a cab, then meet you at O'Shea's. I know where it is."

"You do?" Alana asked.

"We've been there, honey." He turned to Kevin and shook his hand. "Thanks, nice meeting you." He then kissed Alana on the cheek. "Have fun."

Alana seemed stunned as she watched Paul dash into the street to hail a cab. Quick as that, he was gone. She turned awkwardly back to Toni and Kevin. "Well…"

"C'mon, I'm thirsty," Toni said and juggled the boxes. "Good grief, woman, did you really buy the store?"

Alana laughed along with Kevin as his phone went off, signaling a text message. He read it while Toni watched him.

"Don't tell me, the department is now texting if there's a fire," Toni said.

"Kinda. It's Lidia, um…she wants…" He stopped.

"Okay, scram. I'll call you later," Toni said with a wink.

Kevin grinned. "Thanks. G'bye, Alana. Keep this goof under control," he said as he too hailed a cab and was gone.

"And then there were two." Toni looked down into Alana's green eyes.

"And one is stuck carrying all my boxes." Alana winced apologetically as Toni adjusted her packages.

"Then let's keep moving before I start cramping. O'Shea's is just up ahead."

Alana laughed and walked alongside Toni, who was whistling Christmas carols. "You seem happy," Alana said quietly.

Toni looked down and grinned. "I am. I was happy when I saw you."

When Alana looked up at Toni, she stumbled slightly and grabbed for Toni. "Better hold on to my arm, schoolmarm. The crowds are vicious this holiday season."

Alana laughed and slipped her arm through Toni's. As they continued down Michigan Avenue, Toni stopped in front of the Hilton. "The bar's inside."

They slipped into a quiet booth in the back of the Irish tavern. "This is nice." Alana looked around as she slipped off her gloves and blew into her cold hands.

The waitress came up and gave Toni a smile. "Well, hello."

"Well, hello to you, too," Toni said. "What's good for a cold December day?"

"A warm bed," the waitress said as she handed them the menu.

Alana rolled her eyes and cleared her throat. "I'll have an Irish coffee, please."

Toni hid her grin in the menu. "I'll have a Baileys and coffee, thanks."

"A warm bed," Allie muttered after the waitress walked away.

"What? I thought that was clever," Toni argued.

"You would," Allie said as she examined the menu.

Toni laughed as she watched Alana. It struck her then, for the umpteenth time, how much she liked having this woman in her life. "You're a good friend."

Alana looked up and smiled. "Thanks. I feel the same about you. I-I enjoy our time together."

"Me too." Toni rested her elbows on the table. "How are Nick and Jocelyn? Boy, I had such a good time with them at Thanksgiving."

"They're coming in on Christmas Eve. They can only stay for a few days."

"Will you tell them I said hello and wish them a Merry Christmas for me?"

"I will. They like you, though that's not hard to understand. Nick talks about you all the time."

Toni laughed. "He's a fine young man. Jocelyn, how is she doing with school? She's almost done."

"She's doing well. Toni…" She stopped and shook her head.

"What?" Toni asked quickly, slipping out of her leather jacket. She looked up to see Alana watching her. "You can touch it if you like," she offered the sleeve of her jacket. "This cost me a pretty penny. I only take it out on special occasions, like a Chicago winter."

"It's very nice. You look good in leather." She stopped short and looked at Toni, who smiled tentatively. "I just…thank you for taking an interest in my children."

"I love your kids. They're great. Please don't thank me for doing something so easily as liking your kids." Toni then took a deep breath and figured now or never. "Okay, I know Christmas is a still few days away, but I-I got you something," Toni blurted out. She watched Alana, who blinked in surprise.

"You did?"

Toni nodded happily "Yep. Want it?"

Alana laughed. "Of course."

Toni slipped the envelope out of her breast pocket and held it. "When I saw this, I just knew you'd like it. God, I hope I did the right thing." She smiled and slid it over to her. "Merry Christmas, Alana."

Alana smiled and opened the gilded envelope; she read it and blinked several times. "Toni, it's—" She stopped and read it again. "New York?"

Toni nodded with excitement. "The Monet exhibit moves from Chicago to New York next summer. During that same time, Van Gogh and some other guy is there, as well. They say it's the chance of a lifetime, and you won't want to miss it. I guess these guys will never be in the same exhibit again for a long time. That's what they say anyway." She shrugged helplessly. "It's just the cost of the exhibit and the stay at the hotel for a long weekend. It was a package. Sorry, I couldn't get you the airfare. This is something that's just for you." When Alana said nothing, she thought the worst. "God, you hate it. I can take it back, really."

She reached for it, and Alana quickly grabbed her hand. Toni's breath caught in her chest as Alana's cold hand held hers. "It's perfect," Alana whispered. "A chance of a lifetime…"

Toni nodded, searching her face. "That's what they say."

"I'll find a way out there. I can't believe you…"

Toni was shocked to see tears stream down her face. "Why are you crying?"

"Because I'm happy." Alana picked up a napkin and dried her eyes. "Thank you. You don't know what this means to me. How did you…?"

"I was out with Kevin, and I just saw it. I just knew you'd, I don't know."

Mercifully, the waitress came up with their drinks.

"Well, now I'm glad you got me something because I got you something, too," Alana announced.

Toni grinned like a kid. "Ya did?"

Alana nodded and examined the boxes.

"You mean I carried my own Christmas present?" Toni scolded, and Alana laughed out loud.

"Merry Christmas," Alana held the large box. "Now I didn't get a chance to wrap it. Paul and I were on our way to…"

"Oh, gimme. I don't care." Toni itched with excitement.

Alana grimaced and tentatively offered the box. "If you don't like it…" She bit at her bottom lip.

Toni eagerly opened the box and took the tissue paper away. She blinked several times and looked at Alana. "It's Nick and Jocelyn and…me," she whispered in awe.

"I drew that a while ago when I was up late and couldn't sleep. I turned it into a watercolor and had it matted. You can pick out the frame. I'll go with you if you want."

Toni was speechless as she gazed at the picture. Alana continued quietly, "You're just so fond of them and they're fond of you, so I thought…"

"It's beautiful. I heard somewhere that some artists sign the back of paintings. Is that right?" Toni asked, and Alana nodded. Toni grinned and handed the picture back to her. "Please."

Alana took a pen out and struck a thoughtful pose. She then

smiled and scribbled on the back of the painting, then handed it back to Toni.

Toni—

You showed me that beyond the blue horizon there was a rising sun of a beautiful new day.

Thank you for your friendship.

Always,

Alana

Toni could feel her lip quivering as she gently placed the picture back in the box. She almost reverently placed the tissue paper back over it and closed it, running her fingers over the box. "It's the most wonderful present I ever received," she said in a quiet voice.

Alana grinned. "Merry Christmas, Toni." She raised her drink and Toni did the same.

"Merry Christmas, Alana."

They sat in silence for a moment or two. "Can we go get it framed now?"

Alana laughed out loud at the serious look on Toni's face. "Sure, I know where to go."

"I can't believe you've carried all those boxes today and not one gripe," Allie said as they piled into the cab. "Paul was complaining—" She stopped.

"Okay, where is this framing place? I don't care how much it costs, you know," Toni said firmly.

"I know, but it won't cost that much."

An hour later, Allie yawned, the clerk looked at his watch, and Toni frowned in contemplation as she held two frames.

"Lady, please. We have to close in a half hour, just choose a frame," he begged, and Allie hid her grin.

Toni glared at the impudent clerk. "Look, pal. I have the artist sitting right over there. You can't rush an artist. What would have happened if somebody rushed Claude Van Gogh, huh?"

The clerk's jaw dropped; he blinked and looked as Allie shook her head and pointed to her temple, making a circular motion with her finger.

"Toni, I think the one on the right is the best."

Toni nodded. "You think? Well, you're the expert," she said, emphasizing the last word for the clerk, who nodded and took the frame.

"It'll be ready in a week," he said.

Toni was astonished. "A week? I don't think it took her that long to paint it," she said and looked at Allie. "Did it?"

"No."

"See?"

Allie gently pulled at her leather-clad arm while Toni glared at the clerk. "Toni, this is normal. You want it to be right, don't you?"

"Well, yeah, but a week?" she exclaimed and continued glaring at the clerk. "You better not let anything happen to that painting."

"I'll take good care of it. I promise." He handled the painting carefully.

Toni nodded and pointed a finger at him. "I'll be back in a week."

Allie rolled her eyes and pulled her out of the shop. "You didn't have to threaten the poor guy," Allie said as she slipped on her gloves. "Oh, Christ!"

"What? I didn't threaten him, really."

"No, Paul," she exclaimed. "He's got the cell phone."

"Use mine." Toni fished it out of her pocket and watched as Allie dialed the number. Toni's eyes bugged out of her head as she looked at her watch. "Oh, shit, Alana. I'm so sorry. God, he's been sitting there for two hours."

Allie nodded. "I got his voice mail. Paul, Allie. Call this number when you get the message. I'll explain. Bye."

She handed the phone back to Toni, who juggled the presents while she hailed a cab. Two drove right by her. "Merry Christmas, assho—"

"Toni!"

By the time they got back to O'Shea's, it was nearly four in the afternoon. Allie rushed in as Toni continued to struggle. Allie looked around. "He's not here. Can I borrow your phone again?"

Toni handed over the phone and set the packages down and wiped the sweat from her brow. "This is more work than a three-alarm fire."

Allie laughed as she dialed. "Paul, did you get my message?"

"Hey, um no."

"No? Well, I'm so sorry."

"No, Allie. I'm sorry. I'm still at work and…"

"What? You're still at work? And just when did you plan on letting me know? We've been sitting here all afternoon."

"That's not very fair, Alana," Toni whispered and stopped when Allie glared. Toni backed up.

"I'm sorry, Al. I can be there—"

"No, Paul. I'll be leaving. Do you want me to pick you up?"

"No, I'll take the train."

"Fine, take the train. I'll talk to you later." She angrily slammed the phone shut and handed it to Toni.

Toni said nothing as she watched Allie seethe; she breathed heavily through her anger and hailed the bartender. "I'll have a gin and tonic, and she'll have a Guinness, thank you," she said calmly and slid onto a barstool. She looked over at Toni, who was wild-eyed. "Join me."

Toni quickly obeyed and hopped up on the barstool.

They were silent for an uncomfortable amount of time. Allie, still furious with Paul, glanced at Toni, who was nearly finished with her beer.

"You want me to go back and beat up the clerk?" Toni asked quietly. "I will if you want me to."

Chapter 13

The next day was Christmas. Toni stood by her window looking out at the cold Christmas Eve night and drank her coffee.

Kevin and Lidia were at Mass, then they'd go visit Lidia's family the next day. Earlier, they all had dinner, which Lidia made, thank God. They laughed and played Christmas music as they opened presents, and Toni once again had that feeling of belonging, of family. She called Matt and Fran and wished them a Merry Christmas and talked for a while, trying to hold on to that feeling.

Now Toni stood in her living room and snuggled around her the new sweater that Kevin and Lidia had given her. She had that restless feeling again; she felt it creeping up on her. She needed to be alone, needed her solitude. This was the feeling she had after her father took out after her in a drunken tirade. As soon as that image came, she quickly dismissed it.

Instead of dwelling on the past, Toni smiled at the thought of Kevin and Lidia finding each other. Kevin Murphy was a good man. She remembered how good he was to her when she was a young girl. Once her father would pass out and Toni saw that everyone was safe, Kevin would come and sit with her mother and the young ones. It was those times when Toni felt restless and closed in, but Kevin would always find her at the coffee house and take care of her. He let her have her time to gather herself, then take her home. Yes, Kevin was a good man. And when she was younger, Toni sometimes wished her father would die so Kevin could marry her mother. It almost happened.

117

When her father fell from that scaffold, Toni felt a relief she never thought possible. The guilt from this followed for a time, but she was a grown woman by then, and the guilt faded quickly. She was relieved—relieved mostly for her mother who suffered all her life and stayed with a drunk and lived her life as that poet Thoreau said, in quiet desperation.

But Mrs. O'Hara loved her children. Of that, there was no doubt. Toni and the younger ones always felt loved and cared for by their mother, no matter what their father did. She had a maternal instinct that surpassed all her heartache, all her sorrow.

Instantly, Toni thought of Alana and smiled. She took a deep breath and sat by the open fire and watched the flames flicker in the darkness of her living room. Alana, she thought. She loved her children, as well. Lived her life for them and nurtured them, watched them grow into happy, healthy young adults.

She was still smiling when the phone rang. "Hello?"

"Toni, Merry Christmas," Alana's happy voice called out through the line.

Toni grinned widely and sat back. "Merry Christmas, Alana." She heard the Christmas music in the background and the voices of Nick and Jocelyn.

"Now you're sure you're busy with family tomorrow?"

"Yep. Between Kevin and Lidia and…everyone, I'm lucky to be home at all tomorrow. How are the kids? It sounds like you have a houseful."

She smiled as she heard Alana's lovely laugh. "God, yes! Nick invited a few friends he hasn't seen in ages. So I'm…"

"Cooking up a storm," Toni said affectionately.

"Right again. I wish I had you here, though. You make a good taster."

Toni laughed along. "Save me some."

"Oh, I doubt that will happen, O'Hara. These boys have heartier appetites than you do."

They both laughed for a moment. Silence then filled the space between them.

"I miss you, Toni."

Toni closed her eyes tight and took a deep breath. She then

smiled. "I miss you, too. Tell everyone I said Merry Christmas and tell the kids I said hello and I…well, ya know."

"I know. I will. Merry Christmas."

"Merry Christmas."

Toni sat there listening to the dial tone for a moment before setting the phone on the table. She wanted to be with Alana that night. She wanted to see Nick and Jocelyn. However, she knew Paul might not react well, and how could she do that to Alana and her kids on Christmas Eve, for crying out loud? She angrily ran her fingers through her hair, walked out into the kitchen, and opened a bottle of wine.

Sitting back by the fire, she raised her glass. "Merry Christmas, Ma," she whispered and damned the tears that blurred her vision as she gazed at the crackling flames.

On New Year's Eve, Allie sat in the living room watching old Fred Astaire and Ginger Rogers movies. She looked over to see Paul sound asleep in the recliner.

She had taken Nick and Jocelyn to the airport the other day. She missed them horribly now. She missed Toni, as well. She glanced at the phone and shook her head and watched television. She glanced at the phone again, the war raging in her head—to call or not to call. There was no question.

I'm so sure I'm going to call Toni O'Hara at midnight. Like she'll be home. A gorgeous lesbian who is single. Home? On New Year's Eve? I doubt it, she thought.

She pointed the remote at the set and flipped the channels. There was Dick Clark counting down the seconds. "Does he ever age?" She laughed quietly. Paul let out a snore to which she turned up the volume.

"5-4-3-2-1, Happy New Year!"

Allie smiled and watched the fools laughing and singing. "Happy New Year, Toni," she whispered and turned off the television. She glanced at Paul, took the afghan, and covered him.

"Happy New Year, Paul," she said and flipped off the light and quietly walked upstairs.

Chapter 14

With the holidays over and boring January outside her window, Toni found herself in a grumpy mood. Kevin rolled his eyes. "You need to get..."

"Don't say it, you horny old man." Toni growled. She picked up the phone and dialed her friend at work.

"Mrs. Sanders," the soft voice rang through the line, instantly putting Toni in a good mood.

Kevin sighed and walked out. "You're hopeless."

"Hey...I haven't seen you in two weeks. How about dinner some night?"

"Sure, how about Thursday? Paul's working late, as usual."

Toni noticed Allie no longer sounded irritated. Her voice held the tone of resignation now.

"I'll pick you up from school, how's that?" Toni asked.

"Sounds like a plan. I'll be ready."

Toni hung up and smiled. Maybe January won't be such a cold, boring month.

They sat at the same table at the same bistro. Toni noticed Alana was a bit subdued. "Penny for your thoughts."

"You'll get change."

Toni laughed as she sipped her Irish coffee. Alana sighed deeply. "Wow, heavy sigh."

Alana looked at her. "How do you know if your partner is cheating on you?"

Toni had the whipped cream-topped drink to her mouth. She shot a look up, but not before dipping her nose in the whipped cream. Cursing herself, she quickly snatched the napkin and wiped off her nose. "W-what?"

"Seriously. Has it ever happened to you?"

"Yes."

"I'm sorry. That was insensitive of me."

"No, no. It's all right. I've already told you part of it. Gina, remember. The snake woman? It was a long time ago. We were together for almost five years. I came home after my shift was over at the firehouse. She wasn't expecting me, and there she was, in bed with another woman."

"Geez! I'm sorry," Alana said seriously. "What a horrible thing to have happen. What did you do?"

"You mean after I made a crazy ass out of myself?"

Alana chuckled at the mental picture. "Yes, after that."

"I moved out. I probably should have long ago, when she never came to see me in the hospital after I was injured. Anyway, I moved out and never spoke to her again. Until my great luck to run into her when I was with you." Toni shrugged, then eyed her friend. "You, um..."

"I don't know," she said, reading Toni's mind. "We're just not clicking. He's always, and I mean always, working. And when he's not, we're on pins and needles."

Toni listened, thinking that was exactly what was happening. A guy just doesn't work every Saturday. She hoped with all her heart she was wrong.

"Well, I don't know what to think," Alana said, then stopped. "Okay, enough. Let's talk about something else," she said. "It just occurred to me, O'Hara, that I know nothing of your life. I've been blathering all these months about my life and family. Do you have any brothers or sisters? What about your parents? You've only mentioned your father once, and it wasn't very nice. So...give."

Alana leaned forward and waited.

Toni fidgeted for a moment. "There's not much to tell," she said, and Alana shook her head but said nothing. Toni ran her fingers through her hair. "I...well..." She stopped.

Alana rolled her eyes. "Good grief!" she exclaimed. "Okay. Answer yes or no."

Toni tried not to grin at her tenacity. "No."

"Very funny. Do you have a brother?"

"Yes."

"Sister?"

"Yes…all right, look," Toni said. "I'm the oldest, then Matt, then Fran. My father was an alcoholic who used to beat the shit out of me on occasion until I nearly killed him. He died drunk, falling off a scaffold…" She stopped as she saw the look of horror on Alana's face.

Alana blinked rapidly. "Did he abuse your mother, as well?" she asked softly.

Toni swallowed hard. She hadn't talked about this in ages, certainly not to any other woman. What a mood killer that would have been. Only to Kevin who lived through it, as well.

"Toni?" Alana asked quietly.

Toni took a deep breath and let it out slowly. "I-I haven't talked about this in so long. I have no idea why I told you," she said, honestly stumped.

Alana reached over and gently took her hand. "For the same reason I talk about Paul and the kids. Now please, you've listened to me, let me be your friend and listen to you. Please tell me."

Toni looked down at their hands. She took a deep breath. "No, he never raised a hand to anyone but me. Kevin threatened him with murder if he ever laid a hand on my mother. Matt and Fran were too young. I was nearly eight when Matt was born and almost eleven when Fran came along. I don't think my mother, well, I don't think they were conceived out of love," she said quietly.

"Fran…that's a pretty name."

Toni smiled affectionately. "That was Mom. She had three favorite saints. Unfortunately, for me and Fran, all three were men. St. Anthony, St. Matthew, and St. Francis of Assisi. So there you go. I became Antonia and Fran became Frances. Matt lucked out."

Alana smiled thinking of Toni's mother. She watched Toni smiling fondly at some memory. Then her gray eyes grew dark as her brow furrowed.

"Anyway, he would get drunk and want to beat up someone, probably because he hated his life, maybe because we didn't have much money. Or maybe, he was just an asshole…"

Alana cringed at her vehemence. "Why did he only hit you?"

"I was his favorite, I guess," she said with a wry chuckle. "I would run interference. He'd go after my mother, and I'd step in and yell at him, egg him on so he'd come after me. It didn't happen all the time. Just enough to make me hate his guts. When Matt was born, Mom got more protective, but it didn't matter. He wasn't gonna hit his only son. He smacked him a few times but never laid into him like…" She stopped and swallowed. She looked up to see the look of horror on Alana's face. "He only caught me a few times. I got faster as I got older." Her hands started to shake. "Shit, I'm fifty years old, and my hands still shake at the thought of him."

Alana reached over again and took the clammy hand in her own, amazed when Toni held on tight. "Anyway, that was our life. He'd get drunk, I'd take a beating, then he'd pass out. I'd get Matt, Fran, and Ma to Grandma's, then I'd go and hide at Mrs. Walinski's bakery or some coffee house. No one knew where I was, and for just a little while, I'd feel safe…"

There was silence for a moment or two. Toni took a drink of water and looked at Alana. "So…"

"Where is your mother?"

"She died four years ago. Car accident, never knew what hit her."

Alana held on tight to Toni's hand.

"Don't feel sorry for me. I can't stand pity. I mean it," she said, not looking at her.

"I don't pity you. My heart aches for you, but I don't pity you. You seem to have turned out all right. Where are Matt and Fran?"

"Matt is living in Seattle. Fran in Boston. After Ma died, they didn't want to stay in Chicago. They both married and left. I don't blame them for not wanting to come back. They…"

"Wait one minute. You told me you were busy at Christmas with your family."

"I-I…"

"Did they come in for the holiday?"

"Well…"

"Do *not* tell me you were alone on Christmas, Toni O'Hara," she said angrily.

Toni stammered. "Well, not Christmas Eve. Um…ah…"

"What about Christmas Day? Damn it!" she hissed angrily, and Toni winced. "Do you mean to tell me you sat alone on Christmas Day?"

"Um…"

Alana closed her eyes; she looked as though she were counting to ten. Toni waited. "Why did you lie to me? Why?"

"Paul doesn't like me," she started and chuckled nervously. "That sounded so childish. You know what I mean. I'm not an idiot. I know you and Paul are having problems. And while nothing is going on between us, I'm still a lesbian, and to a man who's having problems with his marriage, that's a threat. So I didn't want to be the cause of any uneasiness with your family at Christmas. I'm sorry I lied to you."

"Don't ever lie to me again. About anything, I mean it. We would have worked something out and—"

Toni gave her a curious look. "Why?"

Alana blinked. "Why what?"

"Why would you care to work something out? This is your family. He's your husband. I'm not worth the trouble."

Alana frowned deeply when she realized Toni was completely serious. "Now you listen to me, Toni O'Hara. I will decide what is right for me and my family. You are quite possibly my best friend, and you will always be worth the trouble," she said with such resolution it took Toni's breath away.

In that instant, Toni knew she loved this woman. She wanted her; she needed her. It was the happiest and saddest moment of her life.

"Thank you. That means a great deal to me. You know what I have to do now, don't you?" she asked with a small grin.

"Oh, I'm not sure I want to know."

Toni got up, walked around the table, took her friend's hand,

and Alana stood. "This," she said softly and pulled Alana into a monstrous bear hug, wrapping her arms around her shoulders. "Thanks. You're the best thing that's ever happened to me," she whispered, kissed her forehead, and pulled back.

Alana looked up and grinned. "You're welcome. Being your friend is the best thing that's happened to me in a long, long while."

They took their respective seats again. "But don't ever lie to me again," she scolded, and Toni laughed and agreed.

After dinner with Toni, Allie put on some soft music and indulged herself in a nice hot bath. She lay in the hot steamy bubbles as her mind slipped into nirvana.

She tried not to think of the problems she and Paul were having. In her heart, she knew he was having an affair. She just didn't want to believe it. She thought of confronting him. Maybe she would—if he ever got home before she was asleep.

Suddenly, Toni popped into her head. Well, so much for not thinking. She closed her eyes and chuckled over the times they'd spent together. From dinners to Cubs games, Toni was always there for her. Listening to her, caring about her. Allie felt closer to Toni than she ever did to Paul. Her eyes flew open at the thought of it.

"No. I can't be...not with Toni," she whispered, trying to convince herself. She shook her head, dismissing the thought.

As she ran the soapy cloth over her body, she instantly pictured Toni. God, don't do this again. It was too late. The images once again were there as they had been for several months now. She sighed as she pictured Toni kissing her breasts. She slid her hand down as she parted her legs as far as the bathtub would allow.

Toni's hands were now teasing her, sliding through the warm folds, making her breath hitch. Warm lips kissed up and down her neck. Soft murmurs of love whispered in her ear as her fingers moved quicker and faster.

"Ohgodohgod..." she whimpered as the water began to slosh over the sides. Allie arched her back. "Toni!" she tried not to cry out as the orgasm swept through her. She shivered violently as she came. Quickly, she pulled her hand away and groaned breathlessly.

"What am I doing? Again." She moaned and slid down in the hot water, soaking her head completely.

Feeling extremely guilty, Allie climbed into bed and turned out the light. She must have dozed off; when she heard the backdoor open, she glanced at the clock on the nightstand. It was 11:30. She waited and listened to his footsteps as he climbed the stairs; she heard the creak of the door as he pushed it open. He fumbled in the darkness as he undressed, then he went into the bathroom. Allie heard the shower going and turned onto her back. She stared at the ceiling until Paul came out, wrapped in one towel and drying his hair with another.

"How was your meeting?" she asked, startling Paul.

"Thought you'd be asleep by now." He slipped into a pair of boxers. "What did you do tonight?"

Allie heard his hesitation and was painfully aware he did not answer her question—or maybe he had. "I went out to dinner with Toni."

"That's good," he said quietly. "Did you have a good time?"

"Yes, I did. I always do with Toni." Allie didn't like the snippy tone she was using, and she knew she said this purposely to bush a button. She remembered what Toni had said regarding what a lesbian is to a married man.

"I'm glad you do," Paul said. He truly sounded as if he were.

"Did you have a good time tonight?"

Paul slipped into bed and lay on his back, as well. They lay far apart in the king-sized bed, which spoke volumes about their marriage.

After a long moment, Paul sighed. "A meeting is a meeting, Al. G'night," he whispered and turned on his side.

Tears welled in Allie's eyes as the hollow feeling swept through her. "Good night, Paul."

She lay in the quiet, looking around the dark shadows of their bedroom wondering how the hell they got to this point. She reached over and flipped on the light on her nightstand.

It was time to find out.

Chapter 15

"Wake up, Paul." Allie sat up.

Paul groaned and rolled over, shielding his eyes from the light. For an instant, he looked just like Nick. "What's wrong?"

"Us." Allie grabbed her robe. "Let's go. I'm hungry. I'll make some eggs."

"I don't want eggs."

"Get the hell out of that bed, Paul Sanders. If I have to say it again, I'll be back with a pitcher of cold water." She left him staring at her as she walked out.

Allie put a pot of coffee on, then got the eggs and bacon out of the fridge just as Paul walked into the kitchen and sat down.

"Scrambled?" she asked. Paul nodded as he glanced up.

While she fried the bacon, she poured two cups of coffee and set them on the table. Paul sat in silence, frowning as he stared at nothing in particular. When she had everything done, she divided the eggs onto two plates and sat. Paul got up and got the hot sauce.

"That will be ugly tomorrow," Allie said.

Paul grinned slightly as he sat down. "We used to do this all the time."

Allie nodded. "When money was tight before life and the job got in the way."

Paul looked up. "And you lost interest in me."

Allie blinked and sat back. She was stunned at the defiant, yet sad look on Paul's face. He then continued eating. "I didn't mean that to sound harsh," he said, not looking up.

"I know. Maybe you're right." Allie ate a forkful of eggs. She couldn't taste much. "Is there someone else? You spend so much time away."

Paul's head jerked up so fast, he dropped his fork. He glared for a moment, then smiled sadly. "I could ask you the same exact question. Would that be fair of me?"

"This isn't about Toni."

"I know. And it's not about anyone I may know. What's happening with us has nothing to do with anyone but you and me. Let's keep this right where it belongs, okay?"

Allie nodded. "I agree. So where are we?"

Paul wiped his mouth on a napkin and tossed it down. "I don't know. We could sit here all night." He stopped and looked at her. "I think since the kids are out on their own, we have to really see each other. I mean really see each other. I don't want to do the blame game. I just don't know."

Allie took a drink of coffee, trying to collect her thoughts. Her mind wandered back to college. "Remember when we first met?"

Paul smiled. "Yes. You were doodling on your sketchpad."

Allie cocked her head and smiled sadly. "And that's what you always thought of it—doodling. Did you ever think how much it means to me? I mean deep in my soul."

Paul stopped smiling. "I-I wasn't being—"

Allie laughed ruefully. "Yeah, you kinda were, sweetie. I think that's part of it. You and I never really got each other. You never understood my passion for art, how it touches my soul. And I don't think I ever acknowledged your passion for your business."

"My passion for the business means a lot to me."

"And I never asked you to give it up, which is what I did with mine." When Paul looked as though he was going to scoff, Allie held up her hand. "And please don't tell me that's what the woman does. She gives up for the family, while the man does as he wants."

Paul turned bright red, indicating that's exactly what he was going to say. He drank his coffee.

"Why did you marry me?"

"I thought you'd be a good wife and mother. You were smart and funny and…"

Allie laughed openly. "I'm hoping the word 'love' comes in there somewhere." The moment she said it, she wanted it back. "I'm sorry. I know you love me."

"Why did you marry me?" Paul drank his coffee.

"You were strong and confident. I was not." She chuckled sadly. "Boy, that was lame."

Paul just watched her.

"What?" she asked.

He looked as though he might say something but then stopped as if he thought better of it. "Don't do this. You've been surprisingly open just now. We haven't talked like this…"

"Ever," Paul said. "And before you go off, I know you always wanted to. On this, I will take full culpability." He took a drink of his coffee while Allie toyed with her fork. "Maybe I never really wanted to delve too deeply about the 'why' of our marriage."

"Why are you now?" Allie asked. They may have had their problems, but Allie knew Paul. And this turn in his willingness to talk deeply did not change on his own.

"I've been told I need to come to grips with a lot of things for a lot of reasons." He tiredly rubbed his face. "And no, I'm not seeing a shrink. The main reason is us. To finally, at last find out what the hell happened and how to fix it. If we want to."

He took a deep breath and let it out as if to pull on some inner resolve. It was scaring Allie. "I know about Sue Tucker from college," he blurted out.

That statement felt like a slap in the face. "What?"

Paul groaned. "You heard me."

"How did you know about her?" Allie asked. Suddenly, the room felt small, and her heart raced.

"Her brother Brian. He was a year older than us, and apparently after you and I started dating, Susan had a big problem with it. He said you nearly ruined her."

Allie was stunned. "Ruined her?" Her mind raced back to that time in college. Sue Tucker had the dorm room next to hers.

"I'm not sure I want to hear about this, but tell me anyway." He glanced at his watch. "Too late in the evening to start drinking."

Allie tried to laugh, but her mouth had gone bone dry. She

took a drink of coffee, which was now ice cold. "She was a friend, and I liked her. She was funny, confident. A take-charge kind of person. And you know I was anything but. She told me one rainy afternoon in my dorm that she was a lesbian. She was shocked but pleasantly surprised when her declaration did not turn me off. I..." She wasn't quite sure how to go on.

"Did you sleep with her?" Paul's hesitant tone made it perfectly clear he really didn't want to know.

"No."

Paul's head shot up. "You didn't? Brian seemed to think you had."

"Brian was wrong. But I won't lie to you. There was something there. I-I don't know what I felt for Sue. Looking back on it, I suppose I was very much attracted to her. But I was eighteen and had never been with anyone, man or woman, so how could I know?" Allie stopped to collect her thoughts. "We had brief encounters, kissing and fondling, but I got scared. I can't believe I'm telling you this..."

"I can't, either. You think you know someone."

Allie looked directly at him. "You don't think you know me?"

"Not really. Not after this." He sat forward. "C'mon, Allie. You never, ever spoke of this. You married me, we had a family, and now here we are. I'm not saying it's all about what happened with Sue. I know I have my responsibility."

Allie sat back. "I'm sorry, but I never told you quite frankly because it was none of your business."

"You had a lesbian whatever and you don't think I should know about it?"

"How many girls did you know before me?"

"Oh, don't start that. This is different."

"How so? It's okay for you to have a sex life before me, but I can't, and if I do, I'm obligated to tell you? Why? To make sure it was okay with you? Make sure I was fit to marry you and bear your children?" She got up and slammed her silverware in the sink and turned on the water. "I wish I would have had sex with Sue. At least it would be something worthwhile to talk about!"

She turned the water off and leaned against the sink. "I haven't thought about Sue in years."

"I think you married me because you were scared."

Allie turned to him then. "Perhaps. I was a teenager, and my first taste of sex and love was with a woman. Coming from a strict Catholic family, yeah, it scared me. Being damned in the fires of hell was a terrifying proposition."

Paul nodded, his gaze darting back and forth. "And then I come along. I wish you would have told me back then."

Allie smiled sadly. "If wishes were fishes…" She looked at Paul and sat down. "And why didn't you tell me before we got married you knew about this?"

Paul thought about it for a moment. "I suppose I didn't want to believe it. Maybe Brian was wrong. I suppose I lied to myself." He sat back, suddenly looking very old. "So now what happens?"

Allie thought about it, wondering the same thing. It struck her then, as she looked at the man she married twenty-five years ago, this was a defining moment for both of them. And out of the blue, that winter night with Sue Tucker played clearly in her mind.

They had been lying on Allie's bed in her dorm. Sue had professed her attraction and love for her. Allie remembered how her palms got sweaty and her heart pounded in her chest not knowing what to do; it was all happening far too fast. Sue sat up and looked down at her. "This is a defining moment, Allie. You define it, or it defines you."

Allie realized now, she allowed that moment to define her as a coward, and she ran. Ran into the arms of Paul Sanders and a safe, normal life. From then on, she and Paul had allowed little moments throughout their lives to define them.

Perhaps it was time, at last for both of them.

"We had our time, Paul. We married for our own reasons. I was scared of what I might be, and you needed me to be what I couldn't." She reached out and took his hand. "We've tried, and for a while, we had a good life. We made two fantastic kids."

"Yes, out of everything, no one can take that away from us." Paul's lip quivered as he smiled. "And you made a good home, Allie. And you helped me make a good business."

They sat in silence, holding hands for a long moment.

"I think that's enough for one night," Allie said softly. "What do you think? We'll talk about this again?"

Paul nodded. "Okay. But not tomorrow. I need time for this to sink in." He patted her hand and stood. "I think I'll sleep in Nick's room tonight."

Tears flooded Allie's eyes as she smiled and nodded. "Good night, Paul."

"Good night, Allie."

Allie groaned as she stood and cleared the rest of the dishes. She put them in the sink, then leaned against the counter and sobbed.

Chapter 16

Toni sat on the couch looking out at the snow. It was sleeting and just plain ugly. She looked around her spacious studio apartment and realized how lonely she was. She didn't even want sex! What the hell was happening?

She walked over to the bedroom area, which was hidden by a four-foot wall and flounced on her huge bed—the bed that usually had another woman in it. She groaned and pulled the pillow over her face.

With that, the phone rang.

"What?" she asked flatly.

"Holy cow, what's wrong with you?" Alana asked.

"Nothing, I'm bored, and it's February. It's sleeting and ugly." Toni winced at her whiny voice. "I haven't seen you in three weeks. I gave you up for dead."

"Ooh, somebody needs food."

Toni glared at the phone. "I do not need food, smartass." She did smile, however, at the laughter coming from her schoolmarm.

"Well, the weather is certainly not cooperating. We can't go out and play," Alana said.

Toni smiled as she listened. She put the pillow behind her head and sighed. "So what should we do?" Toni asked with child-like anticipation.

"Well, I've never seen where you live, so invite me over and I'll make dinner," Alana suggested boldly.

Toni stared at the ceiling. Alana? In her home? Hmm. "Is Paul working again?"

"No. He's out with the guys, watching hockey, I think."

"Hmm. The Blackhawks are doing well. What bar?"

"I'll kill you first."

"Very dark, Alana. Okay. Come over whenever you like. I have nothing in my house, though."

"Why does that not surprise me? I'll take care of it."

"I have wine and Guinness."

"Figures."

"Shut up and take down the directions."

After a trip to the store, Allie followed the explicit directions. "She gives good directions." Then she thought of what she had forgotten and laughed. "Key lime pie..."

She took out her cell and called the restaurant. Yes, they had it. Yes, she could buy the whole pie.

She pulled into the restaurant and dashed in, trying not to get soaked. As she stood by the register waiting for the pie, she glanced around the restaurant. Her heart stopped as she stood rooted to the spot.

There was Paul. The waiter was just seating him and a redheaded woman, who reached over and held Paul's hand. Allie realized this was the woman Paul was with at the deli that one afternoon last August. She continued watching as Paul smiled, leaned in, and...kissed her. The redhead placed a hand on his cheek in an intimate gesture and gently ran her fingers through his graying hair.

Allie was stunned. It had been three weeks since their heart-to-heart talk. Allie smiled sadly. So this is what he's doing about it. "Oh, Paul," she whispered sadly, holding the tears back.

"Ma'am?" the waiter gently nudged her.

Allie blinked and took the pie, handing him the money. She glanced back and felt her stomach clench as she watched her husband holding this woman's hand, then kissing it tenderly. Then it happened. She watched him mouth the words, "I love you."

She couldn't swallow as her stomach lurched, felt the bile in the back of her throat. She grabbed the pie and quickly got into her car.

Toni whistled as she stepped out of the shower and towel-dried her hair. She tossed the towel on the bed and dressed. She had just slipped into her jeans and sweater when the bell rang.

"That was quick," she said and opened the front door.

There stood Allie soaking wet, holding a pie in one hand and two plastic grocery bags in the other.

Toni laughed, and as she reached for the pie, she noticed Allie's bottom lip quivering.

"Are you all right?" She pulled her inside. "Alana!" She took the bags from her and the pie. She stripped the wet coat off her and tossed it on the kitchen chair. "Say something. Are you hurt?"

She guided Allie into the living room, easing her down on the deep cushion. She knelt in front of her.

"Alana," she said and gently shook her. Alana blinked, then started to cry. Toni was shocked. She pulled her into her arms and rocked her. Her hands roamed over her body, checking for blood or some sign of injury. Visions of Alana being in some sort of car accident flashed through her mind as she held her.

After a moment, Toni gently pulled back. "Hey, now tell me what's happened," she whispered tenderly and brushed the wet hair off her face.

Allie sniffed and ran a finger under her nose. "I saw Paul."

"Are the Blackhawks doing that badly?"

Allie glared at her.

"Sorry. He wasn't at a bar?"

"No. I stopped to get you a key lime pie, and he was there with a woman."

"A client?" Toni asked. Please say yes, she thought.

"Well, if he kisses all his clients and tells them he loves them, there's no wonder his business is booming."

"Oh, shit. I'm so sorry."

Alana reached in her pocket, took out a tissue, and blew her nose. "So much has happened in the last few weeks. I want to tell you, but right now, I feel numb."

"You're in shock and you're soaked and freezing. C'mon, take a hot shower and I'll get you something to put on. Let's go."

As Toni gently urged her up, Allie looked around. "This is nice."

Toni chuckled. "I'll give you the tour when you come out. Go on now." She gently prodded and pushed her up the two steps into the bedroom area.

"Nice bed." She sighed as Toni propelled her to the bathroom.

"Thank you," Toni said as Allie closed the door. "Not that it's getting much use lately. Oh…" She knocked on the door. "There are towels on the shelf. Take your time, kiddo."

"Thanks," Allie called out. "I see them."

Toni grabbed a pair of sweats and a sweatshirt. She knocked on the bathroom door again. Allie opened it, wrapped in a towel. Toni nearly had a heart attack.

"Here's something to wear," She avoided looking at the soft milky white skin of her shoulders and upper chest or the long neck or the soft skin of her arms or the…

"Thanks again." Allie smiled sheepishly and gently closed the door.

She came out twenty minutes later. Toni looked at her and chuckled. The Chicago Fire Department sweatshirt was much too long as were the sweats, although they clung to her hips nicely.

"Come here, sit by the fire." Toni pulled over a huge overstuffed chair.

Alana sank into its depths and sighed. She put up her feet and wriggled her toes.

"I made some coffee. Would you like that or a glass of wine?"

"Wine, please, then I'll make dinner."

"Skip dinner. We'll order out. You can make me dinner some other time. Don't argue," she said firmly, and Alana nodded.

Toni came back with two glasses of wine. After handing one to Alana, Toni sat on the hearth, facing her. There was a moment or two of silence before Alana spoke.

"A few weeks ago, Paul and I had a very eye-opening discussion."

"That's great." Toni smiled and took a drink of her wine.

"Well, we admitted many things. Paul was uncharacteristically open and honest. I questioned him on it, and he told me someone had said he needed to be open to figure out what was wrong with us and how to fix it. If we can. And after seeing him with this woman tonight, I bet she's the one who was helping him."

"How do you figure?"

Alana took a drink of the red wine. "This is wonderful. Thanks. The woman with Paul didn't look like a hooker or some young gold-digging fling. She looked like an ordinary woman in love," she said softly.

"Maybe she is," Toni said. "Love hits everybody."

They looked at each other for a moment until Toni shrugged.

"I suppose what's got me so rattled is that Paul looked the same."

"Ah, I see." Toni smiled slightly. "So what did you and Paul talk about?"

Alana glanced at Toni but took a drink instead of saying anything. Toni watched her cautiously and laughed as Alana continued drinking. "Don't eat the glass."

Alana laughed along as Toni poured another glass from the bottle. She knew Alana watched her as she poured. The room was deathly quiet when the doorbell rang.

Toni blinked. "Dinner. Hope you like Chinese. Hold that thought. You can tell me more in a minute."

They sat in front of the fire, eating out of the cartons. Toni hid her grin. "You hate eating like this, don't you? You're dying for a plate."

Alana laughed and turned bright red, which Toni found adorable. "I'll be right back."

Toni speared the piece of pork out of the container with her chopsticks while Alana balanced her plate on her lap.

"This is good," she said honestly, and Toni agreed.

"I love Chinese."

"Toni O'Hara, you'll eat anything."

"True, but I love Chinese. Okay, time for your fortune."

Alana happily picked a cookie. She broke it open and read it and turned bright red. "Okay, your turn."

"Hey! Ya gotta read it, goofball," Toni said with a mouthful.

She wiped her hands on her jeans, which Allie tried to ignore, and reached for the fortune. Alana held it away from her.

"Gimme..." Toni warned, and Alana shook her head.

"They're stupid sayings that don't mean a thing."

"Gimme..."

"No."

Gray eyes narrowed dangerously. She snatched the little paper out of Allie's hand. Toni held it over her head, laughing. She looked up and read it aloud. "You will find love right in front of you."

She stopped and finished chewing. "Hmm. What's so stupid about that? Okay, I'll read mine." She broke open the cookie and took out the fortune. "Hmm."

"Hmm what?" Alana watched her.

Toni shrugged and tossed it into the fire.

Alana gaped at her. "Why, you big ass..." she accused and Toni threw her head back and laughed openly. "I can't believe you made me read mine and you tossed yours in the fire."

"I know." Toni got up, still chuckling. "Time for pie."

They sat there staring at the fire, not saying much. Toni ate the key lime pie as Alana watched her. "Aren't you afraid of getting sick again?"

"Nope. I feel fine."

"I should get going," she said in a small voice.

"You don't have to. You can spend the night. Take the couch," Toni added quickly.

Alana's stomach was doing flip-flops—too much emotion for one day. Hell, for three weeks. Alana stopped and put her head back. "God, I'm tired, and I don't want to go home. Is it all right if I stay here?"

"It's more than all right. I don't want you driving in this weather in the state you're in. It's late."

"I'll call home. I don't know now what he'll be doing tonight. But I can't just stay out and not let him know. If he's home, he'll worry."

"What if he's not there?" Toni asked.

"Well, I would hope he'd have the decency to call as I'm doing."

Allie got the home voice mail and left Paul a message, then left him a message on his cell, as well.

Toni watched her as she left the message and saw the sad resignation all over her face. "Okay, that's done. Now let's get you to bed." She came out with a heavy blanket, sheet, and pillow.

Between them, they made up the couch. "I'll keep the fire going for you."

"Thanks." Alana looked around. "I really like this studio. It's huge." She walked over to the big picture window that overlooked the lake, watching the moon as it hung low in the sky. "Nice view."

"Wait." Toni flipped off the lights. From the fourth floor, Toni had a clear view of Lake Michigan with no obstructions. The moonlight flooded the room.

"Very nice. I like this."

"Wait till tomorrow and you see the rising sun on the horizon."

"Beyond the blue horizon," Alana whispered sadly.

Toni stood next to her and put a gentle arm around her sagging shoulders. "Waits a beautiful day. It'll be beautiful again. I promise." She placed a small kiss on her head.

For an instant, Allie leaned into her body.

"Okay, off to bed," Toni whispered and let her go.

"Thanks again, Toni. You're always there for me," she said honestly.

"That's the plan, kiddo," Toni said with a wink. "Good night," she whispered as Alana crawled under the blanket.

Toni sat on the edge of the couch. "If you need anything, you give a holler. Right?"

"Okay, good night," Alana whispered tiredly.

"And tomorrow, you'll tell me what you and Paul talked about if you want." Toni bent down and kissed her forehead, then walked away.

Alana watched her as she walked into her bedroom. In the darkness, Toni could barely see Alana over the small dividing wall. She heard her walking around, then heard the couch move.

Though she knew Alana was just beyond the small wall, she instantly felt the loss and her heart ached.

She wondered if Alana felt the same. What did Alana ache for? Paul? Toni? Anyone? She wanted to go out to Alana, but she knew she needed to sleep, needed to gather her thoughts. And if Toni knew Alana at all, she knew Alana would be thinking of Jocelyn and Nick and what they would think. Toni thanked God they were grown.

After seeing Paul with that woman, Alana and Paul would have to make a decision before too long. Toni's stomach clenched with the idea of Alana confronting Paul.

She said a small prayer for Alana and her family as she drifted off to sleep.

Utter bliss and contentment. That's what Toni felt when she opened her eyes the next morning. She smelled the fragrance of shampoo and sighed as she wrapped her arm around her pillow, pulling it close to her body.

The phone on her nightstand rang, waking and scaring the crap out of her. She bolted up and let out a yelp as Alana bolted up at the same time.

"What the..." Toni rubbed her eyes as the phone still rang. She tore her gaze from the stunned look on Alana's face and answered the phone.

"What?" she yelled. "Kev. Yes, dinner tonight. Sure, sure. Fine. No, I just woke up. Right, yeah, love you. Right, bye."

"I am so sorry." Alana scooted off the bed. "I don't even remember coming in here. Christ, I'm sorry."

"Don't be. It's okay. I was just stunned. Are you okay? I must have been sleeping like a dead woman. I didn't even hear you." She laughed and ruffled her hair. "I'm starving."

Allie raised an eyebrow. "You're hungry?"

Toni bounded out of bed; luckily, she wore something the night before. "Yes. Usually when a beautiful woman spends the night in my bed, I feed her, whether she wants it or not."

"How chivalrous of you."

"That's just how I roll. Lemme get dressed."

Allie drank her coffee and watched in awe as the waitress placed the large platter in front of Toni.

"So about last night," Toni said, buttering her toast.

Allie cringed. "I'm so sorry."

"You said that. And there's no reason to be. You did nothing wrong."

"Oh, no, I know. I just felt like I should be able to…" She shrugged.

"Hey, this is a traumatic thing. You want to talk anytime about this…" Toni said, digging into the eggs. "What do you want to do?"

"I want to go away somewhere and…" Alana started, then took a deep breath and continued, "And all that would be is running yet again."

"Again?" Toni asked.

Allie avoided her as she ate her bagel. "I'll tell you sometime, but just not right now. Is that okay?"

"You can tell me whatever, whenever. This is a lot for you to handle. I'm here. That's all."

"Thank you," Alana said with a sigh. "So when Paul comes home, I'll confront him with it. I have no idea what will happen next."

"Will you reconcile if he wants to come back?"

Alana looked into the gray concerned eyes. "After our conversation a few weeks ago, I don't know, but I don't think so. I know Paul. He and I had our problems, and yes, perhaps we should have talked more, perhaps we would have ended it much sooner. I honestly didn't think he'd go outside our marriage. He and I really need to talk about this."

Toni reached over and took her hand. "You know I'll be here for you. You need anything, anything at all, you call me. I'm there," she said seriously.

Inexplicably, Allie reached over and gently placed her hand on Toni's cheek. Toni swallowed hard and blinked. "I know. You

141

don't know what it means to have you in my corner."

Toni smiled and nodded. "I feel the same way, believe me." She reached up and held on to the hand that touched her cheek. "We'll get you through this. I promise."

"I believe you. Toni, I lo…" She stopped and smiled. "I love you. I don't want you to think…There's so much going on…"

Toni shook her head. "Shh. We don't have to talk about what anything means right now. Let's just get you through this. C'mon now. You failed at dinner last night. At least let me eat a good breakfast."

"I'm sorry. I don't want to interrupt."

Allie wasn't sure why she just said that to Toni, but she felt better saying it. She knew Toni would understand and be there for her.

For now, that was all that mattered.

Chapter 17

Allie's stomach was in knots as she heard the back door open. Paul, of course, was not home when she came home that morning. Being a Saturday, she figured he went into the office. Although after seeing that he lied to her the night before, she was no longer sure what Paul was doing. There were no phone messages for her that morning, but it looked as though Paul slept in Nick's bed.

Paul walked into the kitchen where Allie sat at the table. She looked up from her cup of tea and smiled. "Hi, Paul. At the office?"

He set his briefcase down and took off his jacket. "Yes. We have a new client coming in Tuesday. We want to be prepared." He reached into the fridge for a beer. "Want one?"

"No thanks."

"So you got stuck in the lousy weather?" He sat across from her. "I got your message."

Allie nodded. "How was the game?" She watched as he picked at the label on the bottle and waited.

He glanced up at her, then concentrated on the bottle of beer in front of him. Allie tried a different tact. "Toni wanted to know what bar. She's obviously a sports fan."

"I didn't go out with the guys last night."

"Oh? They poop out on you?" She watched as he took a long pull from his beer.

"I had a last-minute dinner meeting—"

"With a client?"

Paul shook his head. "No, not a client. A prospective business partner. She's a brainiac with numbers, and she's a lawyer." When he stopped, Allie saw the smile flash across his face for just an instant. It was fleeting but glaringly telling to Allie; a feeling of loneliness swept through her that was just as fleeting. She realized Paul was still talking.

"Donna, that's her name. Donna Singleton. She's been the VP of accounting for many years. She's loyal and loves the business. Without Donna, we'd probably be in the toilet right now. So we're discussing her becoming a partner. You had seen her in the deli that one time."

The whole while, Paul did not look at Allie when he spoke.

"Allie..." He stopped and took another drink.

"What? Please, at this juncture, and after all we talked about last month, I think we need to keep talking and be honest."

He looked up. "Are you being honest with me?"

Allie cocked her head. "How do you mean?"

"About Toni."

Allie groaned. "There is nothing between Toni and me. We're friends, good friends. That's all. I've never lied to you."

"Only to yourself."

"Okay, I think I like you better when you didn't want to talk about anything but Notre Dame football and the Cubs." She noticed a smile tugged at his lips when he drank. "Are you reading *Cosmopolitan*?"

Paul nearly spit up his beer. "No."

Allie took a chance then. "Then it must be Donna," she said softly as she poured another cup of tea. She ran her fingers over the top of the kitchen table, oddly remembering when they bought it. No, she thought, she went out and bought it. Her mind raced thinking of all the things she and Paul did separately all these years.

"Hey," he said lightly and tapped his bottle on the table.

Allie blinked. "Oh, I'm sorry. I was thinking."

"Yeah, been doing a lot of that lately."

"With Donna," Allie offered.

"Yes, Allie. With Donna." He sounded exasperated as he ran his fingers through his hair, then took a long drink. Allie knew that gesture; Paul was like Nick in this regard. It was a sign of supreme frustration. In a moment, she was sure Paul would shut himself off. "And to answer your next question. No, I am not having an affair with her. We've had conversations about our lives and how we feel. But I am not sleeping with her."

"That was not my next question," Allie said and smiled. "But it was in my top ten."

Paul chuckled grudgingly. "What's going on with us, Al?"

Allie sat back. "I think we're growing up."

Paul snorted into his beer. "Then we'd better hurry or the kids will catch up to us."

They laughed for a moment before becoming serious once again. "Are you in love?"

Paul's head shot up, completely caught off-guard. "I said I was not having an affair. But I can see where you think it. Hell, the idea of you and Toni together runs through my mind all the time. Are you going to tell me you don't think about Toni? Please remember I'm the one who came home last night."

Though Paul didn't mean to stir it, Allie felt the anger welling inside her. She wasn't ready to talk about what she might feel for Toni, just as Paul was not ready to discuss Donna. "I am not having an affair with Toni O'Hara."

Paul just looked at her but said nothing.

"All right, Paul, you're not having an affair, either."

"And I'm not ready to talk about my feelings for Donna. I'm trying to sort twenty-five years of my life and make some sense out of it, so I don't feel like a fool for loving and marrying a woman I knew was gay…" His voice trailed off as he sat back.

Hearing that out loud for the first time in her life made Allie's heart pound in her chest. Was Paul right? Suddenly, her mind sifted through all the years, all the trouble with their marriage.

Paul reached across and took her hand. "Donna and Toni are not the problem with us."

Allie composed herself and agreed. "But I think they're the catalyst for us to acknowledge what we are and figure out what we want to do."

Paul nodded. "These talks exhaust me."

Allie laughed. "I hear ya."

"What do you think would have happened if we talked like this twenty-five years ago?"

"We probably wouldn't have married and had two wonderful kids."

They sat once again in deafening silence. Allie could hear the clock ticking on the wall—it sounded like a time bomb ready to explode at any minute. She looked at Paul, who was deep in thought. "I'm sorry for this."

He looked up and nodded. "Me too. It's kind of surreal. I feel like I'm in a bad dream. It would be much easier if we didn't like each other."

Allie agreed. "And if we could lay blame at each other's doorstep. But I think we've shown our respective culpabilities."

"Yes. Can I tell you one thing?"

Allie cocked her head. "Only one?"

Paul smiled. "I'm glad neither of us is having an affair, and it's just about us."

"I am, too."

"Are we talking divorce?" Paul asked tentatively.

"Let's think about what that means."

"Okay." Paul sat back. "You mean think about it right now, right?"

"Yes. Right now, if that's okay."

"Yeah. I think we need to talk about it. It's driving me crazy. My stomach is in knots over this."

"So is mine. While it's been a long time coming, it seems like it's happening so fast."

"Too fast? Do you want to wait on it?"

"No. I think it's best we talk honestly about it."

"Well, we have all weekend."

They decided to take the rest of Saturday and think about what a divorce would mean to each other and as a family, then discuss later that night. It was Paul's idea to get out of the house and go to dinner.

"But let's pick a place that doesn't have any memories for us, so we can think clearly," Paul said.

Allie agreed completely. They didn't need any more emotional stress than they already had, so they decided on the new Italian restaurant one of the teachers in the art school talked about. It was quaint but not too quiet so they didn't have to worry about anyone hearing their conversation.

The server brought the bottle of red to the table and poured two glasses. Neither Allie nor Paul wanted an appetizer. Paul toyed with his wineglass as Allie watched him. He looked tired, but his eyes sparkled in the candlelight on the table. He also looked miles away; Allie wondered if he was thinking about Donna Singleton.

Just then, a wave of sadness wafted through her. They were on the verge of divorce, something that was probably inevitable, but she felt sad and lonely now. Even though they had separate lives, Allie had always felt safe and secure. Did she want to give that up? She wondered if Paul was thinking the same thing.

As if knowing what she was thinking, Paul looked up. "Do we want to do this? I mean, divorce. We've been together for so long, and it hasn't been all that bad."

"We have been through a lot together. Building a family, having a home. We've worked hard…" Allie stopped when she really heard what she was saying. She laughed sadly.

Paul cocked his head curiously, but then he smiled. "We sound pretty pathetic, don't we? Neither one has said we loved the other." He shook his head and took a drink of wine. "I do love you."

"And I love you. But it's time we admit to each other what we want out of life. At last, let's be totally honest." She reached across and took his hand, which he held tight. "We have such a long life still to live."

Paul nodded and looked down at their hands. "I think I could be falling in love with Donna."

Even though Allie knew this would happen, her heart ached. But she couldn't deny how Paul looked after he admitted this. It was as if a weight had been lifted from his shoulders.

Allie gripped his hand tighter. "I think you're already there."

When Paul looked up, he had tears in his eyes. "I never meant for this to happen to us."

"I didn't, either. But there it is." She let go of his hand and picked up her wineglass. "What does Donna say about all this?"

Paul sat back, letting out a deep sigh. "She's been after me for months to talk about it with you. She said we can't talk about us until you and I are settled."

"She seems like a steady, intelligent woman."

"Yes, she is."

"One who can help you and love you like you need to be loved."

Paul ran his fingers through his hair. "I hate this!"

"I know." Allie sat back. "But as long as we keep talking honestly, we'll get through this."

Paul nodded. "What about you? What do you want?"

Allie thought about it. "I don't mean anything against you. But I want to fall in love. I want to feel the passion I..."

"You didn't feel with me," he said softly.

"I'm so sorry. This is something I should have said long ago, not kept in that place deep in the back of my mind with..."

"Sue."

"It's so stupid. Why did I have to start thinking about this?" Allie said loudly as the tears came. Paul winced as the server walked by. "I just put it so far out of my mind figuring it was just a thing because I was a teenager. If I just didn't think about it, I'd be fine. Then we had Nick, then Jocelyn, and the years just flew by. Now in a chance meeting, for godsakes, I meet Toni, and all this has me thinking about it all over again. And she's such a good friend and..." She put the napkin to her eyes, trying to stop her inane ramblings.

"It's okay," Paul said softly.

Allie now had a headache from trying not to cry. She wiped her eyes with the napkin and sniffed. "What do we do next?"

"I think we need to talk to the kids. We can talk to both of them at the same time."

"Yes, I think that's the best. God, what are they going to say?" Allie wondered how they were going to break it to them.

"I don't know. I'm sure they have no idea." Paul sat back. "I'm just glad they're grown. This would be devastating otherwise. You know, I could talk to Nick and you could talk to Jossie."

Allie thought about it for a moment. "No. I think it's best if we do this together. You and I are in agreement about the divorce. We should tell them together. Jocelyn's spring break is in a couple weeks. I'll ask her to come home then, and Nick can fly in for a visit, as well."

"I am not looking forward to this."

It was the longest two weeks of Allie's life. Jocelyn and Nick agreed to come home for Jocelyn's spring break. Paul was a nervous wreck the morning he was to pick both up at the airport.

At one point, Allie couldn't take his pacing anymore. "I can't believe I'm saying this, but would you please go to work?"

Paul stopped pacing and glared at her. Allie put her hands on her hips in a challenging posture.

Inexplicably, both started chuckling. Paul sat on the edge of the couch. "You haven't said that in twenty-five years."

Allie washed the same spot on the kitchen table five times waiting for Paul to come back with the kids. She thought of calling Toni; she wanted to tell her so much about what was happening. Was it divine intervention that Toni had a conference in Des Moines that week? Allie didn't know, but she knew Toni could tell something was going on. When she called the other day, Allie could hear the soft concern in her voice. She smiled now, thinking how Toni was always there for her—always caring.

Hearing the car in the driveway had all thoughts of Toni pushed to the back of her mind, but her stomach was in knots. She clasped her hands together and closed her eyes. "Please let this go well, God."

"Mom?"

When she heard Jocelyn's voice, she smiled, and her trepidation stopped. Deep in her heart, she knew her daughter. While she might be surprised, she would understand. Allie tossed the dishcloth in the sink, ignoring the unsettling feeling of what Nick would say.

She hugged both children while glancing at Paul, who looked as though he could use a drink. "Are you hungry?"

"Are you kidding?" Nick said, his head already in the fridge.

"No, I'm fine, Mom. Now what's going on?" Jocelyn asked.

Allie inwardly laughed. Oh, Jocelyn, she thought, always right to the point. She gently pushed Nick out of the way. "Everybody, sit. I'll make you a sandwich." She was glad to have something to do.

As she pulled out what she needed from the refrigerator, she glanced at Paul, who nodded.

"Your mom and I have something to tell you."

Nick grinned. "You're sick of Chicago winters and you're moving to Florida."

Paul winced. "No, son. Your mother and I have been talking for a few months now."

Allie placed a sandwich in front of Nick. She knew Paul would not eat, just as she had no appetite. She glanced from Nick, who concentrated on his lunch, to Jocelyn, who watched her father intently.

"Talking about what, Dad?" she asked quietly.

Allie sat next to Paul, placing her hand on his arm. "Talking about our lives and what we want out of them."

Nick looked up. "You are moving," he said with a mouthful.

Allie and Paul exchanged glances. It was Jocelyn who spoke. "No, Nick. They're talking about what they want out of life." She smiled sadly and looked at Allie. "And I don't think it's the same thing."

Nick had the glass of milk to his lips. He said nothing, just drank his milk.

Allie felt the tears nearly overwhelm her. For an instant, she thought of telling them it was a mistake. Everything was fine. She was fine, their father was fine. Everyone was fine and happy. And in the next instant, she knew she couldn't say that. Not the way Jocelyn looked at her. She was pleading with Allie to tell the truth. To treat her like an adult, not the adorable five-year-old she held in her lap while Allie gazed at the paintings in the museum, wondering what if...

"No, sweetie. It's not the same," Allie said softly.

Paul leaned forward. "Things between your mother and me haven't been right for a long while, kids. And it's time we made them right."

"What the hell are you talking about?" Nick tossed his napkin on the table. "You've been married for twenty-five years. You're just now thinking about this?"

Jocelyn still locked gazes with Allie, as father and son continued.

"No, son. We've been separately thinking about it and not talking to each other. It's only since we've been alone without you kids in the house, we've come to realize…"

"This is bullshit," Nick said angrily. "What about me and Jossie?"

Paul frowned deeply. "What about you?"

"What are we supposed to do?"

Paul sat forward. "You can start by acting like an adult."

Nick stood so fast, the kitchen chair toppled over. He marched out of the kitchen, nearly taking the swinging door off its hinges.

"Well, that went well," Paul said and stood. "I'll go talk to him." He looked at Jocelyn. "Jossie, I'm so sorry, sweetie."

"It's okay. Go after Nick before he strokes out. I'll talk to Mom."

Paul kissed the top of her head and walked out. Allie and Jocelyn sat in silence for a moment. "So?" Allie asked softly.

"You and I had a brief discussion before Thanksgiving, but I won't say I'm not shocked and disappointed. But I have to be honest and say I had a feeling about this. How Dad was always working and never home. Oh, I know he worked a lot when we were kids, but he was truly always there for us. It's just when we left the house, I thought you two would be off and running together. But you never did. I wondered why."

Allie nodded but said nothing. Jocelyn leaned forward. "Is there someone else Dad is seeing?"

"What's happening between your father and me is just that, sweetie. But if you're asking if your father is having an affair… No, he's not."

Jocelyn looked tentative and started to say something, then stopped. Allie smiled sadly. "No, sweetie. Neither am I."

"I'm so sorry. I don't think, I mean, I don't…"

"Honey, it's okay. It's a natural question."

Jocelyn sat back. "You don't love Dad anymore?"

"Of course, I love your father. I'm just not in love with him. If that makes sense." Allie took a deep breath and let it out slowly. "If any of this makes sense."

"It does. I suppose it wouldn't be such a shock to me and obviously to Nick," she said and laughed. Allie chuckled along but let her continue, "if you two fought all the time. But you never did. It's like…" She stopped and thought for a moment.

"What, sweetie?"

"It's like we felt safe and loved and taken care of. But now that I think of it, we never saw you and Dad affectionate with each other."

Allie winced at the truth in her statement. Paul and she were never demonstrative, never affectionate. It was like they were friends and roommates, for lack of a better word. Good God, Allie thought, twenty-five years. She nearly missed Jocelyn's next words.

"You never fought, but you never showed…I'm sorry. I shouldn't be saying this."

"No. No. I want you to say whatever you feel, sweetie."

"Good because you've always said that to us. And I don't want to stop, especially now. So what are you going to do? Divorce? Man, that sounds so surreal to say."

"I know, Jos. I know. But we can't continue living like this. And we have such a long life ahead of us."

"I remember when I was a teenager, when we had a mother-daughter talk, you said something that has always stuck with me."

"God, I hope it was something worthwhile and not something like 'don't forget to wear clean underwear.'"

Jocelyn laughed. "No, that would be something you would have said to Nick."

"True."

"You said never settle for anything but real, true love. Money, fame, none of it matters if you wake up in the morning next to someone who doesn't have your heart in theirs."

Tears stung Allie's eyes as she remembered the exact time she had that discussion with her children. "I feel like a hypocrite." Allie tried to control her emotions.

Jocelyn reached across the table and held Allie's hand. "You're not. You and Dad loved your children more than anything. Maybe now it's your time, both of you. Time to find real love." Jocelyn sniffed loudly and let go of Allie's hand to pick up a napkin. "Boy, that sounds hokey, but you know what I mean."

Allie plucked a napkin out of the holder on the table and dabbed her eyes as she sniffed loudly. "How did you grow up to be such a considerate, intelligent woman?"

"I had two great parents."

"Well, now I have a blinding headache." Allie smiled. "I do love you, Jocelyn. No matter what happens, I will always love you."

"I know. I feel the same. I hope Nick isn't been a total tool to Dad."

"Your father loves you both very much. This is extremely hard on him, too."

"I'll talk with him. And if I have to, I'll talk to Nick, too. He might be older than I am, but Marcie has taught me a couple martial arts moves. If it comes to that."

Allie and Jocelyn laughed at the idea. Allie hoped it wouldn't come to that.

Jocelyn left the kitchen to make sure Nick had not left. Allie sat there, drained emotionally. Though it was the hardest conversation she'd ever have, not counting Nick, she couldn't help but be so proud of Jocelyn. She was grown. No longer was she the tiny girl who always had her hands in the air waiting to be picked up. Jocelyn was beautiful, inside and out.

"Hey, Mom," Nick's soft voice called out.

Allie looked up to see him standing in the doorway, smiling sheepishly. Allie had to chuckle at the child-like posture. "C'mon in. You look like you did when you were six and you threw the baseball through the living room window."

Nick laughed and sat across from her, but Allie noticed he sat back, his hands shoved into his pants pockets in a defensive manner. She only wondered what his discussion was with Paul.

"So," Allie said with a deep sigh. "What are you thinking, Nick?"

"I dunno. It's just a shock, I guess. I mean, hell, Mom, you and Dad? Geezus. What are you going to do? Divorce? Then what will you do?"

Allie cocked her head. "About what?"

"Living alone."

Allie glared. "Your father would be living alone. Are you worried about him?"

Nick seemed taken aback. "No. He's a man."

It took Allie a second for her brain to catch up with what he just said. "Are you kidding me?" Allie leaned forward. "I thought we raised you to be a logical, thinking, and caring human being."

"Well, I—"

"And what makes you think your father can be okay alone and not me?"

"Well, you—"

"Do I not have a job? Have I not taken care of this house and everyone in it?"

"Well, yeah, but—"

"And have you ever had to worry about anything while you lived here?"

"No—"

"And who made you feel that way?"

"You and Dad—"

"Then get that testosterone-laden tone out of your voice, young man." Allie angrily sat back. It seemed everything came to the surface, and poor Nick was the recipient. "I have spent all my life taking care of this house and this family. Your father has worked like a dog to make sure we had a house to take care of. We have loved and cared for you and your sister and now, for the first time in our lives—"

"Mom. Okay, okay. I'm sorry. You're right. I should never

have questioned your ability to live alone. I guess..." He stopped and ran his fingers through his hair, looking so much like his father. "I guess it's just that I don't want to see you lonely."

"Nick." Allie saw the tears well in his eyes. "No one is going to be lonely. I have you and Jocelyn. Your father and I do not hate each other, sweetie. We just don't want the same things in life, and we never really did. I don't want to go into all the reasons, but they really have nothing to do with you or your sister. Our love for you will never change."

"I know," Nick said. He sat back in a dejected heap. "I guess it's just such a big change for me."

Allie raised an eyebrow. "Yes, and your father and I are just breezing along with this. You poor thing."

Nick winced but smiled grudgingly. "You don't have to be sarcastic."

"Too late, don't you think?"

They both looked up when Jocelyn and Paul walked back into the kitchen. Allie could tell it had been very emotional for both.

"Enough talk," Paul said. He grabbed Nick by the scruff of his neck. "C'mon, we're going out for an early dinner."

Allie smiled and stood. "I agree. Things may change, but we're still a family."

Chapter 18

The next week, Nick was furious. He took a cab from the airport and didn't go straight home to his mother. Instead, he went downtown to find her and confront her. He marched to her office, saw the stenciled lettering *Inspector Toni O'Hara*, and banged on the door.

"Geezus! Come in!" He heard her bark.

As he marched in, he saw the coffee spilled all over her paperwork. Toni was mopping up the mess when she looked up. "Nick, what a surprise. When did you get…" She stopped short when she saw the angry look on his face. "What's wrong?"

"Are you fucking my mother?"

Toni looked as though she wanted to faint. Her mouth dropped as she closed her office door. "What in the hell are you talking about?"

"Answer my question, damn you."

Toni stood tall and calm. Nick went on relentlessly. "Last week, my folks decided they were getting a divorce—"

"What?"

"And now, I just get a call from a friend of mine, Joey. His father is my dad's attorney. He said his dad is handling the divorce and told Joey it was probably because of you. My dad told him about the dinners, the Cubs games, the museum, and that's why Dad is filing for divorce. So?"

Toni's mind was reeling. Divorce? What the hell happened? She took a deep breath and gathered her thoughts. "I'm your mother's friend, Nick. I haven't seen her for at least two weeks. And if all this had transpired, that's why. And for you to come barging into my office with ridiculous accusations..." She stopped and took another deep breath. "You'd better leave and talk to your parents."

"If you were a man, I'd belt you right in the mouth," he said angrily.

"And if you were a man, I'd gladly take the punch. Now get out of here before I forget I'm a lady and kick your ass."

For an instant, Nick thought he might break down. His hands shook horribly. Toni softened. "Nick, go see your mother. Talk to her. I'm sure she's hurting pretty bad right now. Believe me, it has nothing to do with me or our friendship, which is all we have."

"I-I'm..." He stopped short.

Toni walked up to him and put her hands on his shoulders. "I don't blame you for what you're feeling, but you're wrong, and that's all I can tell you. You need to talk to your mother. She needs you. Now more than ever," she said, and he nodded. She opened her door and he walked out.

He turned to her and gave her a sad, apologetic look.

Toni smiled. "It's all right, son. Go now." She gently pushed him down the hall.

The front door was open when Nick walked in. "Mom?"

His mother came out of the den. "Good grief. You scared the life out of me. What in the world are you doing home again? Is everything all right?"

"Tell me what's going on."

"What do you mean? Sit down."

Nick sat on the couch. His mother sat in the chair next to him. "Now tell me what's happened to make you fly home."

"I talked to Joey Conroy yesterday. His dad..."

"Yes, he's your father's lawyer."

"Yeah, well, he said his dad told him that Dad filed for divorce. He was shocked and said besides money, the only thing they could come up with is..."

"Is what?" Allie sat forward.

"Toni," he said, not looking at her.

"What?" Allie said angrily. "Your father went to see his

lawyer, just as I got one, and went to her. We discussed this last week when you were in. This is between your father and me." His mother closed her eyes, seemingly to collect her thoughts. "There is nothing going on with Toni."

"Well, that's what she said, but…"

Allie grabbed Nick's forearm. "What do you mean? Have you talked to her?"

"Well, yeah. I was upset. I, well, I asked her if you two were…"

"You didn't? How dare you barge into that woman's office and accuse her of…she is the best friend I have…have ever had. And if you can't understand that, young man, then…"

"Mom, Mom, I do. I was wrong. I…She threatened to kick my ass," he said seriously.

"If she doesn't, I will. Did you apologize?"

"I tried, but she told me to come straight to you and talk. She said you needed me now more than ever and I should take care of you," he said, shamefaced.

He saw the smile cross her face. "She's a good friend, huh?"

"Yes, she's a good friend, and she doesn't deserve what's happening. I have to call her. She must think I'm an idiot."

"Haven't you called her at all?"

"No. I wanted to get all this squared away before I talk to her. William Conroy has a big mouth."

"Do you think Dad told him it was because of Toni?"

"No, I don't. I know Bill Conroy. He's a jackass, but your father thinks he's a good lawyer."

"You're not going to get screwed, are you?"

"Of course not. Your father and I don't hate each other. We'll be fine." She looked at him. "I still can't believe you went to Toni."

"I'm so sorry. But she really looked concerned and shocked when I said you and Dad were getting a divorce. She turned white. I thought she was going to pass out."

Allie cocked her head. "Really?"

"Yeah. She almost had to sit down. I think you need to call her."

"I will right after we sit with our attorneys. Now can you stay?"

"No, I need to get back. I can't believe I flew here for this."

Allie hugged him. "I can't, either, and you're totally wrong about Toni. I'm glad you're thinking about me, sweetie, but I'd like to wring your neck right now."

Allie sat across from Paul, who winked and smiled, albeit sadly. She had not told him about Nick's impromptu visit earlier in the week. They sat in silence as the two lawyers looked over the briefs.

Allie's lawyer looked up. "It seems we have a very amicable divorce here."

Bill Conroy snorted sarcastically. Paul looked up at him with a mixture of curiosity and confusion. "Bill...?"

Bill held up his hand, looking at Allie's lawyer. "My client wants to be amicable. But I'm concerned about this lesbian Mrs. Sanders has been seeing."

Allie was shocked and looked at Paul, who was visibly stunned. When he looked at her, Allie knew he had talked to Bill about Toni.

Paul gave her an apologetic look, then turned to Bill. "That has nothing to do with this."

Allie's lawyer leaned forward. "It's not wise to bring this up, gentlemen. Not since there is a certain VP, one Donna Singleton." She looked at Paul, who again was stunned.

This time, he looked at Allie in surprise. She had indeed told her lawyer of Donna, but only as a point of reference, not to use it as part of the divorce.

"As my husband said, that has nothing to do with this..."

Then all hell broke loose between the two lawyers.

"You have no proof that my client is in a lesbian relationship," she said.

"I'm sure if we investigated..." Bill started.

"You can spend all the money you want on a private investigator and you'll find nothing," Allie's lawyer said.

"Your client stayed at her place overnight," he spat out.

Allie wanted to kill Paul at that moment. He shrugged helplessly and shook his head.

"It was the same night your client lied to his wife and saw a particular redhead, counselor."

Now Allie felt extremely guilty for telling her lawyer about Donna. Paul and Allie looked at each other as their lawyers continued as if they were not there.

"You have no proof, either," Bill went on. "If you go there, this will be a very messy divorce."

Allie's lawyer cleared her throat. "By law, my client gets half of all monies and property."

Bill leaned on the desk. "My client gets his business free and clear."

Allie's lawyer leaned in, as well, challenging him. "That's over a million dollars. If I remember correctly, my client worked for the first five years of their marriage, pregnant while your client had the luxury of finding the perfect job. This woman deserves..."

When Paul started chuckling, at first Allie was nervous. She hoped he wasn't having a breakdown right here at the conference table. But when he winked, Allie suddenly realized what was happening—neither lawyer was listening to what Allie or Paul thought or wanted. They were doing what they thought was best—to make it ugly until one of them gave up.

Allie and Paul had discussed what each wanted and how they wanted the divorce conducted. And what was happening right now wasn't it. Paul rapped his knuckles on the desk, softly at first, to get their attention. When neither lawyer acknowledged him, he banged twice, silencing them.

"Thank you," Paul said. "Allie, what do you want?"

"The house," Allie responded. "It's all I really need."

Paul smiled. "I'll have Bill draw up the papers. You get the house and twenty percent of what my company is worth."

"Paul, that's not necessary."

"You worked for the first five years for me," Paul insisted. "Your lawyer is right about that."

Allie relented. "Okay. What about the kids?"

"They're beneficiaries to my retirement and any insurance policies. I'll continue to pay for Jossie's college. And you and I will discuss anything else."

Allie grinned and agreed. Paul looked up at Bill. "That's about it."

"Paul, twenty percent of your company. And what about this lesbian..." he whispered.

Allie banged her fist on the table so hard she almost broke her hand.

"Now you've done it." Paul sat back and folded his arms. He looked at Bill. "You're on your own."

"Bill, I understand you want the best for Paul, but if you ever, ever do anything to harm Toni O'Hara, I will make your life a living hell. Do I make myself perfectly clear?"

Bill breathed heavily through his nose but said nothing.

"He gets it," Allie's attorney said. "You'll have the papers drawn up and filed by the end of the week. The divorce is official in sixty days."

Bill Conroy, red-faced and angry, jammed the papers in his briefcase. "I'll talk to you later, Paul." He left the room with Allie's attorney.

Allie and Paul sat opposite each other. "So that's it," Paul said.

Allie nodded. "That's it."

"I'm sorry about Bill. I did tell him about Toni, but I swear, Al, I never had an idea he would bring it up like that."

"I know. I'm sorry I told my attorney about Donna. She just asked, and I told her everything. But I feel the same. I didn't tell her to make it part of the divorce."

"Irreconcilable differences," Paul said softly. "Sounds so clinical."

Allie just nodded in agreement. She flexed her hand and winced. "I think I damaged this."

Paul then stood. "You need to get that looked at. Do I have to pay for it?"

Allie glared, then laughed. "Let's get out of here."

"Well, I guess all that's left is to sign the final papers then..."

Allie walked over to him and hugged him fiercely. Paul hugged her and kissed her head.

"Let's get out of here," he said.

She turned, and without another glance back, Allie walked out and headed for her new life.

Chapter 19

"Spring has sprung!" Kevin declared as he walked into Toni's office.

She looked up and grinned. "Has it really?" she asked in a tired voice.

Kevin shook his head. "C'mon, you need to get some air. You've been cooped up in this office for weeks. What's the big idea pulling double shifts?"

"I'm fine, you old nag." She rubbed her face. "I'm just tired and hungry."

"You're always hungry," a voice called from the doorway.

Toni whirled around to see Alana standing there, grinning.

"I'm a growing girl," Toni said in a soft voice. Her heart raced a mile a minute.

"You look tired," Alana said.

Toni reached for her hand and frowned as she saw the elastic bandage on her injured hand. She gently pulled her into the office and sat her on the couch.

"What happened?" Toni sat next to her.

"I'll explain everything. I'm sorry I haven't called you."

"Don't worry. I'm just so glad to see you. So did you punch out your husband?"

"Ex-husband. The divorce is final in another month."

"Already?"

"Yes. Amicable divorces go quickly, we found out. Especially when there's nothing to argue about." She avoided Toni's eyes.

"You're not telling me something," Toni said seriously. "I can tell when you don't look me right in the eyes."

163

"We'll talk. I promise. Now Jocelyn and Nick are coming home next weekend. I'm cooking, so you have to come. You look like you haven't been eating right." She looked into Toni's eyes then.

"I'm fine. It's a deal. C'mon, let's go get lunch or something. I can't believe you're here."

"You've lost weight, Alana," Toni said with a disapproving scowl. She dug into her bowl of chili.

"Stress," Allie grumbled as she ate.

Toni glanced at her sad look. "So tell me about it and why you haven't called me in over a month," Toni said evenly. She tried not to sound upset.

Allie scratched her temple. "Where to start."

"Wherever you like," Toni said, eating her chili. "Maybe by telling me why you're divorcing Paul."

Allie looked up then. "After the kids were grown and moved away, it struck me that we had nothing in common, only the kids. And after talking to Paul, he felt the same way."

"I don't want to get into your business, and if I'm out of line, just say so."

"Okay."

"Is Paul having an affair with that redhead?"

"No, he isn't. And to answer your look. Yes, I'm sure, and yes, I believe him. Just as he believed me when I told him there was nothing between you and me."

Toni blinked as if trying to register the information. Allie smiled slightly. "He likes you, but being a man, he was a little threatened by you and what we have."

"What we have?"

Allie looked into her eyes again. "Yes. I suppose he doesn't think I can have a very attractive lesbian friend, have a great time together, and be friends without sex."

"Why would he think that? I mean, he knows I'm a lesbian, but why would he think you would be in that situation?" Toni watched her spoon as she swirled it in the chili. She looked up when Allie didn't answer. The tears that formed in Allie's eyes took her off-guard. "Alana," she whispered. "What is it?" Not wanting to add to the tense moment, Toni took a mouthful of chili.

Allie blinked and quickly wiped her cheek. "There was a girl in college…"

Toni nearly choked on her spoon. She started coughing and turned bright red.

Allie sat back and waited while Toni wiped off her sweater. "Are you all right?"

"Yes." Toni glared at her. "You do that on purpose. What the hell did you say?"

"You heard me."

"And you will elaborate, please," Toni said. She took a drink of water and cleared her throat.

"When I was in college, I had a friend Sue, who was a lesbian and who loved me, I guess. I don't know why."

"Why she loved you or why she was a lesbian?" Toni's lips twitched. "Sorry, just trying to keep it light. She loved you because you're a good woman. And she was more than likely a normal red-blooded American lesbian." She pushed her chili away and leaned her elbows on the table. "Well, you've got my complete attention now."

Allie saw the crooked smile and felt her cheeks get hot. "Well, I was eighteen and had no idea about love let alone about lesbian love, so I ran. I was scared, and I ran away from her and—"

"Right to Paul." Toni nodded.

"And never looked back." Allie played with her water glass, avoiding Toni.

"And you never thought about it in all these years? Never had any feelings for another woman?"

"I—"Allie shook her head, finding her glass enthralling.

Toni waited. "Can I ask a personal question?"

Allie laughed. "At this point in our relationship, I have nothing to hide. No, I did not have sex with her. Was that your question?"

Toni chuckled along. "Yes."

"But…"

Toni stopped laughing. "But what?"

"Well, we did kiss and do what teenagers do."

"It's been a long time. What do they do?"

Allie glared at her. "You know exactly what I'm saying."

Toni laughed like a little kid. "I know. I just love to see your neck get all blotchy." She took a drink from her water glass, looking at Allie over the top. "Well, you were a kid. This Sue knew who she was and must have cared a great deal to tell you how she felt." She sat back then. "It's not easy to tell someone how you feel, especially when you're not sure how the other woman feels."

"As the years went by, I had the kids, the house. I know I gave up my art, but it was worth it. Now with both of them gone, I'm teaching. It's my passion, and Paul's company is his."

"Okay, but it doesn't explain why he thought we had something going on..."

"He knew about Sue."

"How?" Toni asked, completely surprised.

"Sue's brother evidently told him about it when Paul and I were dating. Paul never said a word to me that he knew. So now when you come along and we're having such a wonderful time and Paul and I are not getting along, he put two and two together. It's stupid, I know."

"Not so stupid," Toni said. "I don't blame him. Now that I know what's going on, I can see where he would think it."

"I know, but I've explained there's nothing, and he tells me now that he thinks he's falling in love with Donna." She answered Toni's curious look. "The redhead. She's a VP in accounting and loves the company."

"And Paul."

"Yes. And Paul."

"So it appears things between you are very amicable. It's okay?"

Allie chuckled at her hesitant tone. "Yes, it really is. It's kind of surreal. I mean, when you hear of a couple getting a divorce after so many years, you automatically think of yelling and blaming and wanting to strafe the other of everything. Paul and

I were never like that. We may not be in love, but we do love each other. It's over and done. We both agreed about the house, which I'll keep. Paul wants me to have a small percentage of his company, which I didn't want."

"Let him."

"Why? I don't need charity."

Toni arched an eyebrow. "It's not charity. I'm sure Paul realizes what you did early in your marriage. You worked while you were pregnant. I think he did the right thing, and I don't think he did it out of charity or guilt. He did it because of your history together."

"I suppose. I don't know why I got angry."

"Maybe you don't want to feel like you're being taken care of."

Allie looked at her then. "You're right. I don't. I've spent my whole life taking care of a family, a house, and for years, holding a job when I had one. I can take care of myself. Nick said the same thing. He worried I'd be lonely but didn't worry his father would."

"He wants to take care of you. As time goes by, he'll realize you'll be just fine. I know you will."

"You do?" Allie smiled. "Thanks. I am happy."

"Good. You know, even though this sucks and it's painful, I think you and Paul acted out of love for each other and your kids. To go on like this would be a waste of your lives."

Allie sighed pensively. "You're right."

"So you have the house."

"That's in good shape." For the first time, Allie felt excited about the future. She felt that fluttering in her stomach—that anticipation of the unknown. "I just need a few things done around the house, like I think the roof. The kitchen sink leaks, and there's something going on with the furnace. I'm not quite sure what that is," she said and Toni chuckled.

"Well, then this is your lucky day, Ms. Sanders," Toni said, emphasizing the "Ms."

Allie grinned suspiciously. "I see the wheels turning, O'Hara."

"I'm a handywoman extraordinaire…" she announced with a mouthful of chili.

"How so?"

"I can fix a leak and check out the roof. I have a few friends who owe me favors. I'll have them come over and give the house the once-over, a good inspection," Toni assured her.

"I can't let you do that," Allie said in a small voice.

"Oh, you're not letting me do anything. You're going to feed me," she assured her.

Allie laughed openly and agreed.

Chapter 20

"Please be careful," Allie begged as she held the ladder.

Toni grinned as she looked down. She adjusted the Cubs hat she wore; she had gathered her hair through the opening in the back, pulling her thick hair off her neck. Allie decided she liked the look and tried to ignore how her heart skipped a beat at the thought of it.

"Don't be a nag. I'm a firefighter, for heavensake," she said as she stood on the roof.

Allie looked up and cringed as she lost sight of her. She let go of the ladder and walked back. Toni stood on the roof kicking at the shingles.

"What's the verdict?" Allie called up, shielding her eyes from the cool spring sun.

Toni shrugged and called down, "When was the last time you got a new roof?"

"Five years ago, I think."

Toni dusted off her hands and nodded. Allie quickly ran back to man the ladder. She watched as the long jean-clad legs made their way down. The hammering started again as Allie watched the muscles in her rear flex. There was a hole in the pocket of the worn jeans, and as Toni's ass came too close to her face, Allie swallowed. She was so close, she saw the dark blue of her underwear peeking through the threadbare denim.

She quickly stepped back as Toni jumped down the last few rungs. "I'd say you're fine. Just a few shingles to replace. I'll go pick some up, be right back," she said and walked away.

"Wait, you don't have to do that. I'll get a roofer."

"You will not. Do you know how much that will cost? Why would you pay when I can do it just as easily?" Toni asked seriously.

Allie had no good reason. "I just don't..."

Toni took an exasperated breath. She placed her hands on Allie's shoulders. "I know what I'm doing and I'm your friend. Why throw money away? Now let me go before you talk us out of daylight," she said as her lips twitched.

Allie narrowed her eyes. "Very funny, O'Hara. Okay, you win. I appreciate your help and accept your offer," she said firmly and grabbed Toni by the arm as she walked away, "on one condition."

"There's always a condition." Toni sighed. "Okay, what is it?"

"I make you dinner whenever you do this. And I pay for any material."

Toni thought for a moment. "You'll go broke feeding me but okay."

Allie laughed as Toni jumped into her car and took off.

Allie was in the kitchen making lunch when the back doorbell rang. "God, Toni, you can come in!"

"Allie? It's Vicky."

Her friend poked her head in the back door. "Hi! C'mon in. Hey, Amy and Jimmy! Hi, kids," Allie exclaimed as she ushered them into the kitchen.

"How are you, Allie?" Vicky asked with a concerned look. "We haven't talked for a couple weeks."

Allie smiled and shrugged. "I feel good. You know things were not good. It was a long time coming. He's happy. I'm happy. The more I think about it, the more I realize how I was just going along all those years. Making excuses for him, for me. I wasted so many years." She wiped the countertop. "Oh, I shouldn't say wasted. It was a good life for the kids. They were always the most important thing. Paul and I agreed on that." She tossed the cloth in the sink and turned back to Vicky. "Now I'm starting over and I'm happy."

"Good for you! Did you take him to the cleaners?" she asked as they settled the two kids at the table.

Allie laughed. "I did not. I wanted the house, that's all."

"But, but the business. He has to be worth…"

"I don't care, don't want it. Now," she said and ruffled Jimmy's hair. "Who's hungry?"

"I am," Toni exclaimed from the back porch.

Vicky whirled around and grinned at Allie, who gave her a scathing glance. Toni stood on the porch wiping her boots.

"You have to work for your lunch, Inspector O'Hara."

Vicky gaped at the two women; Allie loved the flummoxed look and did a little grinning of her own.

"Slave driver," Toni mumbled, then saw Vicky. "Hey, Vicky, how are you?" she asked as she walked into the overcrowded kitchen. "This kitchen is a fire hazard."

"Fine, Toni, h-how are you?" she said self-consciously.

Toni smirked. "How's Mike? I haven't seen you two at the club for a while." She didn't give Vicky a chance to respond. "And I'm doing well. Just doing a little roof repair for the schoolmarm."

"That's right, now get back to work," Allie grumbled playfully.

"Yes, ma'am."

She walked out but not before snagging a handful of potato chips and winking at the giggling children.

Vicky finally closed her mouth and slowly turned to Allie. "She's fixing your roof?"

Again, Allie loved the incredulous tone. "Yep, and the sink and the furnace. She's pretty handy to have around," Allie said lightly and walked away.

"I'll bet." Vicky sighed and sat in a dejected heap and ate a potato chip.

The day had grown considerably warmer for March. Vicky and the kids had gone, and now Allie heard Toni walking on the roof; she then heard a heavy thud. She stopped making the sandwich for Toni and ran through the swinging door.

"Oh, God, she fell off the roof!" she exclaimed and dashed out the screen door and ran into the brick wall.

"Oooff!" Toni grunted as she held on to the out-of-control woman. "Geez, you're always running into me. What's the matter? See a mouse?"

"No, you idiot. I heard something on the roof. I thought you fell," she said, holding her heart.

"You'd have heard me scream like a girl." Toni laughed as she wiped the sweat off her forehead. "The noise you heard was the pile of shingles. I'm nearly done, but I needed some water."

She followed Allie into the kitchen. "God, you're filthy!" she said as she handed her the glass. She watched as Toni gulped the entire glass and asked for another.

Allie nearly fainted when Toni took off her ball cap, then her shirt. She wore a plain gray tank top—a tight-fitting tank top—underneath.

"Man, it got hot!" she said as Allie took the discarded shirt. She found herself staring at the muscles in her arms, and good Lord, she stared at Toni's breasts. Allie could not find enough moisture to swallow. She refilled the glass and drank it quickly.

"Almost done. I'd say another hour or so. Hmm, what's for lunch?" she asked, eyeing the lunchmeat on the counter. Allie gently pushed her out the swinging door, trying to fight the tingling sensation when she touched Toni's firm back.

"I'm going, I'm going." Toni laughed as she walked out.

An hour later, Toni stood by the sink washing her hands and face. Allie tossed her a towel.

"Okay! Your roof should be fine for at least another few years. I'll have a friend of mine come and check it out anyway." She rubbed her hands together and sat down. "I'm starving."

"News flash." Allie set the huge sandwich in front of her.

"Wow, that's a sandwich!" Toni exclaimed and dug in.

Allie shook her head as she set an icy cold bottle of beer next to the plate and sat. "You know the way to my heart."

"Do I?" Allie found herself asking before she could stop.

Toni blinked in midbite, dropping a slice of tomato in her lap. Allie chuckled, and Toni blushed. Neither woman acknowledged the question.

"You really like to do physical work, don't you?" Allie asked as they ate lunch.

Toni nodded. "I do. As a kid, I always wanted to be a fireman. Mostly because of Kevin, you met him. And because I didn't want to be anything like my father." Her voice trailed off. She took a healthy pull on the icy beer. "Kevin was a fireman, and when my father would go on a bender, I'd go to a coffee shop. Kevin nearly killed Dad once. I was petrified, my mother begged Kevin to leave. It was horrible. The kids were crying. I was trying to get them out of the house. My mother was pulling at Kevin, who was so filled with anger..."

"How old were you?" Allie asked softly.

Toni blinked. "I dunno. Maybe twelve. I was big for my age, always passed for being older. It got me into a few places when I was about sixteen," she said, wriggling her eyebrows.

Allie gaped at her. "What did you do?"

"I knew at an early age that I was gay. So I got a fake ID and passed for eighteen; alcohol was legal at eighteen for a while, remember way back then? So I went to my first gay bar, waltzed right in, and ordered a beer."

"You did not! At sixteen?" Allie exclaimed and leaned forward. Toni nodded. "What happened?"

"I got shit-faced and had my first sexual experience."

"No!"

"Yes!"

"Was it..."

"I barely remember, but I remember throwing up," she said lightly. "Ah. First love!"

Allie threw her head back and laughed. Toni joined her.

"How about your first time?" Toni munched on a pickle.

"It was with Paul." Allie shook her head.

"You've only..."

"Yes, don't remind me," Allie said flatly. "We were just about to graduate. Alcohol was involved, as well. If I were honest, looking back on it, I was thinking of Sue and what happened. It was over in a matter of minutes."

"Ouch."

"Though it certainly wasn't all Paul's fault, it was a sign of things to come, or not coming," she said, and Toni spit up her beer in laughter.

"You have an annoying habit of doing that to me when my mouth is full."

"Your mouth is always full," she gently reminded her.

"Too true. So what else has to be fixed?" Toni asked. "C'mon, tell me."

"Well, the sink in the bathroom is backed up. But…" It was too late. Toni already grabbed the toolbox off the counter and bounded up the stairs. Allie got up with a groan. "I wish I had that woman's energy. And her body."

By the time Allie got to the bathroom, Toni was on her back under the sink. Allie raised an eyebrow but said nothing as she looked at Toni's flat abdomen; Allie remembered those days.

"I need a wrench from the toolbox. The real big one."

Allie lifted it out with a groan. "How can you…"

Toni easily took it and started unscrewing the bolt. Allie watched as she took the U-joint off and cleaned it out, then reattached it. "Not sure if this will be enough. I'll come back later and check it out. You may not need a plumber."

Toni sat up, wiping her hands on her jeans. As Toni sat forward, Allie realized she knelt too close to Toni. Their faces were inches apart.

"So you're not a plumber, as well?" Allie asked in a strained voice.

Toni grinned. "I am not." She then stopped grinning and swallowed as she looked into Allie's eyes. "Never noticed how green your eyes were."

"They are?" Allie whispered and quickly shook her head. She noticed the smudge of grease on Toni's cheek and tentatively reached over to wipe it off. "You have grease on your face."

Toni grew serious and just nodded. Allie was painfully aware that Toni stared at her lips, and she took the time to run her tongue over them. When Toni moved her hand and placed it on her hip, Allie tried to control the quivering jolt that shot through her. She allowed Toni to gently pull her closer.

"Alana," Toni whispered tenderly.

At the sound of the soft endearment, Allie's legs trembled. Eyes focused on full lips as they drew nearer.

"God, Toni," she whispered desperately and closed her eyes. She could feel Toni's soft, warm breath against her lips. God, she's going to kiss me...

"Allie! Toni! It's Vicky, where in the hell are you?"

Allie jumped like a scalded hound and scooted back. Toni did not move, but she was breathing as though she had run a race. They stared at each other.

"U-up here." Allie tried to call out, but her mouth was bone dry. She cleared her throat. "We're in the bathroom, Vicky," she called out and stood with Toni's offered hand. Allie had the wrench in her hand, not knowing what to do with it. She looked up at Toni.

The look of pure unadulterated want in the gray eyes melted Allie to the spot. She groaned helplessly and sagged against the bathroom sink, holding the wrench in both hands. "God, don't look at me like that," she begged.

"What are you two doing in the bathroom?" Vicky asked as she looked at both women.

"Fixing a problem," Toni said in a low voice. She squeezed between the women and walked out.

Allie swore she could feel the heat emanating from Toni's body.

Vicky looked down the hall. "God, she is hot!" She fanned herself.

Allie glared at her. "Why don't you take a cold shower while you're in here?" She stormed out of the bathroom.

"What did *I* do?"

"What do you want?" Allie asked as Vicky followed her downstairs.

"I'm making Mike his favorite dish. I need to borrow a couple things," she said as she bounded into the kitchen.

"Help yourself," Allie said absently. She looked out the window at Toni, who dragged the ladder back to the garage. What would have happened if Vicky hadn't come by? She knew the answer. She still felt Toni's warm breath on her lips.

With Vicky gone, Toni came back into the kitchen. "She makes me nervous," she admitted and picked up an apple.

For some reason, Allie was aggravated. Toni watched her absently as she scoured the countertop—twice.

"Maybe it's because she thinks you're hot," she said sarcastically.

Toni stopped in midbite, the apple hanging out of her mouth. She blinked, then quickly chewed. "What did you say?"

"You heard me."

"Alana…"

"Oh, skip it. If you run, you might be able to catch her." Allie immediately wanted the childish words back. Okay, out of control, out of control. Allie looked to the heavens for help.

Toni tossed the apple core in the garbage and grabbed Allie by the elbow. "What's wrong? Why are you so angry?"

"I'm not. Let's just forget it."

Toni let her go and let out a dejected sigh. "I apologize for what nearly happened upstairs."

Allie shot a look into the gray eyes. "Sorry? Why?" She put her hands on her hips. "Would it have been so awful?"

Toni jerked her head in Allie's direction. "W-what?"

"Quit making me repeat myself," she said angrily and stormed out of the kitchen, leaving Toni standing here looking very confused.

Allie stood by the living room window. She stared at nothing in particular. Her heart skipped a beat when she heard the kitchen door creak on its hinges.

"I-I better go," Toni said in an uncertain voice. "To answer your question. No, it would be far from awful."

The hammering started as Allie smiled. "You told me you could fix a leak," Allie said, still staring out the window. She turned to the grinning Toni. "Or was that just a ploy to get me to feed you?"

Toni laughed and tossed her jacket back down on the chair and headed back to work.

Chapter 21

"Alana, are you sure? The last time I saw your son, I threatened to kick his ass," Toni said, regretting her angry words. Nick was only trying to protect his mother. Toni knew the feeling.

"Of course. He asked if you were coming. Nick likes you, so does Jocelyn," Allie said honestly.

"God, I hope so because I really like your kids."

There was silence for a moment. Since the near kiss the week before in Allie's bathroom, neither woman had broached the subject. Toni was too overwhelmed by the possibility of what that kiss would have meant. She wondered if Alana felt the same.

"W-well, good. Then it's settled. They'll be in Friday night and leave Sunday. Saturday, I'm having the barbecue. Stop by in the afternoon. Anytime after two or so."

"Okay. I'll be there. Thanks."

Toni saw Nick and Alana as she walked up the driveway. She thanked God, Nick looked as nervous as she did. Then Alana whispered something in his ear and kissed his cheek. Alana then gave him a gentle nudge, and he met Toni halfway.

"Hi, Toni. It's good to see you again." He stuck out his hand.

Toni smiled as she took the offered hand. "You look well, Nick. How've you been?" She let out a deep relieved breath the same time Nick did. Both chuckled quietly.

"I'm so sorry," he said, still holding her hand.

"It's okay. I know how you felt. She's your mother, and you're a good son."

"Thanks, but I shouldn't have done that. Let me get you a beer," he offered with a grin. Toni nodded her thanks.

Alana walked up to Toni and stood on tiptoes to kiss her cheek. "Okay?"

Toni nodded and held out her shaking hand to Alana. "I was as nervous as a cat."

"Thank you." Alana looked up and smiled.

Toni sported a confused look. "For what?"

"Nothing, everything." Alana cocked her head and smiled. "You mean a great deal to me. You're kind and considerate. You know how much my children mean to me and you want them to accept you. Thank you."

For a moment, they just looked at each other. "Alana. You…"

"Here ya go!" Nick announced.

Alana grabbed Toni by the arm. "What? I what?"

"Mom, you keeping Guinness stocked in the fridge?" Nick asked with a raised eyebrow and handed Toni the black beer. "Hell, I forgot to get me one."

Toni took it and offered a slight smirk to Alana. "Stocking my favorite beverage? Why thank you," she whispered.

Alana tried to ignore the playful flirtation and looked to the heavens. She glanced at Toni and laughed. "Knock it off, O'Hara."

"Toni!" Jocelyn's voice called out.

"And I want you to finish that statement later," Alana insisted.

Toni laughed and turned to Jocelyn. "My God, it's been four months. You look, well, you look twenty-one." Toni reached in her jacket pocket and handed her a small gift-wrapped box.

"For me?" Jocelyn asked.

"Happy birthday," Toni said.

While Jocelyn tore open the small box, Toni knew Alana watched her with Jocelyn. She glanced and saw the happy smile, and Toni almost let out a deep contented sigh like a schoolgirl. She looked at Alana, who wiped tiny beads of perspiration from her forehead. She looked flushed.

"Are you having hot flashes?" Toni whispered. Alana tried not to grin as she glared.

"Hair combs," Jocelyn said. "Toni, they're beautiful. What design is this?"

"Celtic. It's a never-ending circle. I, well, your mother gave me the idea. She says you're always pulling your hair back and could never find something strong enough for your thick hair. I saw them in this shop on Belmont, and I just thought of you. You have thick hair like your mother's," she said with a shrug.

Jocelyn had tears in her eyes. Nick watched and smiled as he drank his beer. "You're just like Mom. So emotional."

Alana's eyes grew misty, as well. It was then Toni realized just how emotional the last couple of months had been for Alana, her children, and for Paul. So much had happened in such a short time, she thought.

"Thank you, Toni. I'm so glad Mom has you," she blurted out and flung herself at Toni, who was stunned. She wrapped her arms around Toni's waist and held on, sobbing.

Nick rolled his eyes. "Women," he said and headed for the cooler.

Alana watched the tender display and wiped the tears away as she lightly slapped Nick in the back of the head as he walked by.

Toni hesitated for an instant, then wrapped her arms in a tender embrace around Jocelyn's shoulders. "You're welcome," she said tenderly. "Now enough crying. If you get your mother going, Nick and I will have to leave."

Nick laughed, watching Jocelyn as she sniffed and pulled back. She reached up and kissed Toni's cheek.

"I'm going to fix my hair," she announced and ran into the house.

"You amaze me, O'Hara."

Toni searched Alana's face. "I do?"

"Yep. C'mon, you need a refill."

Nick manned the grill. Toni sat nearby, talking to Jocelyn about school. Alana escaped to the kitchen.

"So whaddaya think about Mom busting up her hand?" Nick asked proudly.

"She didn't really tell me how it happened," Toni said honestly as she took a handful of peanuts.

Both siblings exchanged glances.

"She didn't?" Jocelyn looked into the kitchen. They could hear Alana humming as she prepared the steaks.

Toni looked at both children, who looked decidedly guilty. "Okay, you two, what gives? I don't know you all that well, but you both look guilty. Now what's going on?"

Jocelyn leaned in and took a drink of beer. Nick shrugged. "You have a right to know, but you can't tell Mom."

Toni shook her head vehemently. "Nope, nope, nope. I learned at Christmas to never ever lie to your mother. She scared the hell out of me." She looked at the giggling young adults. "I'm serious."

"She'll get mad but…okay. Dad has his company, and before the divorce, Mom's lawyer was going to ask for half," Jocelyn started.

"Seems natural," Toni offered as she ate the peanuts.

"Right, but Dad, well, he…"

Nick continued for his floundering sister. "He and Mom had already agreed on a settlement. But then Dad's lawyer spoke up and accused you and Mom of what I accused you of in your office… "

Toni nearly choked on her peanut. She coughed and leaned forward and tried to catch her breath. "What is it with this family? I swear you're all trying to kill me." She felt Nick slam her on the back. She spit up the wayward peanut and took a deep breath.

"Why didn't she tell me that?" Toni hissed angrily.

Nick and Jocelyn pushed her back into the lawn chair.

"Geez! Keep it down, will ya? She'll kill all of us," he said nervously.

Jocelyn gently put her hand on Toni's arm. "I know my mother very well." She stopped and laughed. "Well, not well enough apparently."

"What do you mean?" Toni suddenly felt uncomfortable, like she was on the witness stand.

"Toni, look at it from Mom's point of view. She didn't want

any money. It was never a consideration. We talked about it. Nick and I are in his will, and Mom just didn't give a damn."

"Mom was always more about the feelings than the material. It's the artist in her," Nick said.

Toni noted the pride in his voice. He was right about Alana. She was a good woman with a good soul. That's what she loved about her. God, she said it. She loved her. She looked at the two adults wondering if they had any clue. Hell, she wondered if Alana had any clue.

"Toni, don't be angry with her. She...she cares for you, and she wouldn't stand for Dad's lawyer threatening you over..." Jocelyn chuckled quietly. "Well, not for anything. So she got so angry with him, she slammed her hand on the table and nearly broke it. Her hand, not the table," Jocelyn said dryly.

Toni chuckled at how much she sounded like her mother.

"So that's why she didn't call me for almost a month. Didn't return my messages." Toni sighed and shook her head.

"She was protecting us and you. She was protecting the people she loves," Jocelyn finished in a soft voice.

For a long moment, she locked gazes with Jocelyn. Toni was overwhelmed and couldn't speak.

Nick chuckled quietly as he opened the cooler. "So Mom stuck up for you," he said, sounding so much older.

Toni looked away from Jocelyn and took the offered beer. For an instant, Nick did not let it go. Toni now searched Nick's hazel eyes, finding a good deal of maturity in them.

"I love my mother." He looked at Jocelyn who smiled. "The question is, do you?"

Toni looked from sister to brother. "Look, kids. Your mom and I..." She had absolutely no idea what to say next.

"All I'm saying is you'd better, as well."

Toni blinked as her heart pounded in her ears. Nick then grinned, and Toni started breathing again. "Or you'll kick my ass?"

"Or I'll kick your ass." He held his bottle of beer near hers. "Right?"

Toni nodded and lightly touched the bottle with her own. "Right."

Jocelyn, not wanting to be left out, reached her bottle in, as well.

"The Three Musketeers!" she announced with a laugh.

"You look more like the Three Stooges," Alana called out.

After a wonderful afternoon, Allie walked Toni down the driveway.

"Thanks, Alana. I had a great time."

Allie stopped by Toni's car and folded her arms across her chest. "You're always welcome in my home."

Both women were silent for a moment. "Jocelyn and Nick really like you," Allie said.

Toni turned to her and smiled slightly. "That's good because I'm fond of them, as well." She leaned against her car. "I'm a likable person," she finished lightly.

Allie let out a genuine laugh and leaned against the car, as well.

"Do you like me?" Toni asked.

"Yes," she said quietly. "I do." She looked down at her shoes, feeling the heat spread across her face. She was grateful for the moonlit night.

"Alana," Toni started, then stopped. She absently kicked at the pavement. "The other day, in the bathroom..."

Allie felt her body tremble at the thought. "Yes?"

"I-I'm not sorry I nearly kissed you. I wanted to. I thought maybe you wanted to kiss me, as well. That's what I was going to say when I first got here."

"I don't know what I'm feeling. This is so foreign to me. I haven't thought of anything like this for so long."

"I'll leave it alone if that's what you want. Nothing is worth losing your friendship. I don't want anything to happen to that."

Allie looked up now. "Neither do I." She took a deep breath. "I don't know what to think."

Toni nodded and reached over and pulled her into a warm hug. "I understand. You've been through a tremendous amount of stress in the last few months. I won't add to it. Now thanks for the day. I'll call you during the week. Good night," she whispered and kissed the top of her head, then let her go.

Allie wrapped her arms around her waist and held on for a moment, surprised at the wave of contentment that swept through her as Toni's warm arms tightened around her shoulders. As Allie breathed in the subtle fragrance of Toni's perfume, she realized she had let out a deep sigh. Contentment gave way to inexplicable emptiness when Toni stepped back.

Confused by her feelings, Allie smiled slightly and stepped back, as well. "Good night, Toni. Drive safe. I..." She stopped herself. She wanted to say, "I love you," as she had before, but now, it quite possibly meant something altogether different, something more, and she didn't know what to do about it.

Toni sported a lopsided grin. "I do, too." She gently touched her soft cheek, then quickly got into her car and drove away, giving the horn a short honk as she waved out the window.

Allie chuckled and waved back until the car was out of sight. The empty feeling lingered as she walked up the driveway.

Chapter 22

"Tracy and Hepburn or Bogey and Bacall?" Alana asked as the batter struck out. She pulled her big jacket around her.

Toni contemplated as she sucked on a peanut shell. "Tracy and Hepburn," she said with a definite nod. She looked over at Alana, huddled in her big down jacket. It was opening day at Wrigley Field. Toni got the tickets from her lieutenant friend and could think of no one else to invite but the schoolmarm.

"Hmm. Okay, Tracy and Hepburn or Gable and Lombard?" Alana gave Toni a smug grin. "Aren't you freezing?" she asked, then grimaced as the wet peanut shell found its way to the ground.

"Nope. I have thick blood. And Gable and Lombard never made a movie together. Can't use them." Toni returned the grin.

Alana stuck her tongue out.

"Don't do that unless you're gonna use it," she said with a sly grin. Alana immediately sucked the tongue back in its home with a furious blush.

"Chicken," Toni whispered into her beer.

"You child." Allie grabbed a peanut.

Behind them, the same man shook his head and leaned in. "Aren't you the same women who were talking about your weight last summer? Can't you just watch the game?"

Toni turned in her seat. "You have a good memory, pal." She motioned for him to come closer. "Stay tuned. We're going to talk about menstruating and menopause in a minute."

The guy quickly sat back and drank his beer. Toni laughed when she saw the stern look from Alana. "What?"

"This was nice of you, Toni. I've never been to opening day." Allie sighed happily and shivered.

Toni took the blanket and spread it across Alana's knees. "You're welcome. I'll be right back," she said and scooted out of her seat.

She ran up to the vendor and returned to see Alana shivering. "Here, you're freezing and you're making me cold just looking at you." Toni handed her the huge cup of hot chocolate.

"Ahh, thanks. Hey, you remembered the tiny marshmallows," she exclaimed, and they heard the man grunt behind them.

"Well, at least they won," Alana said with a shiver. "I hope the heat in your car works. Where to?"

Toni slid in and turned on the heat. "My place if you don't mind. You never made dinner for me the last time you were there. You were a bit um, preoccupied."

"But you took care of me." Alana looked out the window.

Toni said nothing as she drove. Yes, she thought, and she'd been fighting the love she'd felt for Alana ever since. When she woke up the next morning to find Alana in her bed, she was as content, albeit shocked, and happy as she had ever been in her life. She knew Alana just needed to be close to someone at the time, and Toni could not deny her the comfort. She never expected to fall in love.

"Toni?" Alana was saying.

"Oh, sorry…what?"

"I asked what you wanted for dinner. What do you have in your house? I'm afraid to ask."

"Hey. I went shopping yesterday, and my refrigerator is full, so don't get sassy, schoolmarm," Toni said with a grin.

"You went food shopping? So you assumed I'd make dinner for you, huh?" Alana asked with a playful glare.

"No, I only hoped," Toni said honestly as she stole a glance at Alana's blushing face.

"Toni O'Hara, you have a way of catching me off-guard with your sincere comments. It's lucky for you I like to cook," she said as Toni pulled into her driveway.

"It's truly my lucky day."

"God, I'm freezing. It's April and I bet we get snow. We were just barbecuing, weren't we?"

Toni listened to Alana, who seemed nervous, hence her rambling. Toni remembered the last and only time Alana was in this apartment. She had just seen her ex-husband in an intimate exchange with the woman he was probably now going to marry. Toni did take care of Alana that night. Though Alana really didn't remember crawling into Toni's bed, she wondered if Alana had thought about it. When she woke, did her body tingle the way Toni's did? She hoped so.

"Good grief, woman, quit yakking. I have the fireplace going. I'll make coffee. If you'd get in the kitchen and start cooking, you'd warm up," Toni said with a playful grin.

Dinner was heavenly. Roasted chicken and mashed potatoes, asparagus, and hollandaise. Toni purred like the well-fed cat she was as she stretched out in front of the fireplace.

"I cannot believe how good that was." Toni sighed, and she turned on her side and looked at the chef. Alana drank her coffee and seemed lost in her thoughts. "Whatcha thinking about?"

Alana grinned. "Two things. First, everything that happened in the past few months. How my life is completely changed…"

"For the better," Toni interjected.

"Yes, definitely for the better. I'm completely content that the divorce didn't affect Jocelyn and Nick. I just thank God they're grown up with their own lives. It would kill me if anything ever happened to them." Her voice was low as she contemplated the possibility.

"But nothing happened to them. You and Paul handled the whole thing with grace. I admire you for that. I'm sorry your marriage didn't work out, but you have so much life ahead of you," Toni said earnestly as she propped her head up on her hand. "Now what's the second thing?"

Alana blushed deeply, which intrigued Toni. "I'm not sure I should say."

Toni snorted. "Oh, now you have to. You know I won't let this go. Now give."

"I was thinking about the night I..."

"Crawled into my bed?"

Alana buried her face in her hands. Toni laughed at the muffled cry. "Yes."

"And..."

Alana took her hands away. "And while I may not have remembered getting into your bed, I remember feeling very warm and contented."

"That's good. I admit it was a shocker but a very pleasant shock. Very pleasant."

Alana sighed and chuckled, running her fingers through her hair. "I...what do you want to do? I mean after the fire department? There is life after that, isn't there?"

"Odd segue, but I'll bite." Toni watched Alana blush once again. "This is going to sound stupid. Remember when I said I used to go to the coffee shops when I was a kid?"

Alana nodded and continued listening.

"Well, I thought maybe I'd have one and there'd be someplace for teenagers to go without heading to the streets. Maybe they'd find safety and peace, even if it's just for an hour or so..." She shrugged again, glancing at Alana to gauge her reaction. "It's dumb, I know."

"I don't think it's stupid at all. I think it's a wonderful idea," Alana said in earnest.

"Yeah? I've...I have an idea of the place, but I'm just waiting for the right time. I have a few years left to work," Toni said, suddenly enthusiastic. She then sat back and grinned. "I'm glad you agree." Toni then cocked her head. "What about you? Are you going to continue to teach?"

"I suppose. I enjoy it, though I'd like to paint more. I miss it, and lately, I've just had the itch to start again and—"

Toni laughed openly and stood. She offered Alana her hand, which she took with a wary look and allowed Toni to lead her to the front door. They walked down the small hall to an adjacent door.

"What are you doing?"

"Keep still and wait." Toni fished the key out of her pocket. She opened the door and flipped on the light.

Alana walked in with a tentative air. It was a large studio situated behind Toni's apartment. She watched Alana as she gazed at the hardwood floors and floor-to-ceiling windows on the south and west side. It looked enormous only because of the landscaping windows.

"Wow, what a view," Alana said. "And another deck outside."

"I know. That's why I bought it. I didn't know what to do with it. I thought storage, but it's too nice just to store my junk. I had no idea what to do until I thought of you."

"Me? What are you talking about?" Alana asked completely confused.

Toni felt like a kid on Christmas morning. "An art studio," she announced happily. She walked into the room and turned around in a circle. "Can't you just see yourself painting away in this?"

Alana looked stupefied. She slowly walked into the room. "An art studio? I can't. This is yours. No."

"Yes." Toni's crooked grin spread across her face.

"Toni, no," Alana insisted as she looked around.

"Alana, yes."

"No."

When Alana grinned, then shook her head, then smiled again, Toni knew Alana struggled with the idea.

"If it makes you feel better, you can rent it. I'll charge you a buck."

"I—"

"Tell me you can't see yourself in this room. Wait until you see the sunlight that streams in here during the day and the sunset at night. Geez, it's begging for an artist." Toni nearly pleaded, and Alana laughed nervously. "You don't have to make a decision now. It's yours if you want. No pressure."

Alan walked away from her and stood by the huge windows. She looked around at the city below and the lake off in the distance. Toni quietly followed her and stood behind her.

"I-I could put my easel right in the corner there. The morning sun would be perfect natural lighting." She turned around to Toni and stuck out her hand. "Okay, O'Hara, you have a deal."

Toni took the offering. "Oh, what am I doing?" She pulled Alana into her arms. "Good, that's done. Now the question of rent." She sighed thoughtfully as she guided Alana out of the room. "My favorite used to be Chinese, but after that wonderful baked chicken...."

"I think you're right. I will go broke feeding you," Alana assured her as they settled once again in front of the fire in Toni's apartment.

Toni tossed a few large pillows on the floor and stretched lazily. "Ah, I'm so comfortable right now," she said with a yawn. She looked up at Alana, who was smiling slightly. Toni found it difficult to swallow. "Are you chilly?"

"A little," Alana said, looking down at her hands.

"Come down here beside me," Toni said in a soft low voice.

The tone sent a shiver through Alana as she swallowed, hoping her legs would move. She slid off the chair and knelt next to Toni, who scooted over. Alana shifted.

What happened next was amazing and completely natural. Alana lay next to Toni, who wrapped her arm around the shivering shoulders and pulled her close to her side. Alana nestled her head in the crook of Toni's shoulder and lightly placed her hand on her chest.

"Is this all right?" Alana asked breathlessly.

"It's more than all right. It's perfect," Toni whispered.

Neither woman spoke for a long while, both watching the dancing flames, lost in the comfort and peace of the quiet night.

"What are you thinking?" Toni whispered.

"In my wildest dreams, I never thought I'd be lying next to another woman in an intimate embrace. And I certainly never thought I'd enjoy it as much as I am." She stopped, seemingly to collect her thoughts for a moment. "I was thinking how comfortable and natural this feels. And I thought about my life and what it would have been like if I had the courage to tell Sue I cared for her when we were in college. That I felt comfort in her arms just as I do at this moment with you. It's amazing I put it so far back in my mind all these years." She stopped and lightly ran her fingertips up to Toni's chin. "Sue's brother had told Paul I nearly ruined her life, then I married Paul and nearly ruined his, as well."

Toni quickly turned on her side to face Allie. "Don't do that. You were eighteen, a baby. You knew nothing of love or sex. And I like Paul, but remember, he knew about you and Sue and he married you anyway. He wasn't an innocent. Please don't take the burden of this completely on your lovely shoulders. No one ruined anyone's life."

Alana smiled. "Lovely shoulders?"

Toni grinned. "Yes, very lovely."

Alana looked into Toni's gray eyes. "Do you feel as comfortable as I do right now? I mean, I know you've been in this position before, a million times, but this is new for me, and I don't know what you're thinking. I-I mean, I don't have to know. You…"

Suddenly, Toni loomed over her. "Listen to me for just a minute and stop yakking."

Alana frowned and opened her mouth. Toni reached down and placed her fingertips against her lips, quieting her.

"I have been in similar situations." Toni looked down into her eyes. "But I have never been in this position before. I've been trying to avoid my feelings for you for a long time now. I don't want to hurt you or scare you off, but my life is so different now with you in it. I can't imagine it before you. Whatever happens between us, please always know that I would never hurt you. You can trust me. I…"

Alana reached up and gently pulled her fingertips away, holding Toni's warm hand in her shaking one. "Toni, would it be wrong if I asked you to kiss me? I—"

Toni needed no more invitation. She lowered her head and gently quieted Alana with her lips. The kiss was warm and tender. A chaste kiss really. Nothing more.

Allie's heart continued to race as she felt Toni's warm lips gently brushing against hers. She heard the groan from Toni when she placed her hand on the back of Toni's neck and gently raked her nails through the dark hair. She pulled back, and Allie whimpered so slightly that Toni barely heard her.

"One more, please." Alana sighed and pulled her back. Toni smiled slightly and obeyed.

This kiss had a little more oomph. Toni lowered her body over Alana and kissed her deeply. Her tongue lightly touched Alana's lips. Allie parted her lips with a deep moan and took the offering, amazed at the feel of Toni's satiny tongue gently exploring...

After a few minutes, both women were groaning, their bodies melding together. Finally, Toni pulled back breathlessly.

"Maybe we should stop. I'm so aroused I think I might implode in a minute." Her voice came out in a raspy growl that sent a shiver down Alana's spine and settled right between her legs. Her body was on fire. Allie let out a low growl and gently pushed Toni back.

"I don't know what I want!" she said helplessly and quickly stood, pacing in front of the fire.

Toni grimaced as she watched her. "Alana."

"I can't believe how you make me feel," Alana said from across the room. She was staring out toward the horizon. "My body is on fire," she said helplessly. "And don't you dare joke about being a fireman," she added when she heard the small chuckle.

Alana turned to her. Toni still sat on the floor, her knees drawn up to her chest and her arms wrapped around them. She sported that helpless grin.

"Stop looking at me like that," she pleaded.

Toni jumped to her feet and walked over to her.

Alana caught her breath as Toni placed her hands on her shoulders. She looked up into tender gray eyes.

"We don't have to solve everything tonight. This was a good beginning. You have a great deal to think about here. So...so do I," she added, and Alana nodded and touched her forehead against Toni's chin. "Now it's late. You certainly can stay," she said, looking into the green smiling eyes.

"N-no, I'd better go home. I-I..." Alana pulled her into a fierce hug.

"Don't worry, we'll work through this. I'll always be your

friend. You will never have to worry about that." Toni kissed her forehead.

"I know that. I feel the same way."

Toni slipped her arm around her shoulders and walked her to the door. Alana stopped and turned to her. "I had a marvelous time. Every bit of it."

Toni grinned and gently cupped her warm face. "Me too. The best time I can remember. It's because of you, Alana Sanders." She kissed her tenderly.

Alana sighed into the kiss. Toni tried to pull back, but Alana threw her arms around her neck and held on for a smoldering kiss. Toni moaned helplessly and felt her body shivering.

When she pulled back, Toni had her eyes closed; she swayed precariously and leaned against the door. "Good God, woman," Toni whispered in a ragged voice.

Alana chuckled nervously and kissed her cheek. Toni couldn't move.

"Good night, Inspector," Alana whispered and walked out.

"G'night, schoolmarm," Toni countered and closed the door.

Chapter 23

"You kissed her?" Lidia put her hand to her heart and grinned. "Romance. Is goot!"

Toni had her head buried in her hands. She looked up. "Is not goot."

"Why is it not?" Lidia shook her head. "You need pastry."

Toni watched her disappear into the kitchen and waited. She thought about what she had done with Alana, and she thought about what pastry Lidia would bring back. She groaned loudly, causing a few customers to glance her way. "I'm so stupid!"

Lidia came back with a plate and set it in front of her. "Eat. I have customers, then I come back, we talk."

"I don't want to talk."

"You will talk," Lidia said in a threatening voice and walked behind the counter.

Toni looked at the plate and her mouth watered. "Apple strudel," she whispered happily, but she had no coffee. As she looked up, Lidia stood over her with a pot. "Thank you."

"You are like child. You know where the pot of coffee is." Lidia poured a cup for her. "Baby. Eat."

Toni knew Lidia did not use the word baby as a term of endearment. It didn't matter right then as she concentrated on the hot pastry. By the time she was done, Lidia had taken care of her customers and sat across from Toni.

"My feet, they are killing me."

"You need to hire someone to help you. Your clientele has grown in the past few years, Mrs. W. You've worked all your life. Isn't it time you retired and relaxed?"

"I am relaxed when I work. But you are right. I do have more customers now." Lidia sighed tiredly. "We will see. Now tell me of the kiss with Alana. And do not leave a thing out."

Toni looked from her empty plate to Lidia, who glared. "You get no more until you spill the beans."

So Toni explained…everything. She had told Lidia and Kevin about Alana's divorce, with Alana's permission, of course. And now, she had to tell them about the present situation. A situation that was much more pleasurable for Toni, and she could only hope it would be for Alana, as well. If their brief encounter the other night was any indication, Alana was happy right along with Toni.

Lidia listened while Toni went on, waving her hands and being very animated. "Why are you so…?" Lidia struggled for the correct word. "I don't know…" She waved her hands like a bird. "Flapping, like bird. What is wrong?"

"We've talked all week, but Alana seems almost too casual, like nothing happened. And now I'm worried if I'm reading this all wrong. Mrs. W., Alana had only a brief encounter with another woman, and that was over twenty-five years ago. And even then, she ran from it."

"She was scared and just a baby."

"I know."

"And Alana did not divorce Paul for you. She is grown woman and did right thing for her and family. Is no goot to stay in loveless marriage, you know that. You sent Gina away when you realize this and you had no one waiting for you in the wings." Lidia sat back and watched Toni, who stared at her empty plate. "What worries you, Antonia?"

Toni looked up then, tears flooding her eyes. "I'm in love, Mrs. W.," she whispered in a helpless voice. "Like I've never been in my life."

"And now it is your turn to be scared," Lidia said. "Is goot."

"How can this be good?"

"Because you are not thinking of sex…" Lidia wagged her finger in Toni's direction.

Toni chuckled. "Well…"

"Stop. You are in love, at last. And you want her for all time, no?"

"Yes."

"Then you must tell her and you must love her like you never have in your life." She leaned across the table and took Toni's hands. "And like you never will again."

Toni felt the tears creep up in her throat so quickly she couldn't speak. Lidia walked behind Toni and gathered her hair, pulling it behind her, gently running her fingers through it.

"Mom used to do that all the time when my hair was longer."

Lidia placed a kiss on top of Toni's head. "You are goot woman. Your mother would be very proud of you. Proud of her daughter who took care of brother and sister and took care of her until the day she died."

Toni's bottom lip quivered as she covered her face with her hands.

"And proud her daughter brought love into an old woman's heart once again."

Toni turned around then, wiping her eyes. "You're in love, too?"

Lidia blushed and nodded. "I think Kevin will poop the question soon."

Toni grimaced. "It's pop. Pop the question. I'm so happy for both of you." She stood and pulled Lidia in a fierce hug.

"Poop, pop. Who cares? Thank you, darling. Now you go and tell Alana."

"I talked to her and asked her out for dinner. She said she was fine but didn't want to go to dinner. So I figured I'd give her the day to be alone. I don't want to push her. God, Mrs. W., what if I did it again and fell for someone who…"

She reached up and cupped Toni's face. "Do not be afraid of love. And do not take no for answer."

Allie sat at her kitchen table staring at the phone on the counter. *What is wrong with me? I want to see Toni so bad, my teeth ache,* she thought. *Why did I say no?*

Because I'm scared shitless, that's why. Be honest, Allie. It's a completely different lifestyle. Oddly, she thought of what her friends would say. They probably would think she was nuts…

Allie needed to talk. She thought of Vicky and rolled her eyes. "That's all I need," she said openly and called the only person she trusted, besides the object of her terror. She picked up the phone and dialed.

"Hey, Mom, what's up? Do you need money?" Jocelyn teased happily. "You kids don't know the value of a buck."

Allie laughed heartily. God, how she adored her children.

"No, I'm fine. Thanks for the offer. I…So how are you? How are the classes coming? You're graduating in a month. It's almost over."

"Mom, you're rambling. What's going on?"

"Nothing, everything is fine." She bit at her bottom lip.

"I don't believe you." Before Allie could answer, Jocelyn asked the million-dollar question. "How's Toni?"

"Toni? Why? Why do you ask?"

"Hmm. Well, she's your friend. And you usually start a conversation mentioning something she's done or said."

"I do?"

"Yes," Jocelyn said. "So. What's wrong?"

"Nothing. She's…she's fine."

"Speak to me. Something's wrong," Jocelyn said softly. Allie heard the heavy sigh. "Mom…" she gently prodded.

"I have no clue where to start."

"Is this about Toni?" Jocelyn asked in a quiet voice.

It's now or never, Allie thought. Her stomach was in knots and her mouth was dry. She walked over to the sink and got a glass of water.

"Okay, now tell me why your mouth is so dry you needed a glass of water."

Allie looked out the kitchen window as the summer breeze blew through the oak tree in the backyard. She smiled at all the memories that flashed through her mind.

"What's going on with you and Toni? You can tell me. And you need to say something, so I know you're still there."

Allie laughed then. "I don't know how you'll take this. I don't want to hurt you or Nick." She bit at her lip when Jocelyn was silent. "You know I love you both very much."

"Yes, I do. I wish I could be with you right now. But I just can't get away—"

"No, no, sweetie. Don't worry. You might want to sit down."

"I am. You're scaring me."

"Then I'll sit, too." Allie took a deep breath and walked outside to the back porch and sat on the swinging bench. "I think I have deep feelings for Toni." She winced and waited.

"Deep like friendship deep or deep like…?"

"Deep like…"

Allie could only hear Jocelyn's soft breathing. "I kissed her."

"Kiss like friendship kiss or…"

"Oh, for godsakes, sweetie. I kissed another woman and not as a friend."

"Holy shit, Mom."

Allie looked at the sun as it filtered through the tree. "Holy shit is right."

"Is this why you and Dad divorced?"

"No, it's not. What happened between me and your father was a long, long time coming. Toni was after the fact, just as Donna was for your father. How are they, by the way? I talked to your father a couple weeks ago, he didn't say much."

"They're fine. I think he's in love with her."

"I think so, too." Allie smiled then. "I hope he is. It would be good for him to be happy."

"Are you?" Jocelyn asked. "With Toni?"

Allie grew silent as she thought about it. She then smiled thinking of Toni and all she'd done and all she had meant to Allie. "Yes, sweetie. I think I am."

"You always sound happy when you talk about her. And when I've seen you together, you both, I don't know, you look happy and content."

Neither said a word until Allie asked, "Are you there, or did you have a heart attack?"

Jocelyn laughed quietly. "I'm still here. I'll always be here."

Allie sniffed quietly.

"Don't start crying yet. I won't be able to understand you. Well, do you want my opinion?"

"Always." Allie sniffed and looked around for a tissue.

"What does Toni say?"

"I'm not sure. We've talked. Well, honestly, Toni has tried to. I've been evasive all week."

"Why?"

"Because I'm scared to death. This is a total change of lifestyles here. She has to understand that."

"And you don't think it's a change for Toni?"

Allie frowned and stopped swinging. "How is it a change for her?"

"Mom. You're straight, or you were, or you've always been gay, and heck, I can't believe we're having this conversation," she said with a nervous chuckle.

"You and me both, sweetie."

"Marcie and I have had several conversations about this very topic. She said straight women are the kiss of death."

Allie blinked in horror. "Thank you. That makes me feel much better."

Jocelyn laughed on the other end. "What she meant is that you don't fall for straight women. They usually only want the novelty, to experiment and move on. Maybe Toni is thinking that about you. Don't you think she's scared, too?"

"Oh, Christ, I never thought of that. You're right. God, what am I going to do?"

"Want me to ask Marcie? She's right here."

"Oh, God, no…" Allie heard the muffled conversation on the other end. "Jocelyn?" Allie could just imagine poor Marcie's eyes bugging out of her head.

"Mom, you know Marcie is gay and very out. Maybe she can help. Hold on." She put her hand over the phone again.

"Jocelyn, oh, my God. Wait!" Allie said quickly and groaned. Her stomach was doing flip-flops. Fine, a young woman who could be my daughter is giving me lesbian advice. Oh, God, I told my daughter I was involved with a lesbian. Allie heard part of their conversation and looked for a hole to crawl into.

"Oh, my God! Your mother? With another woman? Is she a hottie?"

Allie hung her head and listened to Jocelyn. "Big picture here, Marcie...but yes, you met her. It's Toni."

"Jocelyn!" Allie said loudly when she heard Marcie squeal with delight.

"Mrs. S. How's it going?" Marcie asked happily.

"Marcie. H-hello, honey. H-how are you doing?" Allie nervously pulled at the collar of her blouse. It was getting warm—too warm.

"Apparently, not as well as you are. Now I understand you need my advice."

"No." Allie took a deep breath. "Well, I...yes."

"You only have to ask yourself one question, Mrs. S. Are you in love with her? Nothing else really matters. You've been telling Jocelyn that since I met her. I know this is different, some of your friends may not accept it. Then you have to ask yourself if they're really your friends," Marcie went on as if giving a lecture. Allie smiled reluctantly.

"Try to imagine the rest of your life without her. If you can, then it's just a fling and you'd better call it off now. This woman is probably afraid of that anyway. The first rule in the lesbian world is, 'Do not fall for a straight woman'—no one listens, but it is a rule. She's probably a nervous wreck. So are you. You have to decide if it's sex or love...hell, Mrs. S., it's what you old folks have been preaching all along."

Allie frowned, then laughed quietly at the "old folks" comment.

"This is just a different kind of love. The Big Man put us all here. You decide. Good luck, I have faith in you...your daughter is a wonderful human being. She'll make a great nurse. It's because of you, you know. Well, I've talked long enough. Hope I helped a little," she said seriously. "But I do have a question if it's not too personal. Don't worry it's not about sex."

Allie winced in motherly fashion hearing the word sex from

Jocelyn's roommate. "Go ahead, honey. Just be gentle." She heard Marcie chuckling.

"Okay, here goes. I'm just curious because I worry about straight women saying they suddenly 'turn gay.' How do you know you might love Toni if you've never had the experience of another woman? You don't have to answer to me. It's just something for you to think about. If you need to, of course."

Allie smiled, knowing Marcie did not want to come out and ask if she had any lesbian encounters. "I know what you're saying and you've helped a tremendous amount. Thank you, honey."

"You're welcome. Here's Jos. Oh, wait. Toni, she's a hottie."

Allie heard Jocelyn grabbing for the phone. "Yes, Marcie, she is definitely a hottie."

"So are you! Well, I mean..." she stammered, and Allie laughed.

"Thanks, I know what you mean."

"Mom, geez! Sorry."

"Don't be, sweetie. Marcie was very enlightening."

"She's right. You've always told me to give love and I'd be loved in return. I won't say this is expected, but seeing you and Toni together, I don't know, I can't help but think it...well, you look right together. Is that odd?"

"I hope not, darling. Because I think I'm really in love, probably for the first time in my life." She sat in stunned silence along with Jocelyn. "Oh, shit, Jocelyn, did I just say...?"

"Yes, you did. This is a more than a little freaky, I have to admit. It'll take a little time to adjust to this. God, does Dad know?"

"He knows the basics, but I haven't talked to anyone else about my feelings for Toni to anyone but you, sweetie."

"Thank you for that. I'm glad you feel we can talk about anything, and no matter what, we will always love each other."

Allie's tears caught her by surprise. She couldn't hold them back any longer. "God, I love you so much." She heard Jocelyn crying on the other end.

"I do, too."

"I think I'm in love with her," Allie said, sobbing into the phone. She said it. There, she said she was in love with Toni O'Hara, another woman. She stopped crying, took a deep quivering breath, and looked around the backyard. "Well, I said it, and the house didn't collapse."

Jocelyn laughed while she cried.

"The sky is still blue. The sun is still shining. God is in His heaven."

"Maybe all *is* right in the world," Jocelyn said through a huge sniff.

"Maybe just in my world. What else was there? Your father and Donna. You, Nick, and Toni."

"God. It sounds weird to hear you say it like that. I have to be honest, but I love you and Toni. You deserve to be happy. So do Dad and Donna. I suppose all this was just meant to be. I know that sounds so simplistic, but I want you to be happy, and if this is it, I'm glad it's Toni."

That did it. Allie started bawling all over again.

"Are you trying not to cry?"

Allie nodded as the tears ran down her cheeks.

Jocelyn laughed quietly on the other end. "Okay, you can't speak, so I'll let you go. I love you, and whatever you decide, I will back you up one hundred percent. So will Nick, we…we kinda figured this might happen."

"What!" Allie exclaimed when she finally found her voice.

"We, um, we kinda…" She stopped and laughed. "You're gonna think this is funny."

"I doubt it."

"Well, we had a talk with Toni and…"

"A talk? When? Oh, God, I'm going to be sick. Jocelyn, you tell me this minute."

"Okay, okay," she said quickly.

Allie listened and sighed heavily. "She didn't tell me you spoke. I'm going to murder the three of you."

"She loves you." Jocelyn giggled.

Allie heard Marcie giggling along with Jocelyn and blushed furiously at the thought. "Oh, stop giggling like two children, for heavensake. I'm hanging up. I-I love you, darling." She rolled her eyes as the two giggling women laughed into the phone.

"Mrs. S. has a girlfriend," Marcie sang in the background.

"Goodbye, Jocelyn. I love you," Allie said with all the maternal dignity she could muster.

"Bye, Mom, I love you, too." She laughed and hung up the phone.

Allie shook her head and sat there, contemplating all that Jocelyn and Marcie had said.

Now what?

Chapter 24

Allie sat at the kitchen table still thinking when she heard Marcus Gillespie's dog Max barking incessantly next door. "Geez, Max, relax."

With that, she heard someone banging on her front door. She ran to it and threw it open. There stood Toni, wild-eyed and panicked.

"Toni!"

"Hide me," she said quickly and stepped into the living room.

"Hide you? What on earth...?" Allie exclaimed and noticed Toni's appearance. Her navy blue T-shirt with the Chicago Fire Department emblem above the breast pocket looked baggy and hung out of her faded denim jeans. "What...?"

Toni looked back and chuckled. "Don't let him take me to the slammer, sweetheart," she said in Jimmy Cagney fashion. Allie didn't know what to think. They both heard someone coming up the steps.

"Oh, shit!" Toni exclaimed and dashed around her, hiding behind the front door. She held her fingers to her lips, then folded her hands as if begging.

Allie was totally confused. "What are—?"

"Allie?" she heard Marcus's voice called out.

"M-Marcus, hi," she said quickly.

"Did some dumb kid just run across your front yard?" the old man asked as his dog barked in the background.

Allie blinked and glared at the front door. "A dumb kid? No, Marcus, no dumb *kid*," she said emphatically and heard the small chuckle from behind the door.

"Well, some kid was in my yard and…" He laughed evilly. "Max nearly got him."

Allie heard a snort from behind her door as Marcus held out a large swatch of navy blue cotton. Allie took it. "Did Max?"

"Nah." Marcus laughed. "The kid must have gotten stuck on the fence. All I saw was ass over legs as he jumped it. I thought he headed in this direction. He must not be from the neighborhood. Everybody knows Max," he said proudly and again—the low growl from behind the door.

"You're right. He must have been from the city. You know those Chicago kids," she said sarcastically and pushed the front door farther, which emitted a stifled groan.

"Yeah, well, anyway, I'm sure he won't be back soon. Max nearly took part of his ass with him." He still chuckled. "Bet he peed himself. Well, g'night, Allie, better lock your doors anyway."

"Thanks, Marcus. Good night."

She closed the front door. Toni stood there grinning. Allie folded her arms across her chest, still holding the navy blue material. "Start talking. By the way, that was a horrible imitation of Jimmy Cagney."

Toni chuckled and pulled the tattered shirt around her. "Well. It's pretty much like the old geezer said. Max, by the way, is not a dog. He's some vicious snarling beast. He nearly got me."

Allie asked the obvious. "What were you doing in Mr. Gillespie's backyard?"

"Well, how else was I supposed to get the lilacs?" Toni asked as if Allie were nuts.

"Lilacs?" Allie asked slowly.

"Lilacs."

"S'plain yourself, Lucy," Allie said dryly.

Toni laughed at that one. "I saw the lilacs and I was going to take a few, but they were too far away from the fence. I had it all planned out in my head," she explained seriously. Allie grunted sarcastically, which Toni ignored. "I was going to hop the fence, get the lilacs, and hop over. Easy as pie. Who knew—Mr. Gillespie was it?" Allie nodded slowly. "Who knew Mr. Gillespie had the dog from hell? Good grief, you suburbanites are paranoid. Anyway," she continued, "the old geezer was right. I nearly soiled myself. The beast came out of nowhere. I backed up and snagged myself on his fence. I may sue," she added thoughtfully. "I hopped the fence and barely got away with my life." She finished obediently and bowed slightly.

Allie hid her grin. She held up the swatch of material. "Feel a draft?"

"I thought there was something missing." Toni laughed quietly as she tried to keep the shirt from falling off.

"That does not explain the lilacs," Allie informed her.

Toni blushed from head to toe and pulled out a lonely sprig of lilac from her back pocket. "As I was coming up your walk, I remembered you liked getting flowers. It was too late to find a florist. So I took some from Mother Nature," she said in a quiet voice and held the limp lavender flower up in a peace offering. "It's a little worse for wear. Sorry…"

Allie blinked and swallowed with extreme difficultly. All the moisture left her mouth and pooled elsewhere. She took the flower with a slightly shaky hand.

"Can I have my shirt?"

Allie laughed openly as Toni struggled with the tattered remnants of her T-shirt. "Don't laugh. This was my favorite shirt. I had it for six years, just broke it in."

Allie shook her head. "I've got a shirt you can wear. That one is now for dusting. Go into the kitchen. I'll be right down."

Toni grinned and obediently sat at the kitchen table.

Allie walked in and tossed her a T-shirt. "It's Nick's. I'm sure it'll fit."

Toni laughed and plucked it out of the air. "Thanks." She proceeded to strip off the tattered shirt.

Allie blinked and tried to look away—no, she didn't. Toni was in excellent shape. Her taut abdomen flexed as she slipped the T-shirt over her head and tucked it into her jeans. As she turned to sit down, Allie's eyes widened in horror. Printed in big red letters—*Remember my name, you'll be screaming it later*—was written on the back of the black shirt.

Toni sat and looked up at the flushed, red face. "What's wrong?" she asked seriously.

Myriad sexual images bombarded Allie's poor brain. She shook her head roughly. "N-nothing, nothing. Have you eaten dinner?"

"No. I haven't had much of an appetite this week." Toni played with the salt shaker.

Allie nodded in understanding. "Neither have I, to tell the truth," she said in a soft voice.

Toni looked up with sad eyes that broke Allie's heart.

"You must be hungry after your mission, Inspector O'Hara. It's a little late, but how about some bacon and eggs?"

Toni nodded with a small grin but said nothing.

They sat across from each other as they ate. "This is good. Thanks," Toni said quietly as she finished.

"What were you doing in Oak Park?"

Toni shrugged. "Just went for a drive."

"And found yourself in my driveway?"

"Car had a mind of its own."

Allie nodded. "So you hopped a fence to get me lilacs."

Toni's face turned an adorable shade of crimson. "Uh-huh," she agreed, playing with her fork.

Allie smiled happily. "Nearly got your ass bit off because I love flowers?"

Toni swallowed, then chuckled nervously. "It would appear so," she replied. "I didn't like this week, Alana. I was miserable the entire time. I couldn't work. I couldn't eat. Well, that's not exactly true. Mrs. W. made some killer apple strudel. But even working out did nothing for me," she said helplessly.

Allie said nothing. She needed to know exactly what Toni felt.

"I never thought I'd be in this position again," she said.

Allie looked up then and watched her. She knew what she was thinking. God, Marcie, you should go into psychiatry. Toni floundered for a moment.

"What position? In love or in love with a perceived straight woman?" Allie asked, and Toni's head shot up and her mouth dropped to the floor. Allie sported a superior grin as she drank her coffee. "I understand that straight women are the kiss of death to you lesbians."

Toni just blinked. She looked like a poor deer stuck in the headlights of an oncoming pickup.

"You're afraid because I'm newly divorced, that I'm vulnerable and looking for a change of pace. That I'll tire of you and revert to the straight life. Am I right?"

"I know you had a brief encounter in college but nothing since." Toni shrugged and grew silent.

"I understand your fear. Mine comes from a different angle. I'm scared to death because it is so totally opposite of what I've experienced. True, I've been married for over twenty-five years. I have only known biblically," she added and Toni hid her grin, "one man and no women. I don't know what it is about you, Toni O'Hara that stirs something so deep in me that no one else ever has. Does this and one brief time in college make me a lesbian?"

Toni offered a tender smile. "I can't answer that for you. I don't like putting labels on people. Gay, straight, black, white, who cares? We are only on the earth for such a short time," she said in a low caring voice. She then leaned in and smiled. "What does your soul say to you?"

Allie blinked several times. She cocked her head in contemplation and looked into Toni's eyes. Suddenly, she had tunnel vision. All she saw were the gray sparkling eyes pleading with her.

All her life, she'd wondered if a beautiful day did indeed wait beyond the blue horizon. She had lived her life for her children. If she were honest with herself, she would admit she never contemplated her soul before this. She was too afraid. If she had, she and Paul would have been divorced long, long ago. But perhaps now it was time to live.

With that, Toni's beeper went off. "Toni, your ass is beeping." Allie laughed as Toni grudgingly pulled it out of her belt and looked down.

"Shit!" She read the number and frowned deeply. "Just a sec." She pulled out her cell and dialed.

Allie saw the worried look and nodded.

"O'Hara, what's going on?" She listened and muttered an expletive under her breath. "Right. On my way." She set the phone down.

She looked at Allie's worried face. "There's a fire. A big one. They're calling everyone in on this. I gotta go, damn it."

Allie put her arms around her. "Please, be careful."

Toni gave her a tight hug. "Sure, I will. We still have a few things to talk about." Toni kissed her deeply. "I have to go," she whispered and let her go.

Allie nodded and stepped back.

"I'll call you later, not sure when, though," Toni said, quickly kissed her, and ran out the door before Allie could say another word.

Chapter 25

Allie watched the news in horrified amazement. It was a horrendous fire downtown. The eight-story building was an inferno. She watched as the news showed the blaze and the amazing number of firefighters. She hoped to get a glimpse of Toni, to no avail.

She fell asleep with the phone on her chest and the remote in her hand and had no clue what time it was when the phone rang. Bolting up, she answered it. "Toni?"

"No, this is Kevin Murphy," the tired voice said.

Allie's heart sank. "Kevin…Toni…It's Toni, isn't it?"

"Hold on, Allie. She's at Northwestern Hospital at the emergency room. Now I—"

"I'm on my way." Allie hung up the phone.

She never drove so fast in her life. It was three in the morning, not a soul on the streets. Please don't let me be pulled over, she begged frantically as she fought the tears blinding her vision. She parked the car and ran into the emergency room and up to the desk.

"I'm looking for a firefighter, Toni O'Hara. I believe she was brought here," she said in a panic.

The nurse leafed through the admittance records and shook her head. "We've had a few this evening. But I'm sorry. I don't find the name."

"You've got to. They told me she was here." Suddenly, she thought of what would happen if Toni didn't make it to the hospital. "Please, look again. Please."

"Alana," a low gravelly voice called from behind her.

Allie whirled around to see Toni standing there. She looked exhausted, her face smudged with soot and dirt, the hair on the right side singed and frayed.

Allie flew into her arms as Toni groaned. She pulled back. "Are you all right? Don't lie to me."

"I'm fine." She ran her dirty hand through her hair. "I wanted to cut my hair anyway."

Allie tried to laugh, but it came out a strangled cry as she covered her face with her hands.

"Alana," Toni whispered and pulled her into her arms again. "Please don't. I'm just tired. Why are you here? Didn't Kevin call you?"

"Well, yes. He said you were here and I just…"

Toni gave her a scathing look. "You didn't hear him out. You just took off, didn't you?"

Allie blushed and nodded. Toni chuckled quietly and kissed her forehead. "I came here in the ambulance with another firefighter. He's in bad shape, and I wanted to stay with him until his wife got here."

Allie let out a small sob of relief and buried her face in her hands once again.

"Don't cry now." Toni pulled her into a fierce hug.

Allie sobbed quietly as Toni gently rocked her. "Is your friend going to be all right?" Allie sniffed and pulled away from the warm embrace.

"Yes, Ruthie is with him now. Let's get out of here, okay?"

Allie nodded. "I'll drive you to your place. It's closer."

"It was a nightmare. I'm getting too old for this." Toni sighed as they walked out of the emergency room.

"You should retire and get your coffee shop."

"Okay, a hot shower, then bed," Allie ordered as Toni nodded obediently and headed for the bathroom.

She emerged from the hot shower, clean and exhausted, wrapped in a huge terrycloth robe. Allie pulled back the covers. "Give me that towel and sit down," she gently ordered.

Toni sat on the bed and Allie stood in front of her. Toni

210

instinctively parted her legs, and Allie quite naturally stood between them as she toweled her wet head. Grinning as she heard the muffled groan of pleasure, Allie gently rubbed the damp thick hair.

She then brushed her thick mane as Toni swayed and sighed happily. "Nobody's ever done this for me before," she whispered tiredly. She then groaned as she felt Allie's nails gently raking through her hair. "Good Christ, you have a marvelous touch."

"And you need to stop moaning. Lie down before you fall asleep sitting up," Allie whispered and started to push her against the pillows. Toni was already there, sound asleep. Allie chuckled quietly as she brushed the graying raven hair off her forehead and pulled the covers over her.

"Sleep well," she whispered and kissed her dry warm lips and turned out the light.

Allie stood by the windows in the dark living room, looking out at the Chicago skyline. Off to the south, smoke still billowed through the night sky. Allie glanced back at Toni's room and said a prayer of thanks that Toni was safe in her bed. It was a terrible fire, big enough for the department to need all firefighters, including inspectors. When her cell phone went off, she quickly looked at the caller ID. She frowned curiously and answered. "Hi, Paul. What's wrong?"

"Nothing. I just heard on the news about the fire and how they called out every firefighter, and I thought of Toni. Was she there?"

Allie smiled in surprise. "Yeah, they called her. She's fine. Exhausted and singed but otherwise okay. I can still see the smoke from here."

"Good." Paul breathed a sigh of relief. "Wait a second. How can you see the smoke from Oak Park?"

Allie hesitated for a moment. "I'm not at home. I'm at Toni's."

Now Paul hesitated. "Oh, um. Are you…"

"Yes, I am."

"Hmm."

Allie heard the smile in that grunt. "What hmm?"

"I guess I was right about you and Toni, huh? I mean, for a guy, I'm pretty perceptive. Wouldn't you... Hey!"

Allie heard the slap through the phone and laughed. "Please tell Donna thank you for that. And I'd like to thank her in person, but never having met her..."

"I know. I'm sorry about that. It's just that it was so soon, and we've been so wrapped up in everything." He stopped and chuckled. "I'm getting the evil eye. That's not entirely true. It was awkward, I guess with you and Donna. I wasn't sure how it would go."

"You worry too much."

"That's what Donna says, too. She, um, she wants to meet you."

Allie heard the slight trepidation in his voice and laughed. "That would be fine. Whenever you're ready."

"I'm glad you're happy, Allie."

When she heard his voice catch, she fought the tears, as well. "Maybe we both deserve to be happy."

"We did good, though, didn't we?"

"Yes, we did." Allie swallowed her tears. "We made two wonderful children and no one can take that away from us."

"You're right. Out of everything, we have that. I'm glad Toni's okay. We were worried."

"Thank you, and thank Donna for me. Good night, Paul."

"G'night, Al."

Allie quietly closed her phone and gazed once again at the city below. "Toni's city," she whispered. She thought of Toni safe and sleeping, and an overwhelming feeling of contentment settled into her bones. She walked through the dark living room to Toni's bed.

Toni lay on her back, her arms stretched out and her mouth slightly open. Allie chuckled when a small snore escaped. She had intended to sleep on the couch, but right now, her only thought was to be safe and warm next to the woman she loved. She slipped out of her slacks and shirt and crawled in next to Toni and snuggled as close as she could without waking her. As she rested her head on Toni's shoulder, Allie reached over and brushed her singed hair away from her face and kissed her cheek.

"Good night, Toni."

Toni woke slowly as she opened her eyes. Sunlight streamed into her loft. Good grief, I passed out, she thought and smiled, remembering how Alana took care of her. Glancing next to her, she saw the rumpled blanket. She turned over and hugged the pillow, inhaling the sweet scent of Alana.

"She slept with me," Toni said with a happy grin, then looked around the room. "And she's gone."

She dragged her body out of bed and looked around her apartment to find she was indeed alone. Fighting the wave of insecurity, she took a quick shower, then slipped into a pair of shorts and a tank top.

It was nearly four in the afternoon. "God, I slept the day away." She picked up her phone and walked out onto the deck. She started to dial Alana's number.

"Well, you're awake!"

Toni turned to see Alana standing on the adjacent deck attached to her new art studio. Toni grinned wildly. "Gimme a minute. I'm calling you to find out where you are."

Alana laughed and leaned against the railing. "I know where I am."

Toni's grin grew exponentially. "Ya do, huh?" She walked over and leaned on her railing.

"I think so. Come on over and I'll show you." Alana disappeared into the studio.

Toni raised an eyebrow. She nonchalantly took a few steps, then ran next door just as Alana opened the door. Alana grinned and stepped back to let Toni enter.

Toni was shocked—pleasantly, happily shocked.

Alana had brought all her artwork and set up her new studio. She placed the large easel in the window where it received the wonderful sunshine she predicted with paints, canvases, and brushes all placed strategically around the studio.

A painting was already coming to life on the large canvas. Both gazed at it.

"Isn't it horrible?" Alana asked happily.

"It is not."

"Oh, it's bad. But I don't care. It won't be for long."

"Well, you're the artist. So when did you do this?" Toni asked as Alana dried her hands off and grinned.

"While you slept like a log." She looked around. "What do you think?"

"I think it's wonderful. You did so much. Are you happy?" She walked over to Alana, who put the towel down.

"I am extremely happy. Are you rested?"

"I am extremely rested and…"

"Hungry," Alana added the obvious.

They sat outside in the beer garden of the North Side pub. It was a gay-owned restaurant, and Allie knew Toni brought her here purposely.

"Nice little place," Allie said honestly. "Come here often?"

Toni laughed as she perused the menu. "Yep, when I want a disgustingly greasy burger. I'm starving." She eagerly rubbed her hands together. "So tell me. How is it that you are a wealth of lesbian information all of the sudden?" Toni asked as she constructed the huge burger.

Allie was astounded at the size of the burger the waiter set in front of this woman. She watched in awe as Toni precisely added the tomato, lettuce…

Allie chuckled at the question, remembering her conversation. "Jocelyn."

Toni shot her head up from her construction work. "Y-you told Jocelyn?" she asked in amazement.

"Yes, go figure, but it wasn't Jocelyn who informed me. It was her roommate, Marcie."

Toni nodded while Allie told her the whole conversation. Toni listened and laughed as she finished her masterpiece, adding the top bun.

"Kids these days, where do they get it?" Toni asked playfully.

Allie smirked but said nothing.

"So what do you think?"

"Are you honestly going to get that thing in your mouth?" Allie asked dryly.

Toni winked as she held up the burger and took a healthy bite. After swallowing, she wiped her hands on the napkin, which Allie was happy to see, instead of the blue jeans.

"Answer my question," Toni prodded and sipped the chocolate malt through the straw.

Allie watched her. After the previous night, when she was petrified of losing her, she realized how much she loved the woman who was making a pig out of herself right now. She raised a curious eyebrow. How in the world did this happen? She no longer cared. She only knew she loved her.

"Last night, you asked me what my soul was saying," Allie said quietly. Toni looked up from her burger and blinked several times. "My soul speaks to yours, Toni O'Hara. It has never spoken to another." She blinked back the tears that leapt into her eyes.

Toni looked as if she couldn't believe what she was hearing. "God, are you sure?" She reached across and took Allie's hand.

Allie grinned and nodded. "For the first time in my life, yes."

"Good. I feel the same," Toni said honestly.

"We're a pair, aren't we? Discussing our lives over a greasy hamburger..." Allie reached across and snagged a fry. "And French fries."

"So what now?" Toni tried not to show her hands shaking. She picked up the burger and took a bite. As Allie was about to speak, she held up her hand to quiet her. "Wait, my mouth is full." She quickly chewed and swallowed. "You're not going to make me choke this time, schoolmarm. Okay, go ahead."

Allie smirked inwardly. "While you were sleeping, I decided to do a few things around my house."

Toni was confused. "Like what?"

"Well, I'm changing the living room, getting new bedroom furniture," she said absently.

Toni shrugged and picked up her burger, figuring it was safe to eat now. "That's nice. How come?" she asked as she took a healthy bite.

Allie leaned in. "Because when I take you into my bed, O'Hara, I want to make sure it's on virgin territory," she whispered in a low seductive voice.

That did it. Toni was stunned as she gaped at her, dropped her burger in her lap, and started choking.

Allie chuckled as the waiter came running out. Toni sounded like a goose as she honked, trying to catch her breath. The waiter slapped her on the back, and Toni coughed up the remainder of the burger.

"Damn it, you do that on purpose!" she accused as she sat down.

"Well, you had so much in your mouth," Allie reminded her.

Toni narrowed her eyes as she drank her ice water. Allie laughed happily as Toni sat back and offered a sexy smile. "So about this new bed…"

Chapter 26

"Do you want to stop?" Allie asked breathlessly. She ran her fingers through Toni's thick hair. This is so right, so natural, she thought helplessly. "Because I don't want to…" She pulled Toni down once again.

Toni groaned and was helpless to argue. The feel of the woman was amazing. Never had Toni O'Hara been so aroused. Never had she wanted nor needed anyone more. This feeling of love was new to Toni. She adored this woman.

Allie reveled in the soft, yet muscular body over her. She never thought she'd feel this much passion for anyone, especially not for another woman. She loved Toni and only her.

The new bed wasn't the only virgin territory to be explored. Passion now took over.

"Kiss me again, Toni, please," she begged, and Toni pulled her into her arms and kissed her—good.

Allie took Toni's hand and brought it to her breast in a bold move that left Toni gasping.

She gently cupped Allie's breast and ran her fingers across the hard nipple. Allie moaned into her mouth as she pulled Toni incredibly close.

She lowered her head and nibbled at Allie's ear. "God, Alana," she whispered, then smiled as Allie shivered uncontrollably in her arms.

"Don't stop," Allie pleaded as she ran her fingers through her hair. Toni slowly kneaded her full breast, then quickly slid her hand under her sweater and in one movement, had the front closure opened.

Allie hissed and arched her back as the warm fingers danced across her breasts. "God, Toni," she whimpered as her hips twitched with anticipation. Toni was murmuring into her ear, kissing and nibbling the tender lobe. Allie ran her fingers down Toni's back and slipped them under her shirt, feeling the strong back, now covered in a sensual sheen of perspiration. The feeling was intoxicating to Allie as she pulled her close.

Toni lifted the sweater, Allie leaned forward, and in one movement, Toni had the sweater and bra discarded. "Oh, God," Allie cried out as Toni growled and took the aching nipple into her mouth.

"Alana, Alana," Toni said desperately as she continued. Her hands roamed over Allie's soft skin, her arms, her breasts, her stomach. "God, I love the feel of you." She slipped her hand farther, her fingers swirling around Allie's navel. Allie arched her back and instinctively parted her legs.

She was frantic for her touch. Allie tried to unzip her own jeans, and Toni pulled back and gently pushed her hands away. She sat back on her heels and looked down at the woman she knew she loved.

Allie's breathing was ragged and coarse. She looked up into the want in Toni's eyes and felt all the moisture pool between her legs.

"I want you, Alana, more than I've ever wanted any woman in my life. I want you to know that this is not just about sex, not with you. It can never be just that with you."

Allie just swallowed and nodded, she couldn't speak if she wanted to.

Toni unbuttoned her shirt, never breaking eye contact. "I've thought about this for such a long time now. Thought if I had the chance, how I would love you," she whispered as the shirt came off. Allie was amazed as Toni easily slipped out of her bra. "How would I show you just how beautiful you are? How you make me crazy with desire," she continued. She then reached down and gently ran her fingertips along the side of her arms, smiling as the gooseflesh instantly appeared. She took Allie's arms, raised them over her head, and kissed her deeply. Allie whimpered and squirmed as she allowed this woman to love her.

"I've noticed how soft your skin is. How it begs to be touched," Toni whispered, no longer looking into the green eyes, but raking over her prone body. She knelt next to Allie and ran her fingers once again over the quivering flesh. She gently traced the line of her waist, to the outside of her breast, feeling the fullness of Allie's heaving breast. "God, you are beautiful," she whispered in awe. Allie was biting her bottom lip not to cry out. She could see where the ladies loved this woman...

Her hands felt every curve, every line of her upper torso. She closed her eyes and smiled as if committing it to memory.

"Kiss me," Allie pleaded. Toni shook her head.

"Soon," she promised. "I just need to know you." Allie groaned and twitched once again.

Toni bent down and lightly placed a kiss on her stomach, smiling as the muscles fluttered against her lips. God, she's kissing my stretch marks, Allie thought. She shifted a bit uncomfortably, and Toni sensed her apprehension.

She moved her body over Allie, so she was nearly nose to nose. "I know what you're thinking. Please don't. I love your body. I love how you gave it up for your children. It is truly the sexiest thing I can think of...you pregnant, alive with life growing inside you. God, you're amazing."

Allie stared into the gray eyes, dark with passion. "You're unbelievable. My God, I see what the women love about you."

Toni shook her head. "No more. I only want you to love me." She kissed her dry lips, then ran her tongue sensually across them before kissing her way down the length of her torso, stopping to feast on the full heaving breast. Allie was squirming and gasping as she felt strong, gentle hands unzip her jeans. Lifting her hips slightly, she opened her eyes and watched Toni slip the jeans down her legs. "Remarkable," Toni whispered and slipped her fingers in the waistband of her panties and gently pulled them down, discarding them, as well.

Completely naked, Allie was now quivering uncontrollably. She felt the moisture running down between her legs. "Toni, please," she begged quietly. Never had she felt such a need to come. God, if she doesn't touch me soon, I will die, she thought.

Toni stood next to the bed, and Allie watched in awe as she unzipped her jeans and pulled them down over her hips. Allie's eyes were glued to the magnificent body before her. If she thought Toni had a nice body in clothes, she was near apoplexy as she gazed at the muscular, yet unbelievably soft and feminine body before her. She didn't know what to expect, never really thought about it.

Toni O'Hara was like a sculpture...muscles defined, curves soft, breasts small but firm. "I'm going to paint you," she whispered stupidly. Toni chuckled and Allie shook her head. "I mean it. You're stunning," she whispered in awe. "I need to feel your body against mine."

Toni swallowed and lowered her body over her. Allie instinctively parted her legs, and Toni, as if she belonged there all her life, easily and naturally lay between them. Both women gasped at the feel of skin on skin, breasts compressing, lips blending into a heavenly kiss.

Toni shifted and lay next to Allie, her hand immediately wandering to the soft dark curls. "Yes..." Allie hissed and parted her legs farther.

"I need you now," Toni said. Allie shivered at the low timbre of her voice. Toni wanted her, needed her, and she wasn't asking. Her fingers lightly danced and entwined in the saturated curls, then dipped lower between the plump folds.

"Oh, God," Allie whispered as she clung to her. Toni kissed her neck, gently nibbling at the soft flesh. So many sensations flew through Allie. Toni's teeth, her tongue, her fingers.

Toni slipped her fingers through the wetness. "God, you're so ready," she whispered sensually.

"You did this. I..."

"What, Alana? What do you want?"

"You're asking?" Allie asked nervously.

"I won't know unless you tell me." Toni licked her ear. Allie groaned and held on as the muscle invaded her ear, sending a shiver through her body. She felt the strong fingers dancing and teasing but not satisfying.

"I want you to touch me. I want you to make me come," she

whispered frantically. Toni smiled and immediately parted the thick folds and slipped her fingers up and down the length of her, causing Allie to cry out at the contact. The pressure between her legs built as she felt herself rising. "Oh!" she cried out as she arched her back. "Don't stop, please," she begged as her hips started moving of their own volition.

Toni felt her clitoris harden as she stroked back and forth. "God, you're beautiful," she murmured against her ear as Allie hung on, lifting her hips, wanting and needing more.

"Toni, inside, please..." She whimpered as she thrust her hips shamelessly higher.

"You want to feel me inside you? Deep inside?" Toni asked in a low growl and inserted one finger deeply, then drew it back. Allie whimpered. God, she needed to come.

"Toni!" she cried out as she reached down to pull her hand into her. Toni quickly pulled her hands above her head and held them both with one hand.

Toni continued and easily slipped two fingers into the warm soft haven. She let out a low groan of pleasure, feeling the walls clamp around her fingers.

"More?" she asked in a coarse voice. She was panting, trying to keep up with the bucking hips.

"Yes, more!" Allie cried out, and Toni responded with a third finger, spreading them out as much as she could, filling her completely. Allie groaned her pleasure as Toni thrust furiously. "God, almost," she cried out.

Toni continued, then pressed her thumb against the engorged clitoris, and that was it. Allie screamed out her name as the orgasm raked through her body. Wave after wave swept through her, and Toni slowed, bringing her back down.

Allie was a mass of quivering flesh as Toni gently held her. "Ohgodohgod." Allie sighed helplessly as she clung to the strong shoulders. Toni kissed her damp hair. "You're...well, I don't know what you are," Allie whispered and heard the small chuckle. "God, Toni. That was remarkable. I've never felt anything like that."

"Neither have I." Toni kissed the salty flesh beneath her jaw line. Once again, she needed this woman. Allie held her close as

Toni nibbled at her neck, her teeth lightly nipping. Allie shook, her legs clamped shut as the jolt of electricity shot between her legs. She felt the moisture cascading once again. Allie then thought of the fantasy, picturing Toni…

She gently pushed on her shoulders, and Toni smiled into her task. She nibbled her way down to her breasts. "Alana?" she whispered into her soft flesh.

"Yes?" Allie voice was a mere whisper. Toni moved completely over her and looked down into the green eyes filled with desire. She kissed her slowly and deeply, her tongue teasing her lips, then slowly seeking entrance. Allie parted her lips, welcoming the satiny muscle as it flicked and explored. Allie moaned, desperately wanting to feel that tongue…

"May I taste you?" Toni whispered against her lips. Allie immediately felt the moisture seeping from her. She couldn't speak. "Tell me," Toni repeated as she slid down her trembling body.

"Yes, please, I need to feel your tongue on me, please," she begged and pushed on the strong shoulders.

Toni kissed and gently licked her way down the quivering torso, settling herself between the soft thighs. She sighed and groaned as she lifted Allie's legs over her shoulders. "God, Alana." She moaned as she kissed her inner thigh, her cheek brushing against the saturated curls. Alana's scent invaded her senses and Toni could wait no longer. She leaned in and gently kissed the dark curls. Allie groaned and reached down gently to rake her fingers through the graying hair.

Toni felt her own arousal start as she slowly licked up and down the length of Allie. Hearing the woman moan and hiss with pleasure, Toni moved farther and snaked her tongue through the thick folds, tasting the love that flowed from her. She groaned against her, causing Allie to cry out and pull the dark head closer to her.

"Oh, God, Toni. This is amazing." She sighed and closed her eyes. Toni's tongue artfully lapped back and forth, teasing her, causing her to squirm uncontrollably. Just when she thought she would start, Toni would ease up and barely touch her. "Please," she begged quietly and tried to pull her head closer. Toni resisted and growled lowly as she backed off.

Allie stopped, realizing that Toni wanted control of her. This excited Allie even more. She placed her hands above her head and held on to her new headboard. Toni looked up, realizing that Alana was offering herself.

"Thank you," she whispered into the curls. "Now keep them there," she said in a low growl. Allie let out a small groan and held on.

Soon, Toni had her writhing on the bed. Only Toni's strong arms around her thighs kept her from flying off the newly christened bed. "Oh, my God!" Allie cried out as the orgasm tore through her body. Toni's tongue was pure evil as it relentlessly milked her orgasm for all it was worth. With every flick of her tongue, Allie jumped and shuddered, helpless to do anything but come again and again.

"Please, enough!" She nearly sobbed as her hands flew to Toni's wet hair and roughly pulled. "Please!" she begged as her body quivered and shook.

Toni relented and quickly moved up the trembling body and held her close. Allie's body jerked with the aftershocks of the powerful orgasm. In a few moments, she quieted as Toni gently held her.

"You just had to make me beg, didn't you?" Her ragged voice squeaked.

Toni laughed and held her close, pulling the covers up over them. "I read the back of that shirt you gave me," she scolded the well-satisfied woman. Allie chuckled wickedly. "I got a helluva lot of ribbing from the guys at the firehouse."

"You'll live," Allie assured her as she shifted and rolled Toni onto her back.

Toni swallowed and looked up into the passion-filled green eyes. "I never thought I could feel so alive, Toni. My body is still humming...I want you to feel that way, too," Allie said, and Toni noted the hesitant quaver in her voice. She gently reached up and took Allie's hand, bringing it between her legs. Allie gasped as she felt the heat between her legs.

"You did this to me, as well. Touch me, please." She gently guided the innocent fingers through her drenched curls. She groaned and closed her eyes, and Allie gently pushed the hand away.

She kissed her then, taking Toni's tongue into her mouth, tasting her own arousal. It made her shiver all over again. She moaned into the sensual kiss, then lowered her head and kissed the small firm breast, loving the feel of the soft skin against her lips. Tentatively, she took the small nipple and sucked it between her lips, smiling as the more experienced woman arched her back into the touch. "God, yes, Alana." She moaned and ran her fingers through the silky blond hair. "Wonderful," she whispered her encouragement.

Filling Allie with confidence, Toni lay back and parted her legs. "Touch me now, please," she said in a low voice that went right through Allie. She slid her hand down the taut abdomen, pausing to allow her fingers to tease around her navel. Toni's stomach muscles clenched and quivered, much to Allie's delight. Seeing this confident woman succumbing to her touch was intoxicating. She grew bolder and slipped her fingers through the saturated black curls. Toni groaned deeply, her breathing was ragged and her body immediately broke into a cold sweat. "Geezus," she growled as she arched her back.

"Does this feel all right?" Allie kissed her breast. God, who knew I would love this so much, she thought happily. Toni couldn't speak; she merely nodded.

Where Alana Sanders found her boldness, she didn't know. Perhaps it was from Toni, who lay there, trusting her with her body and soul. Knowing that Toni knew Allie would never hurt her filled Allie with such love and desire to please her.

"Toni, look at me," she whispered firmly. Gray eyes popped open as they gazed into the ocean of green. "I want to please you as you have pleased me. I want to know your body, what makes you tremble, what drives you crazy. I want to know all of it." She kissed her deeply. Toni groaned as Allie plunged her tongue deep into Toni's awaiting mouth. She slid her fingers through the hot moisture, amazed at Toni's state of arousal. Her fingers slid back and forth, gathering the moisture with her fingers. Toni was gasping and bucking her hips.

"Now, Alana!" She groaned, and Allie felt her clitoris distend and harden. She flicked her fingertips over the swollen shaft, and Toni's body stiffened tight as a bow. Allie watched in awe as muscles contracted and bulged. The strong body glistened, rigid with the onset of her orgasm.

"You are magnificent. Now," she whispered in her ear. "Come for me," she ordered sensually. She plunged three fingers deep within her, amazed as the warm plump flesh clamped around her fingers.

"Oh, God!" Toni cried out as she felt the orgasm knife through her body. "Alana!" she cried helplessly as she came. She rode Alana's hand, bucking into it, feeling her wetness pouring out. She was slightly embarrassed. Never had she let go with such abandon before. Never had she felt this much passion and desire.

"God! No more!" Toni cried out and roughly pulled her hand away. She was near hyperventilation. Allie grinned as she loomed over the helplessly spent Toni, who was trying desperately not to faint.

Allie ran her fingers through the wet head, and Toni opened her eyes. She looked at the woman she loved with amazement. "Shit!" was all she could say.

"I did good, huh?" Allie asked, grinning wildly. Toni gave her a horrified look, then laughed.

"Good? I nearly fainted. If this is what you're like in bed, woman, I *will* have to retire early," she said and pulled her close.

Both women lay in each other's arms, souls and limbs entwined.

"We are definitely keeping that shirt," Allie mumbled, and Toni laughed and pulled her close.

Epilogue

Lidia stood behind the counter watching as Toni proudly stood outside of the new Rising Sun Café looking up at the sign across the top of Lidia's bakery.

"Crazy woman got me. Now we have a bakery and coffee shop. I still do not know what a smoothie is."

Behind her, Kevin leaned in and kissed her neck. "It's a good thing, Lidia Walinski. Now with Toni as your business partner, you don't have to work so hard, and you'll have more time with me."

Lidia leaned back against Kevin and grinned. "You are lazy Irishman, but I love you."

"My good luck." He wrapped his arms around her waist.

Lidia laughed and pulled away. "Enough of the Irish charm. I have things to do. They will be here soon."

Toni walked in, sending the bell tinkling over the door. "Love that sound," she said and looked around. She picked up a towel and wiped off the tables and rearranged the sugar and creamer, the silverware, and napkins. "All set. I hope we get some new customers with this grand opening, Mrs. W."

"We will, Antonia. Do not worry."

It was the end of summer in Chicago. The streets teemed with vacationers; Toni hoped some of them would be sitting in her coffee house. This will work, she thought positively. Perhaps the younger ones would stop by instead of heading for the streets. Perhaps some wouldn't. Remembering her own miserable childhood, Toni vowed to make a difference, even in a small way.

She sighed happily and walked around the counter. The aroma of fresh-baked pastry filled her senses and had her stomach grumbling. They had tastefully decorated the coffee house with artwork of an up-and-coming artist. Beautiful scenery and bold colors expressed the passion of the artist. Toni grinned, forever grateful she was the lucky recipient of some of that passion.

With that, the object of her musing walked into the coffee house. Alana stood there, smiling and happy. Toni watched her, grinning like a schoolgirl.

"May I help you?" Toni leaned on the counter.

Alana walked up to her and chuckled. "I'm looking for a place that has great coffee and conversation," she said, mirroring her lover's position.

"Well, you've found it. Welcome to The Rising Sun Café," she said. "And we have some wonderful artwork from a local. She's a bit on the eccentric side, but you know how odd artists are."

Allie hid her grin. "Yes, they tend to befriend other crazies."

Toni laughed. "Thank God for that." She pulled Allie into her arms and kissed her. "Are you nervous? Paul and Donna said they'd come by for the opening."

"No, not really. I just want this to be a success for you and Lidia."

"It will. I—"

The tinkling bell had them looking at the door. There was Paul, smiling and looking decidedly happy. Allie hadn't seen him in almost four months. He looked well, and Allie couldn't help but be happy for him. Donna stood next to him, but she walked up to Allie.

"Hi. I'm Donna."

"It's nice to finally meet you. I'm Allie. This is Toni." Allie stepped aside as Toni took the offered hand.

"It's good to meet you, Donna."

"Same here." Donna looked around. "You know, I've come here so many times. It looks the same but different somehow. Oh, it's the artwork on the walls." She looked at Allie. "Yours? They're beautiful."

"Thanks," Allie said, feeling a little awkward.

"And for sale," Toni added and grunted when Allie elbowed her ribs.

"Get used to that," Paul said, leaning into Toni.

Lidia came out of the back with Kevin behind her; he carried a large tray of pastry. "Welcome," Lidia said, wiping her hands on her apron.

Toni made the introductions, and soon, everyone arrived for the opening.

Nick arrived with his new girlfriend. He was on the verge of taking the plunge and getting married. Toni laughed as she remembered sitting in the backyard with Nick, discussing the topic. Nick was as nervous as a cat, while Toni was the picture of calm reassurance. It was only afterward, Toni revealed to Alana she was the one who was sick to her stomach. It was sweet of Alana to hold the cold cloth to Toni's forehead.

When Jocelyn walked in with her boyfriend, Paul and Toni gave him a wary look.

Donna leaned into Allie. "I'm going to kill Paul if he doesn't leave that poor boy alone."

Allie agreed. "I feel the same. Toni gave him the third degree when Jocelyn brought him over for dinner. I had to explain to that goof she'd get arrested if she kept skulking around the hospital watching the poor kid."

Donna grunted and glanced at Allie. "Men."

Allie shot her an incredulous look, then both women burst into laughter. "Sorry. I couldn't resist," Donna said.

"I have to remember that one," Allie said, still laughing. "You know, when Jocelyn graduated and started at Loyola Hospital, I had already moved in with Toni and wanted to just give the house in Oak Park to Jocelyn. Paul agreed, but Jocelyn wanted to work out a payment plan to buy the house when she could. I refused to take money from her." Allie looked at Toni, who was talking with Paul and her children. "It was Toni who gently explained how I needed to treat Jocelyn like an adult. This was her right as a grown responsible woman to make her own way. I'm a lucky woman, Donna."

"We're both lucky," Donna said softly.

Allie smiled. "Yes, we are."

Jocelyn came up to them, giving them both a kiss. "Donna,

can I steal you for a minute? Truman wants to talk to you." She pulled Donna away as Paul walked over to Allie.

"Who names their kid Truman?" he asked, watching them.

Allie rolled her eyes. "Stop being a protective dad for a moment."

"Okay." Paul snorted. "Like that will happen."

"Look at her, Paul. She's in love."

All color left Paul's face. "You think so?"

"Yes, I do."

"Well, if that's love, what about Nick?"

"He looks ill."

They laughed as Toni walked up with two glasses of champagne. She handed one to Allie, then Paul. "Thanks for coming, Paul. It means a lot to us."

"You're welcome," Paul said. "I hope it works for you. It's a good idea. And I like the new name of the place." He looked at Allie, who grinned. He then glanced at Toni. "Does she do her cleaning routine to that song and—"

"Yes," Toni said, hiding her grin. "Every Saturday." She laughed at the glare from Allie. "Well, I think I'll go talk to Nick and Jocelyn." She then lowered her voice. "What kind of a name is Truman?"

"Go," Allie said, gently pushing her away.

Paul and she stood in silence for a moment. Paul swirled his glass of champagne. Allie watched Toni as she laughed and talked to Nick and his girlfriend. They watched Donna with Jocelyn and Truman.

"You're happy."

Allie looked up at Paul. "Yes, I am."

Paul nodded and finished his champagne. Unexpectedly, he leaned over and kissed Allie on the cheek. "At Thanksgiving when Toni came over, I wanted so much to hate her guts. But she was too nice. I saw that right off. And then she called you 'Alana.' When she said it, Allie…" He stopped and thought about it for a moment. "It sounded right. Like she had tapped into a part of you I didn't know, and part of me resented her for it."

"I can understand that." Allie looked up at him and smiled. "But you're happy now, aren't you?"

229

Paul grinned and took a drink. "Yes." He looked at Allie then, tears rimming his eyes. "It's okay, isn't it? I mean, it's right that you and I can find love after all this. And I don't mean to say I didn't love you."

"Paul," Allie said quickly. "It's okay. We raised two great kids and tried so hard for so long. We're due some happiness. Without any guilt. We've found real love, at last. I for one am going to build on it and be grateful for the rest of my life that Toni came into my life when she did. I think you might say the same."

"Yes," Paul said and laughed. "God help me, Allie. I'm happy." He pulled her into a strong embrace. "We'll be okay. The kids are fine."

As he pulled back, they saw Toni standing there. She held two glasses of champagne. As Paul reached for one, Toni pulled back. "Ah, ah. You've got your gal over there with a glass for you." Paul chuckled as Toni looked down at Allie and said softly, "This is for my gal."

Paul quietly slipped away unnoticed as Allie took the fluted glass. "So I'm your gal, huh?"

"Yep." Toni raised her glass up to Allie. "We've found the beautiful day, Alana," she said with a tender smile.

"At last," Allie whispered softly.

They leaned in for a soft loving kiss filled with the promise of more beautiful days to come.

Behind them, the bell tinkled as the door opened. Several young people walked in. "Are you open?" one asked.

"Yes," Lidia said. "Welcome to The Rising Sun Café. Come to the counter, please. What would you like? Please don't ask me to make smoothie."

Toni held on to Alana and watched the young people as they sat huddled around the small table by the window. With steamy cups in hand, they laughed and talked of their lives and passions, their misfortunes, and their hopes.

Each of them looking beyond the blue horizon for the rising sun.

About the author

Kate Sweeney, a 2010 Alice B. Medal winner, was the 2007 recipient of the Golden Crown Literary Society award for Debut Author for *She Waits*, the first in the *Kate Ryan Mystery* series. The series also includes *A Nice Clean Murder, The Trouble with Murder,* a 2008 Golden Crown Award Winner for Mystery, *Who'll Be Dead for Christmas?* a 2009 Golden Crown Award winner for Mystery, *Of Course It's Murder* and *What Happened in Malinmore.*

Other novels include *Away from the Dawn, Survive the Dawn, Before the Dawn, Residual Moon,* a 2008 Golden Crown Award winner for Speculative Fiction, *Liar's Moon, The O'Malley Legacy, Winds of Heaven, Sea of Grass,* and *Paradise.*

Born in Chicago, Kate moved to Louisiana, and this Yankee doubts she'll ever get used to saying y'all. Humor is deeply embedded in Kate's DNA. She sincerely hopes you will see this when you read her novels, short stories, and other works. E-mail Kate at ksweeney22@aol.com.

Also by Kate Sweeney

The Kate Ryan Series

She Waits
A Nice Clean Murder
The Trouble With Murder
Who'll Be Dead For Christmas
Of Course It's Murder
What Happened In Malinmore

The Moon Series

Residual Moon
Liar's Moon

Also

The O'Malley Legacy
Winds Of Heaven
Sea Of Grass
Paradise

Published by
Intaglio Publications
Walker, La.

You can purchase other Intaglio
Publications books and ebooks online at
www.lgbtbookshop.com, Amazon/Kindle or
at
your local bookstore.

Visit us on the web and read excerpts from
upcoming novels
www.intagliopub.com